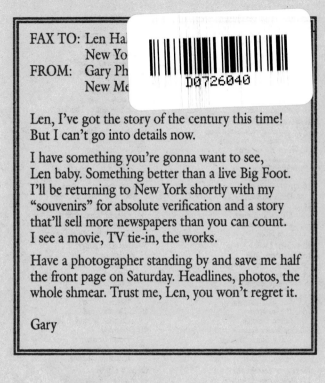

FAX TO: Len Ha...
        New Yo...
FROM: Gary Ph...
        New Me...

Len, I've got the story of the century this time!
But I can't go into details now.

I have something you're gonna want to see,
Len baby. Something better than a live Big Foot.
I'll be returning to New York shortly with my
"souvenirs" for absolute verification and a story
that'll sell more newspapers than you can count.
I see a movie, TV tie-in, the works.

Have a photographer standing by and save me half
the front page on Saturday. Headlines, photos, the
whole shmear. Trust me, Len, you won't regret it.

Gary

Please address questions and book requests to: Harlequin Reader Service
U.S.: 3010 Walden Ave., P.O. Box 1325, Buffalo, NY 14269
Canadian: P.O. Box 609, Fort Erie, Ont. L2A 5X3

WESTERN *Lovers*™

LYNN ERICKSON

WEST OF THE SUN

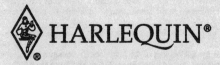

TORONTO • NEW YORK • LONDON
AMSTERDAM • PARIS • SYDNEY • HAMBURG
STOCKHOLM • ATHENS • TOKYO • MILAN • MADRID
PRAGUE • WARSAW • BUDAPEST • AUCKLAND

HARLEQUIN BOOKS
225 Duncan Mill Road, Don Mills,
Ontario, Canada M3B 3K9

ISBN 0-373-30186-3

WEST OF THE SUN

Copyright © 1990 by Molly Swanton and Carla Peltonen

Visit us at www.eHarlequin.com

Printed in U.S.A.

CHAPTER ONE

WITH THE SUN hot on her back, Julie Hayden squatted and took a closer look. If she tried really hard to keep her breathing shallow, she wouldn't be able to smell it, but the fat, iridescent flies that lifted from the carcass were impossible to ignore.

"Wow, Miss Julie, somebody sure did a job here." Deputy Sheriff Ken Lamont whistled and shoved his sweat-stained Stetson back on his head. The thought flashed through Julie's mind that Ken Lamont, what with his Gomer Pyle looks and less than keen intelligence, wasn't going to be any help at all, but the notion dispersed with the swish of the hot wind through the bunchgrass and the gummy buzzing of the flies.

Coyote, Julie's big yellow dog, got a little too close, his nose busy sniffing the dead horse that lay on the dry, cracked earth of her ranch. She held Coyote's collar and pulled him back absentmindedly, wiping her forehead with the back of her other wrist.

"Damn," she muttered. "She was my best brood mare."

"What's that, Julie?" Ken Lamont asked.

Julie twisted her neck to look up at him, squinted into the sun and repeated her statement.

"Just what you needed," he replied sympathetically.

Julie straightened up and stood with her feet apart, hands on hips, studying her dead mare. The animal's death hadn't been caused by disease or predators or injury or old age—or any cause that might have been expected. No, it was dead because someone—some *thing*—had cut off the mare's head, clean as a whistle, right behind the ears. More gruesome yet, the horse's head was nowhere to be found. It was gone, as if it had disappeared into thin air.

"Miss Julie," Ken Lamont ventured cautiously, "do you think it's beginning again?"

"I figured *that* was coming," came Brady's voice from behind her. He'd been looking for tire tracks or blood or anything at all to help explain this grisly killing. Brady Tasavuh was her forty-five-year-old foreman, her good friend, a Hopi Indian who'd been working on her ranch for years, and his cynical tone of voice was typical. Brady had a way of viewing events with elaborate sarcasm.

"Well now, Brady, it sure looks like nothing from *this* world coulda—or woulda—done such a thing," Ken said.

Brady looked down at the sad carcass and frowned. "You've got a point there, Ken," he offered, uncharacteristically amenable.

Julie wasn't so sure she agreed with either of them. But one thing she *was* sure about: it was beginning again. It had been nearly seven years since this kind of mutilation had occurred on her ranch—stock with their heads cleanly cut off—neat, as if a surgeon had done it—and she recalled with sudden clarity the rumors that had circulated back then. She'd been twenty-eight years old, and her father had been still alive and running the ranch when several animals had been found decapitated out on the mesa—just like this mare.

"Summer of '83, wasn't it?" Ken was saying. "Hell of a year. Bad drought that summer."

Drought. Julie looked out over the parched rangeland, the grass burnt brittle and yellow by the sun, the fissures in the thirsty soil, the few scrubby trees whose leaves were drooping and dusty. It was only July, but already the high, arid mesa of New Mexico cried out for rain. This part of the state in the remote northwest, San Juan County, was never verdant, being on the eastern edge of the huge southwest desert, but it wasn't usually this dry.

Coyote was running in circles, nose to the ground, tongue

hanging out like a pink flag. "Crazy dog," Brady said. "It's too hot to run around."

Hot. It sure was hot. And dry as a bone. Julie squinted across the brown, humped land to the west, where the clouds always came from, those afternoon clouds that boiled up over the horizon in the summer and dumped their precious load then moved on. But the sky was clear and bright, an impeccable blue, and the sun hung huge and heavy, suspended in the middle of it like a baleful eye.

"I *sure* hope people don't start spouting that UFO business again," the deputy said, shaking his head.

"Yeah," Brady agreed, his breath stale from last night's beer. "If it's not UFOs around here, it's that Indian spirit stuff."

Julie shot him a look. He was in rare form today, probably hung over. It was only his bitterness showing through, she knew. His bitterness with his life, his wife leaving him, his hopes gone, his son, Hank, too much like him, heading nowhere fast. She felt pity wash over her. But Brady would hate her pity.

Brady Tasavuh. His last name was the Hopi word for the Navajo Indians. It meant "head pounder," because that's what Hopi tradition thought of the newcomers, the barbarian Navajos from the north. He must have had some Navajo blood in his family somewhere, but he looked pure Hopi—a shortish man, who sported two braids as a deliberate statement, a man who gave the impression of being sturdy and likable, also of being damaged goods. He'd been educated in the white man's schools, and like many Indians, walked a fine line between the two worlds, Indian and white. He'd had aspirations to own a ranch and had saved his money for years. He was careful, a hard worker, equally good with horses and cattle and recalcitrant farm machinery. But Patsy, his wife, had left him to return to the clan on the Hopi reservation, and a more traditional life, which he scorned. Now he rarely left the ranch, squandering his savings, drowning his disillusionment in hard physical labor and too much beer.

"Spirit stuff or UFOs or whatever," Julie said decisively, turning from the carcass. "This time we're calling in an expert, and quick, while the evidence is fresh."

"An expert on Unidentified Flying Objects?" Brady remarked caustically.

"Yes, as a matter of fact. My dad looked into it the last time, in '83, but it was too late by the time he got hold of them."

"Got hold of who, Miss Julie?" Ken asked, still gawking at the dead mare.

"The UFO investigating team at Holloman Air Force Base, right here in New Mexico," she said. "In Alamo-gordo."

"Oh sure, I heard of them, but I kinda thought they were only interested in hocus-pocus and little green men and lights in the sky," Ken said.

"Well, this time it's a horse with no head," Julie said. "And I just want somebody to come up here and investigate, maybe find the damn head and who's killed my mare. Enough is enough." She helped them secure a canvas tarp over the carcass, whistled for her dog, then strode over to the old pickup truck she'd driven and slid behind the wheel.

Brady looked at Deputy Lamont and arched an eyebrow. Lamont shrugged, "Guess the lady's ready to go," he said. "Come on, Brady."

It was six hot, dry miles back to the ranch house. Julie drove fast, bouncing over the ground, leaving a plume of dust hanging in her wake. She was upset by the loss of her mare. God knows, she couldn't afford any losses at all in a normal year, but with this drought...

She hit a rock and the truck rattled and bounced. Lamont mumbled something and eyed her sideways. "Sorry," Julie said, and tried to hold her speed down.

The flat adobe ranch house finally came into view, with the rusted hulks of farm machinery and leaning outbuildings on the perimeter of what her mother had tried to make into a lawn. Now it was hard-packed dirt, cracked from the lack of moisture. A lonely cottonwood tree drooped dispiritedly over the front porch. Julie was so used to the sight that it usually looked familiar to her—and welcome. Today the place looked suddenly decrepit.

Coyote leaped out of the back, Deputy Lamont climbed down slowly, while Brady swung himself out. "I'll keep in touch," the deputy said. "You make sure and let me know if you find any more animals, uh, like that. And I'll get hold of that there team at Holloman, Miss Julie. Sure hope they don't think I'm loco."

"Thanks, Ken. And, hey, listen, don't spread this around if you can help it." She hesitated, embarrassed. "Well, it's just Thatch Fredericks at the bank. He's been pestering me with this loan that's coming due. If he hears I've lost that prize mare, well…"

"Sure, Miss Julie. I'll do my best, but Trading Post is an awful small town, you know. Somebody's bound to get wind of it sooner or later."

"Oh, I know. But the later the better, Ken." She tried to smile, but it came out a little lopsided, so that even Ken could tell she was upset.

Hank ambled over from the bunkhouse to see what they'd discovered. Brady's son was never in a hurry, not in work or play. But then, when a guy had nowhere to go, why should he hurry?

"Find anything?" he asked.

"No," Julie told him. "No head, no car tracks, no footprints, nothing."

"Bummer," Hank said. He had a narrow face for a Hopi, high cheekbones, a broad mouth and wide-set eyes. One of his black brows had healed over an old split. He was a good-looking boy, built sturdily like his father, but taller. The only unattractive thing about him was the utter lack of animation in his expression, his stance. He lacked even his father's cynical wit.

It was as if nothing of significance ever touched Hank. The single thing Julie had ever seen him show any interest in was the old pickup truck, and that happened only when he wanted to drive somewhere. He was hidden to her, as unreadable as a statue. Yet she knew he must feel things inside. Everyone did.

Ken Lamont climbed into his own car and nodded at the boy. It was not a friendly nod either, it was more of a warning. "I know you, boy," the look said, "and you're a trouble-maker. You stole a car once when you were fifteen, and you drink too much. I've got my eye on you." What Lamont said out loud, though, was, "Be seeing you, folks, take care."

"I fixed the irrigation pump again," Hank said sulkily when Ken was gone. "It's about done in."

Julie sighed. That's all she needed. No irrigation, no hay for winter feeding. She certainly couldn't afford to *buy* hay, not with that loan coming due. Thatch Fredericks at the bank wouldn't lend her another penny. He'd said that he wouldn't even renew her present loan, not unless she paid something on it. Oh well, she'd think about it later, figure out what to do.

"Thanks, Hank. Just try to keep it running until it rains. Then maybe we can give it a rest and replace some parts."

"Until it rains," Brady repeated. "And when's *that* going to be?"

"Aren't you Indians supposed to know that stuff?" Julie asked lightly. "You're the ones who're close to nature and all that."

"Not this Indian," Brady said. "How about you, son?"

Hank shrugged.

"No rain dances up your sleeves?" Julie asked wistfully.

"I can't even do the Texas two-step, Miss Julie," Brady said with a straight face.

Lonely was a word that never entered Julie Hayden's head. She'd been raised on the ranch and loved the land fiercely, as her father, Bud, had taught her in his stalwart way. She'd had her parents, and Brady, his wife Patsy and school. She'd even gone away to college in Colorado to study animal husbandry. She knew every rancher for miles around and every inhabitant of Trading Post, the closest town. She even knew a fair number of folks in Farmington, the city twenty miles north of her place. She lived alone on her spread, whimsically named the Someday Ranch, perfectly content to stay that way since she'd divorced Mark. Alone wasn't lonely. Alone was free.

If only the ranch weren't in so much financial trouble. If only her dad were still alive. He'd always known what to do. Why, he'd bought the ranch for peanuts and made it pay for years. Somehow Julie just wasn't as good at running things, she guessed. She'd made mistakes, trying to grow the wrong kind of grass for hay and losing the whole crop to aphids, buying that high-bred, expensive mare that she admired, the one that was going to be the basis of a new bloodline, the one that was now lying dead out on the dry mesa.

Julie felt her throat tighten in that way she hated. Head down, she went into her house, let the screen door slam behind her, threw her hat onto the kitchen table and sat down in the old wooden rocker in the corner. It was cool inside, cool and dim, because the thick adobe walls kept it that way. The kitchen was a big room, centered on the old pine table. The green linoleum on the floor was scratched now, the sink faucets leaked and the screen door needed a hinge fixed.

Was this all there was to life? she wondered. Worrying? Growing older and feeling burnt out like an old engine? Probably she was losing her looks, too. Or maybe she just didn't take care of herself anymore. Too frequently she stuck her heavy, waving golden hair up under that old straw hat and just let it go. Rarely, once in a blue moon, did she bother to put makeup on her eyes, eyes that were wide-set and pretty— or they had been when she was younger—ice-blue and transparent with thick dark lashes fringing them. Her nose that was slightly turned up was now sprinkled with freckles, and her wide mouth, with the heavier lower lip, were too often sunburned. Of course, she thought, there was no one to dress up for, there was no reason to pamper herself.

She still had a good figure, though. It was from so much hard work, naturally, but her waist was narrow, her hips firm from horseback riding and her shoulders straight. Once she'd been called pretty, but that seemed so long ago, eons ago. And now, now, she just couldn't take the time to care.

The phone began ringing at dinnertime. First it was Mabel, an old friend of her mother's, who'd heard the rumor from Mrs. Hickman, who rented space in the back of her store to the deputy sheriff, Ken Lamont. "Is it true? A horse with its head cut off? Did you see those kind of scorch marks on the ground like people always see?"

Then it was Ken's cousin, Darlene, whom Julie had gone to school with. "Did you really see the spaceship? Everyone says they give off this green unearthly light. Weren't you terrified?"

"It was a laser," announced Terry, who ran the gas station and curio shop in Trading Post. "The government's experimenting with laser weapons, but it's top secret, so they'll never admit they did it. You know, Star Wars and all that."

Even Julie's mother, Amanda, called. "I couldn't get through. Your line was busy all evening, dear. You know, I heard on the local news that you'd found a dead horse, and they thought it was some kind of crazy stunt or that a UFO had done it. Are they really going to start that all over again, Julie?"

"I hope not, Mom."

"Why, I remember that last time. It almost drove Bud out of his mind. All that silly business about men from outer space." Her mother paused for a moment. "Julie, do you know what killed your horse?"

"No, Mom."

"Was it...I mean, was the head gone, like last time?"

"Yes."

There was a silence on the line, then Julie's mother spoke again in a hushed tone. "What do you think did it? Do you think it really could have been—"

"No, Mom, I don't. I'm sure there's some explanation."

"You be careful. This old world holds more secrets than people realize. You never know. And you all alone out there."

"I'll be careful, Mom."

"Come up and visit soon. I miss you. I'll introduce you to some very nice people, dear. We'll go out to dinner, okay?"

"Okay, you take care now."

After that call Julie unplugged her phone and went outside to sit on the porch. It was dark out, a warm velvety blackness that hid all the faults of the ranch. The moon was rising, a full moon, spreading a silver glow in the east. The bunkhouse showed lights in the windows, and she was almost tempted to go over, knock on the door and see if Brady and Hank wanted to play a few hands of poker. But they were probably drinking beer, too much by now, and they would be surly. Never mind.

Yet her thoughts dwelled on the two men in the bunkhouse. Brady had a drinking problem, all right, although he kept it under control most of the time. But his son was another story. Julie worried about Hank. Where would he go? What would he do? He had no education, no real friends, no goals in life. You couldn't reach Hank. Nobody could, not even his father. Often enough, Julie wondered if Hank would become one of those statistics: deceased male, Native American, early twenties, death due to a car accident, a knife fight or liver disease. What a terrible waste, she mused, frowning.

She swung her gaze around to the west where the jagged walls of Red Mesa rose, just discernable as a dark bulk against the star-filled sky. And it seemed to Julie then that there was a faint glow of light, a tiny point of brightness out there in the distance against the base of Red Mesa. But, of course, it was only the moon reflecting off some mica in the rocks. A quick gust of wind swept across the yard, rattling the leaves on the cottonwood, then dispersed. Julie shrugged mentally as the warm darkness enfolded her again.

THE NEXT DAY dawned just as hot and bright. The announcer on the Farmington radio station said that the humidity was at nine percent and that lawn watering restrictions were in effect for all of San Juan County. He gave various theories as to why there was a drought, but Julie had already heard them all before: the Pacific current off South America, *el niño*, was too cold, the greenhouse effect was warming up the earth, the jet stream was in the wrong position. Everybody had his own theory, but maybe it was the Indians who were right. They declared that the gods were angered by something man had done wrong and had withheld rain. Hey, it made as much sense as any other theory, and she had just about as much control over the gods as those other, more scientific causes—none at all.

She and Brady spent the day rounding up the rest of the horses and herding them into a fenced-in area closer to the ranch house, so they'd be safe from whatever might or might not be out there prowling around and cutting horses' heads off.

She had plenty of time to think, sitting on a horse's back, a bandanna over her mouth, driving her animals back toward the house. A human being had killed her horse. But who? And why? Oh, she'd read about those devil cults that teenagers were joining in cities like Denver and Albuquerque. They killed animals as part of their rites—and people, too. The news was full of ghastly tales. But there wasn't a kid around Trading Post that she could think of who was involved in anything like that. And besides, there had been no tire tracks. How would the kids have gotten way out by Red Mesa? They could have ridden horses, she supposed. There *had* been hoof prints all over, but then, her own horses had grazed there, so the tracks could be, and probably were, theirs.

Who on this earth would want to do a thing like that? If it wasn't kids, who else had a motive? Did somebody want to make her go broke, sell out? Did somebody want to get rid of her?

"Brady," she finally asked, "do you think somebody deliberately killed that horse to get me to give up the ranch?"

"I thought of that already," he said, kneeing his animal closer to her. "But it sure doesn't seem likely."

"No," Julie mused.

"Of course, there is that fellow, Murdock," Brady said carefully, putting her thoughts into words.

"I know."

"He wants the ranch. He gave you a good offer for it. Maybe he's getting impatient."

"But Jack Murdock is so rich he can afford any ranch he wants. All those Western books he writes! Even Terry has them in his store," she said. "And he's a nice man. He'd never kill a horse. He loves horses."

"People do strange things to get what they want."

"Well, he can probably just wait until the bank forecloses," she muttered. "That's a lot easier than killing a horse and carrying its head off somewhere."

Brady said nothing, just swung his lariat at a horse that had wandered a little.

"No, Jack Murdock would never do such a thing. How would he get there? What would he do with the head? That's crazy, Brady."

"It sure is, Miss Julie."

The phone rang that afternoon when Julie got back to the house. It was Ken Lamont, apologizing for the gossip getting out. "Gosh, Julie, I'm sure real sorry, but this story hit the wire service, and it seems everybody wants to do a piece on it. I don't know *how* it got out so fast."

Julie was silent for a moment, frowning. She knew darn good and well how the story got out. Ken had driven back to town yesterday and told everyone in sight. He wasn't a bad man, Ken, he'd just been in a small town all his life and was probably bored to distraction. This mutilation was news, a great source of gossip at Gracy's diner. Oh well, she thought, what was done was done. "It's okay, Ken," she said, "it was bound to get out eventually."

"I just don't know how…"

"It's *okay*. But let's try to play it down if we can," she said meaningfully.

There was a long pause on the line, then he cleared his throat. "I got some bad news," he said sheepishly. "There's, ah, this guy here already, a reporter from the *Nation,* you know, that tabloid paper. He's been asking tons of questions all over town. He's bound to find out where your ranch is and come snoopin' around. Thought I better warn you.''

She pursed her lips. Great. She remembered all the trouble her dad had with the yellow press back in '83. And, oh, those headlines! Men from Outer Space Experiment on Cattle. Humans Next?

"And I got hold of that team at Holloman. They're sending someone up here," Ken said. "All top secret stuff. They didn't want to let me talk to anyone on the team at first, but I refused to leave a message. It was the missing head that really got their interest."

"Well," Julie said, "at least *there's* some good news."

"You bet."

"But that reporter, I just wish…oh, never mind."

"I sure know what you mean," he said. "Guys like that'll drive you nuts."

"Um," Julie said. "Well, I'll watch for him. Don't worry about it. I can handle some dude from the city."

"If you need me now, Miss Julie, you just give a call. Day or night."

She hung up and stared at the phone absently, already putting the nosy reporter out of her mind. Someone was coming from Holloman. Good. Maybe they'd set to rest all the crazy rumors. Maybe they'd find out who killed her horse. She'd sure like to know, because then maybe she could take the person to court and get some money out of him. That mare had cost her three thousand dollars!

She stared at the phone a little longer, weighing her choices. She *should* call Thatch at the bank and give him a definite date and an amount she was going to pay toward her loan. She knew she should call, but she didn't know where the money was coming from. She didn't have it, plain and simple. She felt a tightening in her chest. She *could* lose the ranch.

It was the first time she'd really admitted that to herself.

She could lose it—either through the bank foreclosing or by being forced to sell to Jack Murdock, who wanted to own a real working spread as far away from the city as possible.

Her mind flitted from one problem to another as she sat there crossing and uncrossing her legs. A reporter...well, if he showed up, she'd let him know who was boss around here. Sure she would. And she'd scare the pants off him, too. He wouldn't dare show his face around Someday Ranch again.

She wondered how long it was going to take this other fellow to arrive from Holloman Air Force Base. Maybe the government wasn't really interested in her problem. Maybe it would take weeks of red tape for them to assign her case to someone. Maybe they'd decided not to investigate at all.

She sighed deeply, feeling an edge of impatience slice through her. She wished she could just stop worrying for once, just let things come as they would and quit forcing everything. So what if no one showed up? She'd find her own answers. And besides, Julie wasn't exactly looking forward to some stranger, or maybe a lot of strangers, nosing around her place. Especially men, she thought. Men made her feel downright uneasy. Maybe she was becoming a hermit. Maybe she *wanted* to be one, because she sure as heck didn't need anyone around, not anymore. She'd had someone once, hadn't she?

Mark Hayden. An image of him knifed through her brain, almost a physical pain. Oh yes, she'd had that normal life once and all its complications. She'd married Mark when she'd been young, too young. She'd only been twenty-two when Hayden had shown up in Trading Post and been hired as a cowhand by her father.

Mark Hayden. She'd kept his name, as it was too much trouble to get it changed, but that was all she had from Mark. He'd been older, thirty, blond, handsome and charming. He'd liked the boss's daughter, too. A wonderful guy, she'd thought, flattered and swept off her feet. Mark had been as smooth as a desert rose in those early days, and she'd married him too fast.

Julie stood and paced, rubbing her arm inadvertently. Mark had turned out to be a real bad case when he got back after a night in town with the boys. Not a month after her father died, Mark had come home raging drunk and slapped her around. She hadn't known how to handle it. He'd apologized the next day, kissed her and held her, and young and foolish as she'd been, she'd forgiven him and accepted his promise that it would never happen again.

Until the next time.

Then it had been sunglasses to hide her black eye, and her humiliation. But she hadn't been able to tell anyone, and he made all those promises again.

Julie hadn't known it at the time, but she'd been growing harder and harder inside, trusting only herself, growing afraid to feel emotion. Her dad had died and left her, her mom had moved to Farmington soon after, and Mark…he'd become a drunk, a mean, abusive drunk.

There'd been other problems, too, with the marriage. Remembering, she felt a sinking sensation in her stomach. She'd never physically enjoyed their unions. Oh, at first a girlfriend had told her that was normal, in time she'd reach that height— some women just took longer than others. But after Mark had begun to knock her around, she'd put up walls in her mind, barriers to protect herself. In her body, too.

She wondered if she was frigid. She'd didn't know and, in truth, she didn't care, because her experiences with Mark had been enough to last a lifetime. There'd been no more men, no more pain. No one was ever going to hurt her like that again.

Julie paced, rubbing her arm unconsciously. In a way it was lucky that Mark had busted her arm, because she'd finally woken up and handed him his walking papers. Brady had seen to it that he'd stayed away, too, laying Hayden out flat when he'd shown up back at the ranch once. And then, finally, Mark had disappeared, drifting away from Trading Post like a bad seed on an ill-gotten wind.

She'd been left with bitter memories, a toughened outlook

and the feeling that she was destined to spend her life alone with only hard work and Brady and Hank to see her through. Julie was aware of a deep vein of loser's anger in her. She couldn't get rid of it, but she could make it work for her, strengthening her. She knew there were a lot of things she couldn't have, but she *could* have her ranch, her stock, her independence, her privacy.

That's why she knew she'd take care of her financial problems somehow. She *had* to.

Julie grabbed her hat, swallowed a last mouthful of cold lemonade from her mug and started out the screen door back into the bright golden heat of the July afternoon. There was still work to do, and all this reminiscing and worrying was no way to get it done.

The door slammed behind her, the sun hit her in the eyes, the heat rose up around her like a living creature.

She banged on the bunkhouse door. "Come on, Brady. Siesta's over. Hank! We've got work to do."

It was Brady's voice that rumbled thickly through the window as she turned to cross the yard. "Sure, sure, in a minute. Come on, Hank, get a move on, boy, and pick up those beer cans."

Julie paused, grimacing, then squared her shoulders and headed toward the barn.

CHAPTER TWO

BEN TANNER felt excitement churn in his gut, a hot pulsing excitement much like that he'd known seconds before banking an F-16 fighter jet into a heart-lurching ninety-degree roll. He stuffed an extra T-shirt, a couple pairs of clean socks into his military duffel bag, checked his cramped bathroom one more time to make sure he wasn't leaving behind any essentials, and did his damnedest to relax.

A mutilation, he thought. It was probably nothing, predators gnawing on a dead carcass, or maybe, just maybe, this was a repeat of the inexplicable slaughters of nearly a decade ago.

He'd have to remember his old beat-up aviator's jacket. It might be ninety-eight degrees in the daytime sun, but at night the high New Mexican desert could grow downright cool.

Laurie. He'd darn near forgotten to call and tell her where he was going.

In a two-room apartment, living room and bedroom, Ben had crammed half a lifetime of memorabilia. There was barely a corner that wasn't stacked with papers, magazines, junk he'd collected in the Air Force when he'd been stationed in the Philippines, odds and ends from his fifteen-year marriage. Even some of Laurie's stuff was still around, in closets, under the bed. He'd have to get her to box it up sometime.

Ben sat on the couch and dialed the dorm in Albuquerque, Laurie's new home at the University of New Mexico. He could have stopped on his way up to—where was it, Trading Post?—but he was too anxious to get to that mutilation site for any side trips. It was going to take him most of the day to get there as it was.

Did Laurie have summer classes this morning? Darned if he could remember.

But she was there, sounding sleepy. He sure hoped she was going to classes and not partying too hard at night. The freshman year was tough enough.

"Geez, Dad, it's awfully early, isn't it?" A stifled yawn came over the line.

"It's almost nine, kiddo. Don't you have any place you have to be?"

"Not today. And besides, you know I wouldn't skip my classes." There was an exasperated sigh, saying, *Let me grow up, okay?*

"Sorry," Ben said. "Look, I'm leaving Holloman in a few minutes, heading up north to a place called Trading Post."

"I know where it is. I went on a field trip near there in high school."

"Fancy that. Anyway, I've got a new assignment up there, and I don't know how long I'll be."

"What is it this time?" Finally she was awake.

"A dead animal that's missing a head. A few years back there was a whole series of strange mutilations up in the desert in the Farmington area. No one ever did find out what happened. And then the killings just stopped."

"So they're starting again?"

"I haven't any idea. It might be nothing."

"UFOs," Laurie said firmly.

"Wanna put your money on it, kid?"

"Sure. I'll bet you next month's allowance."

"Forget it. I'll bet you a buck it's something perfectly logical."

"Like what?"

"Like I'll call you and let you know."

"You're a skeptic, Dad."

"Learned a new word, did you?"

"God."

"Don't cuss. It's unladylike."

"Sure. Well, you better get going. Love you."

"Love you, too, kid. Behave yourself. If you need me, get in touch with the deputy up there. Got that?"

"Right on."

The hardest thing Ben Tanner had ever done in his life had been to tell Laurie, when she was only twelve, that her mother had cancer and wasn't expected to make it. Then, that following year, when it had just been Laurie and Ben and no more trips to the hospital, their lives had been hell. Carol had been their whole existence; she'd been wife and mother and friend and lover, the center of their universe. And suddenly there'd been a black hole.

Hard and painful. At first, for Lord knew what reason, Laurie had blamed him for the runaway tumor in Carol's head. If he hadn't been in Asia that last year, if he hadn't been a pilot, if he'd been like other dads.... There had been blame and guilt and anger. How could a void hurt so bad? But then had come the slow healing, the little talks at night, the dinners out, the movies together and finally a smile or two, a genuine laugh. They were going to make it.

Ben tried to remember when Laurie had first had the courage to bring up the subject of his flying. She'd said, "Dad, why do you *have* to fly? What if something happens to you, too? Can't you get a job on the ground?"

She'd needed him. Without Carol, Laurie had needed someone there, close by, not a dad who went popping off to some test site in northern England or off to Japan for three months at a time to go over specs for a new engine, while a neighbor kept his daughter.

He'd balked at the idea. Flying was his life. What was he going to do at a desk job, fade away like an old soldier? And if Ben were being honest with himself, he'd have admitted that Laurie's pressing him to retire had made him feel resentful. And for a time he'd even felt anger toward his dead wife for putting him in that spot.

A few months had passed. Laurie had been with friends while he'd been in California, testing a new model fighter jet for Lockheed Aircraft, and when he'd gotten home to New

Mexico, he'd been hit with a double-barreled shotgun. The first barrel had been Laurie. "I want you *here*!" she'd wailed miserably. And two weeks later his commanding officer had been the second barrel. "Face it, Tanner, thirty-six is too old to be flying around like a kid. Leave the testing to the youngsters. Come on back into the real world."

"Are you grounding me, sir?" Ben had demanded in shock and anger.

Well, he hadn't been grounded exactly, but the orders to fly those cumbersome military transports had not been his cup of tea. It was about that time Ben had run into Jon Reveal at a party in Alamogordo, New Mexico. Reveal, who was head of the UFO investigating team stationed there, had made him the offer to retire from active duty and join the elite unit, and to Ben it beat the hell out of a desk job or flying railroad cars in the sky. So he'd taken the job, and it hadn't been too bad; it was, at least, different. And his daughter? She'd been delighted.

Laurie had grown from a gawky thirteen-year-old into a tall, slender, dark-haired young woman. Their talks at dinner had become more sophisticated, and Ben had worried about her first real dates. To be honest, he'd worried about sex. Carol should have been there. But then, thank the holy Lord, his sister, Nan, had visited from Seattle and had a few chats with Laurie, off-the-cuff stuff, but effective. Ben had felt foolish not being able to say, "Hey, look here, Laurie, don't go letting that guy get too fresh, kiddo, because at his age, that's all he's thinking about." So Ben had let Nan do it instead, and then he'd felt cowardly. Worse, he'd felt like a failure.

And Laurie's comment when they'd dropped Nan back at the airport in Albuquerque? "You know, Dad," she'd said, "you didn't have to invite Aunt Nan down to tell me all that junk about sex and boys. I already knew it."

He'd had a few dates himself over the years since Carol's death, though very few. They'd always been blind dates, too, a fellow pilot or a UFO team member acting as matchmaker.

"You've got to get over Carol," Elena Redding had said

after a few wines at a barbecue, "and find someone else. You can't go through life alone, Ben Tanner, not a big hunk like you. And think of Laurie."

Well, that's just what he *was* thinking about, himself and Laurie. And about the last thing the two of them needed was complications. Life had taken on meaning at last. There was no pain; there was finally a tomorrow again. There were great memories of a great marriage. It was enough.

Ben locked up his apartment and headed out into the bright New Mexico sun. Was he forgetting anything? He'd called Laurie. He'd packed his kit—a suit-case-size black box full of a hodgepodge of equipment: test tubes, an assortment of chemicals, fresh surgical gloves, a Geiger counter, thirty-five millimeter camera, flash, a microscope, a flashlight and silver duct tape. His work was odd to say the least, and it required a wide assortment of tools, chemicals, measuring tapes, special film. He'd been at this job for almost five years now, and he'd found uses for the darnedest things, from paper clips and envelopes to plastic wrap, thermoses and little toy magnets.

Naturally computers came in handy, too, although he usually sent his fieldwork data on ahead to the base at Holloman and had the official technicians there enter his findings and graph the correlations for him.

Ben warmed up the Jeep—didn't take much time, as the temperature in Alamogordo was already ninety-two degrees—and quirked a black eyebrow in excitement. A mutilation. The guys, his fellow team members, had been jealous as hell when Jon Reveal had called him very early this morning and given him the assignment. But then Ben knew there was really no favoritism involved. In truth, he had one of the best track records at Holloman for finding answers to the mysteries. And, too, Ben had his top security clearance, had had it since his test pilot days, and that clearance saved him weeks of hassle when it came to information gathering. It seemed that all the UFO sightings for the past four decades were classified. And there had been plenty of sightings, all right. Not just Air Force and other military pilots had come forward with bizarre tales, but hundreds of commercial and civilian pilots had reported close encounters up in the blue, cloud-filled expanses, as well. The Air Force had taken over investigations back in the fifties, and since then thousands of hours of interviews and even some film of the sightings had been locked up, away from the populace, classified as top secret. Wouldn't want to alarm the poor, unsuspecting public.

Ben turned the canvas-topped Jeep north toward Interstate 25 and grinned cynically. It was okay for a handful of military men to possess all that material, but Lord help the good old U.S.A. if a civilian got his hands on classified documents. Often he marveled at the military paranoia—not that he didn't work for the military, himself—but he wondered what everyone feared so much. Little green men invading from Mars?

There weren't any little green men, as far as Ben was concerned. Nor were there translucent-skinned, massive-headed aliens with huge, intelligent dark eyes roaming the skies, either. In fact, Ben was certain, there was a logical, earthbound explanation for everything under the sun. That explanation only had to be searched out, reasoned, explored.

Ben cruised past the taco stands, movie theaters and used car lots and headed out onto the open highway. His track record for unraveling the mysteries of the skies was all but unblemished. He was the one who'd used modern computer science to study, frame by frame, that fuzzy home movie of a UFO over Catalina Island in California, and he'd proved beyond a shadow of a doubt that the film was nothing more than a shot of a twin-engine plane circling in the sun at an unusual angle. What a disappointment that had been for the true believers. But, Ben often thought, it was better that they faced reality.

Then there was that symmetrically burned grass in the Vermont field that turned out to be a hoax perpetuated by a bunch of clever high school kids. A good hoax, but nothing the townspeople shouldn't have discovered for themselves. Still, it had been autumn, and Ben had gotten to see the fabled colors of New England for the first time.

His easiest assignment to date had involved multiple UFO sightings over Phoenix, Arizona, on March 30, 1989. Of course the UFO's darting across the inky black night sky had been nothing more than an unscheduled meteor shower, but the Phoenix city council had nevertheless called Holloman, producing an expert from the Air Force, just to silence the local alarmists.

Ben had had his tough assignments, he'd had his easy ones. But each one had been explicable, and the few answers that had eluded him, Ben decided, had merely been because he'd been lacking pertinent facts. The answers had been there, the time to find them had simply run out.

They called him the devil's advocate at Holloman. Actually, taking the job Reveal had offered had been a convenient way to avoid the embarrassment of being grounded or transferred to flying those lumbering transports. There was, of course, the fact that he had seen some damn odd things in the sky as a pilot and become as curious as the next guy. The job had at least provided some excitement—not exactly like flying at Mach two, but it had its moments.

Actually, Ben thought as he adjusted his wire-rimmed sunglasses, he'd been waiting a hell of a long time for a call like this. A mutilation. For over a decade, since the first mutilations were reported in Wyoming and Colorado, then New Mexico, no one had come up with a single clue as to what or who had done the strange killings. Not a scrap of evidence. At first it was believed that the U.S. government—doing some kind of classified research—was behind it. But Ben, and many others who had access to top secret documents on government tests being run, knew otherwise.

He steered the little Jeep easily, one booted foot up on the open doorjamb, one hand resting casually on the top of the wheel. Overhead a trio of sleek-nosed jets heading out from the air base did acrobatics in the blinding morning sun, spinning out over the desert, separating like a flower blossoming. They were good, he thought, but the pivot could have been a hair cleaner. They'd never make it up against the Navy's Blue Angels or, for that matter, some of the flying he'd done.

Ben had been good. A better test pilot than an acrobat, though. He'd had all the daring of youth, the thrill-seeking in his blood, the guts to push the edges of the envelope up there, to expand the horizons of the greats, the Chuck Yeagers. Of course his commander had been right—the limits of the sky were for the young, the *very* young. And Ben had Laurie to think of. Still it did twist his guts to see those kids up there, soaring, pushing, silver streaks thundering out over the great desert, the world at their fingertips...*damn*.

Well, one of these days he was going to buy himself a little two-engine Cherokee of his own. Just to tool around in. To have fun. It wouldn't be a fighter jet, but it'd still be flying. It'd still be a test of his reflexes.

He drove north through land that opened out into wide, nearly horizonless expanses. He had to admit that the desert was a little like the sky, open, boundless, full of surprises, free. But whereas the sky was blue, and white at the horizons, the desert offered a cacophony of color: red twisted mesas, green irrigated fields, silver-and-olive prairieland, golden meadows of sunflowers, purple mountains beneath that piercingly blue sky. There was something about the desert air, too, a quality of sharpness, of diamond-clear definition. Poets wrote of it, artists flocked to the Southwest to reproduce it, Indians praised it as creation and Ben felt a kind of peace surrounded by its bountiful beauty.

Trading Post. It was in the northwestern corner of the state, he knew, dead center of nowhere. He prayed this call from Deputy Ken Lamont wasn't a false alarm, another predator attack on a drought-weakened horse. Still, Lamont had told Ben's boss that the head had been cut off with the skill of a surgeon's hand. Did this deputy know what the skill of a surgeon's hand looked like?

Avoiding the congestion of Albuquerque and Santa Fe, Ben drove the back roads north and west through the centuries-old Spanish pueblos and Indian villages that dotted the isolated regions of the high desert. He'd only driven through parts of the state like this once before, and then, as now, he was struck by the timelessness of the towns and the people. Oh, there were gas stations and roadside stands selling everything from fresh fruit and vegetables to tacos, silver and turquoise jewelry. There were Indian women in colorful skirts and Mexican ladies in rebozos. The Catholic Church was ever-present even in the most remote pueblos. How could a pueblo be complete without the bell tower of an aged adobe church patiently squatting in the center of town? It was a peaceful land, a land singularly unmarked by modern society. The summer tourists came and went; the Native Americans looked upon them with amused indulgence.

Ben stopped at one of the pueblos and grabbed a steaming hot burrito at an outdoor stand. It was laced with jalapeños—red-hot chopped green chilies. He drank two orange sodas then pulled out his map.

"Is this the road to Farmington?" he asked the man who'd served him.

The man studied the map while Ben mopped his neck with a blue-and-white bandanna. *"Sí,"* he said, pointing. "It is easy to miss." He folded Ben's map and handed it back. "Perhaps you should take the big highway. It is quicker."

"Not in my Jeep," Ben said, nodding toward his somewhat battered red vehicle. But for all its slowness, its tendency to guzzle gas, it was ideal for desert driving. There'd been many a time when he'd flown out to an assignment and then had to rent a four-wheel-drive vehicle when he got there. Laurie had dubbed the old Jeep Nelly. And it had stuck.

Checking his watch, Ben figured he'd make Trading Post, just south of Farmington, by three-thirty or so. It was daylight till eight, so he'd have plenty of time to locate the mutilation site before dark. He had his camping gear with him, too, and bottled water, so barring any unforeseen hang-ups, he'd be able to really dig into his work just after sunrise. It occurred to Ben that this Deputy Ken Lamont might not have roped off the area or kept someone on guard, but no one would be that foolish, would they?

It was hot as Hades by two, but even if Nelly was without her doors, Ben had left the canvas top on. Still, the heat from the sun rose off the stretch of road ahead in shimmering waves, causing the distant mesas to be distorted, floating on the horizon like great red ships on a colorless ocean.

Ben took off his aviator-style sunglasses and mopped his sun-browned forehead. Damn, but it was *hot* out. He reached for his water bottle and took a long gulp, feeling the tepid water trickle down his stubbled chin and onto his already damp T-shirt. It was blistering out, and the summer drought wasn't helping, either; he could see the trail of dust from his tires hanging in the dry air behind him. Yet he loved New Mexico. It was wild, free, seemingly untouched, despite the many centuries of occupation by the Indians, then the conquering Spanish and finally the whites who'd poured in on the famed Santa Fe Trail. He might have been born and raised in the cool, damp northwest, but this was now home.

In La Jara he gassed up and checked his directions. It was still a good hour's drive up to Trading Post. And there was nothing between here and there but strange, desolate country, dry and unforgiving. Every so often he spotted a tiny pueblo, a ranch or two in the distance, but that was positively it. The earth baked and cracked under a blazing desert sun, and there wasn't a single wisp of cloud on the horizon.

The dead horse. What was really behind it? A true UFO? No, Ben wasn't about to buy *that*. Many of his fellow workers did believe in UFOs, would have staked their reputations on them, in fact, but no one had proven their existence to Ben yet. More than likely this killing, and maybe even the multiple killings of a few years back, were the work of a devil-worshiping cult or something like that. Regardless, it was Ben's job to find out, to gather every scrap of evidence he could and solve this mystery.

For all Ben Tanner's dedication and drive, he knew he could be overbearing, appear too sure of himself. At forty-one, he was still in good physical shape, except for an occasional headache, a result of having endured so many brutal Gs as a pilot. He was just short of six feet two, had smokey blue eyes and unruly dark hair. Carol had always teased him, telling him that he was lean and strong-featured, like Sam Elliot, the movie star. "But you're better looking," she'd said, and he'd felt like blushing, because he couldn't have given two hoots what he looked like. If he could have changed anything about himself, though, Ben would have opted for a lighter beard; as it was, he really could have shaved twice a day.

Trading Post was what Laurie called an eyeblink town. "If you blink, Dad, you miss it." There was a small grocery and feed store, bank branch, thrift shop, gas station, curio shop and hairdresser. A fifteen-seat breakfast diner dubbed Gracy's closed after 2 p.m. The deputy sheriff—the sheriff was up in Farmington, twenty miles away—occupied an office in the back of the grocery, a one-room cubicle with a telephone, two-way radio, desk, filing cabinet and only one chair. There was no jail. Again, like the sheriff's department, restaurants and motels, the lockup was in Farmington.

"You Ken Lamont?" Ben asked, sticking his nose into the cubicle.

"That's me." The middle-aged deputy stood, hiked up his official khaki trousers and hooked his thumbs in his snakeskin belt. "Can I be of service?"

"I'm Tanner, Ben Tanner," he said, closing the door behind him, "from Holloman. You called my boss."

"Well, so I did, now. Didn't expect you so soon, though. You musta been pressing it pretty good."

Ben smiled and took off his glasses slowly. *Small-town cop,* he thought. "Yeah," he said, "I made really good time. Took the back roads."

"Good, good. Well, say, want a cup of coffee? A Coke? Holloman, huh? You a fly-boy?"

"I was." And Ben left it at that.

"Is that so? You know you boys used to buzz this town

every so often till Mrs. Hickman, who owns this here grocery store, complained to the Air Force about the broken jars. How fast do those jets go, anyway?''

"Fast," Ben said, growing impatient. "Some faster than others. But I can promise you, Lamont, I never broke any of Mrs. Hickman's jars." *I don't think I did, anyway.*

"You want some coffee, Tanner?"

"That's very kind of you, but I think I better get out and see that dead carcass of yours." He put emphasis on the "yours," because he'd found people were oddly possessive of their little finds. It was times like this that Ben's assertive demeanor could be a drawback. He wanted to press, he *was* pressing, but he tried very hard to come off slow and casual, easygoing.

"Well, that dead mare was one of Miss Julie's," Lamont said, turning to the map on the wall behind him. "That's Julie Hayden. She owns this here ranch—" he pointed "—'bout eight miles out on county road five. You take this left off the dirt road and three miles up go left again at the fork. Take you directly there."

"I see," Ben said, going around the desk to study the map. "I don't suppose Miss Julie Hayden would mind if I just drove straight to the site of the killing?"

"Wouldn't do that if I were you. Between that damn yellow dog of hers and Brady…"

"Brady?"

"That'd be her Indian foreman, Brady Tasavuh. He and his boy are mighty protective of Miss Julie and what's hers. Have been ever since the divorce. They like their privacy."

"I see."

"Yep, you best go straight to the house. Can't miss it."

Couldn't miss an armed fortress, either, Ben thought, envisioning an eccentric old maid, an Annie-get-your-gun sort of female who surrounded herself with slavering dogs and big strong Indians who never smiled. *Swell.*

"Sure you don't want that coffee?"

Ben shook his head. "I'll just gas up and head on out there

while there's still daylight.'' He turned to go, then paused. ''By the way, Lamont, you folks have any theories about this mutilation? About the other killings a while back?'' It sounded casual enough, but Ben's question was in dead earnest. Frequently locals knew a whole lot more than they were telling.

Lamont kneaded his jaw. ''Some say it's one of them there UFOs.'' He shrugged. ''I don't cotton to those stories, myself.''

''Neither do I,'' Ben said and headed on out.

He had to admit it, he thought as he drove, this land was about as barren as he'd seen. Of course he'd flown over this corner of the state, and he'd always known how sparsely populated it was but, ye gads, it took a tough soul to make it here. There were a few head of cattle hither and yon on the dry rolling land, and road signs that warned of open range, a couple of sheep, but that was about it. They grazed seemingly on nothing, small bunches of brown vegetation that dotted the land every ten feet or so. And as for water, not only was there a drought this summer, but New Mexico was reportedly the driest state in the country, anyway. The tenacity of these people absolutely amazed him.

Julie Hayden. *Miz Julie Hayden*, as Lamont put it. He had a mental image of a Western-style Amazon, a strong, big-boned woman, tan and weather-beaten, with arm muscles bunching under a plaid shirt. God, he hoped she just let him do his job.

As Lamont had promised, the Hayden ranch was easy to find. It was hard to make a wrong turn where there were no roads. He moved slowly up a long drive, an extension of the unpaved county road, really, and spotted three structures, an adobe-style ranch house with a lone tired tree drooping over the porch, a leaning barn and what looked like a bunkhouse. Was that where those unsmiling Indians lived?

Ben pulled up alongside the bunkhouse and turned off the motor. Somewhere he could hear a dog barking. He took off his glasses as he stepped down onto the hard ground, then mopped the sweat off his neck with his bandanna, glancing around as he did so. There wasn't much to look at. A corral, a few sheds that had seen better days, some rusty farm machinery, an old water pump from a well, a broken-down washing machine sitting in back of the bunkhouse, a useful-looking blue pickup truck that had hay sticking out of the rear gate. He put his dark glasses back on. It was a poor looking place, functional but poor. Yet there was something here. Maybe it was the land. In the distance, to the west and south, a mesa jutted straight out of the valley floor, a long, flat-topped mesa the color of rose that shimmered in the afternoon heat. And if it weren't so dry this year, Ben could imagine the array of summer color that would blanket the earth. It would be wild and boundless, dazzling the eye, beckoning. Maybe it wouldn't be so bad to sit on that front porch in the evening and watch the huge orange sun set on the mesa....

His boot heels seemed to echo too loudly as he mounted the three steps up to the porch. Where was everyone, anyway? Hadn't Lamont let them know he was coming? Ben rapped on the door, once, twice. *Come on.* Finally he heard that barking again, the door swung open, and he found himself staring down at a hundred-and-twenty-pound yellow monster of a dog and the twin black eyes of a double-barreled shotgun.

CHAPTER THREE

DARN CITY SLICKER REPORTERS, Julie thought to herself as she squeezed the trigger just a hair for effect. Of course, she wasn't really going to shoot—heck, she'd been around guns all her life—but *he* didn't know that.

"You're not welcome, mister, so just turn yourself around there and get off my land. Now."

As if on cue, Coyote raised a lip to show a white tooth. A low growl rumbled in his chest.

The man, still unmoving, his face hard and unafraid, looked at the shotgun then switched his gaze to the dog. Julie was sure he curled a lip right back at Coyote.

"Excuse me," the tall stranger said coolly.

"Like I told you, you're not—"

But he stood his ground, not flinching at either Coyote or her shotgun, and inadvertently, she let the barrel of her gun waver a little in her hands.

"Look, I don't know who you were expecting, but I'm here because you called me," he said in an angry voice. "And didn't anyone even tell you not to point loaded guns at people? That is *if* it's loaded?" Deliberately he reached out and pushed the gun barrel aside, and his smokey blue eyes met hers in challenge.

Julie swung the barrel right back with a jerk and scowled. "Who do you think you are? What're you talking?..." she began but then suddenly fell silent. What *was* he talking about? *She* called *him*?

For an uneasy moment she stared at him, and then abruptly it came to her. This was...it must be the man from the Air

Force base. Quickly she lowered the gun and gave Coyote a curt command, whereupon the big yellow beast crept into a corner.

Julie felt like a fool. If she'd looked at the stranger instead of assuming too much, she would have realized immediately that an eastern reporter would not have shown up at her door in dusty jeans, scuffed boots and a T-shirt. This man was far too rugged, too sun-browned to be a big-city reporter.

"Well," she began, letting out a breath, all too aware that she owed him an apology for shoving a gun in his face. Unfortunately apologies were not her strong suit. "Well," Julie reiterated. "Look, I honestly thought you were someone else...someone I really don't want around here."

He was stone-cold silent. He wasn't going to make it easy for her, was he?

"Never mind," she said, "it was just some reporter I thought was coming."

"I see," he said with studied derision.

"Anyhow, I'm sorry about this," she got out, glancing down at the lowered gun, aware that she didn't sound in the least sorry. Finally she set the big heavy thing against the wall, realizing that she was twice as uncomfortable with nothing in her hands. "Well," she said, wanting to bite her tongue off, "I'm Julie, Julie Hayden." She stuck her hand out for him to shake.

"I guessed that," he said and stepped on inside. "Tanner, Ben Tanner. From Holloman." He took her proffered hand and gave it a firm shake.

"Some coffee? A soda? Water?" It was the least she could do, considering.

He shook his head. "I'd rather skip the amenities," Tanner said, "if you don't mind, and head on out to see that dead animal of yours."

"Well, sure," Julie said, "right away if you like."

"I'd like," he replied.

"Let's go then." Julie grabbed her straw cowboy hat from a peg, pulled it down over her brow and closed the door after them, locking Coyote in the house. This was awkward. She'd threatened this guy with a gun, and now she was supposed to talk to him in a civil manner, show him around, be polite. Should she say something else, offer more of an explanation, another apology? But that would only make things worse.

"We'll take the pickup," she said, leading the way.

"I'd rather take my Jeep," he said, his eyes fastened on hers, "if that's okay. I've got equipment I'll need out there."

She didn't like it one bit, and she stood there in the hot afternoon sun feeling as if this stranger had barged in and, in the space of five minutes, taken control of her life.

"Is there a problem?" Ben Tanner asked abruptly. "I mean, if you don't want to come along, you could point me in the direction."

"No," Julie said, looking down at her feet for a moment, thinking, "it's no problem. The terrain's just rough. That's all."

"Nelly, my Jeep," he said, "can handle it."

While Tanner moved his gear from the passenger seat, Julie pinned a note on the bunkhouse door for Brady to see. Brady would have found it mighty peculiar to have returned from the range and found the pickup there with no Julie in sight. And as it was, she hadn't a clue how long they'd be gone. Now that his anger over her greeting had subsided, she could see that this Ben Tanner had a single-minded determination about him. He might be poking his nose around out there in the desert for hours.

Holding on to the bar in front of the passenger seat with one hand, Julie indicated the way with the other. He drove well. Obviously he was used to backcountry terrain, steering around rocks, through low brush, easing the Jeep—Nelly, he'd called it—down the side of steep washes.

"How far out is the site?" he asked, calling over the grinding noise of the engine.

"About five miles, six tops." She turned to make sure he'd heard and then found herself strangely reluctant to look away. He was actually a very good-looking man, she noted, rawboned and lean. Good-looking, but clearly arrogant. And that superciliousus expression on his face, the impatience, the way a muscle worked in the hard line of his jaw—who needed it? Plus, he'd been awfully condescending to her. She hated that in a man.

She sat there coolly assessing him. He must have been around forty, forty-one, but he had all his hair, lots of it, the curling dark stuff coming right up out of the neck of his T-shirt. There were dark hairs on the back of his capable hands and on his strong-looking forearms.

He had a face, Julie decided, that would turn a woman's head in most situations, with a generously curved nose and a dimple in a whiskered, cleft chin. A long, chiseled face, a rugged face. Too bad his personality didn't match it for attractiveness.

"Where to?"

"What?" Julie asked.

"Which way?"

He'd stopped. Just now—or had he stopped moments ago? Had she been staring at him all along?

She shook her mind free. "Head up that cut." She pointed. "But be careful, the land's tricky here, it falls off to the right."

Tanner shifted into first. "I believe I can manage it," he said dryly.

It was some distance out to where her mare was. Had they been driving on a highway it would have taken ten minutes, but this trip was going to take a good part of an hour. The sun was lower in the sky, resting heavily on Julie's right shoulder, causing perspiration to form on her brow and upper lip. She took off her straw hat and wiped the dampness away with her forearm, then realized Tanner was watching her out of the corner of his eye. Did he think she was unladylike, a backcountry hick? Defiantly she hoped so.

It *was* hot out. And dry. Both of them drank from time to time out of the canteen he carried, the water dripping down their chins, wetting and cooling their shirts. Once Ben Tanner poured some down the back of his neck, the droplets hanging there on his dark hairs, gleaming diamondlike in the sun. She saw then that not only was his shirt damp at the neck, but he was soaked in a dark line down the front and under the arms, as well. An odd thought flashed through her mind. She'd been around the Indian men on the ranch so long she'd forgotten how profusely a white man sweated in this awful heat, forgotten how a man like Tanner sweated on the neck and brow, down his long back, his chest and belly. She'd forgotten how a man might wipe that glistening sweat off his brow and then flash her a look from a sun-browned face. It *was* odd, Julie thought, how she'd forgotten these things so easily.

She put her eyes and thoughts back on the road, forcing them there, willing them to obey. She might have money problems and problems with that Western novel writer, problems with Brady and Hank and Lord knew what else, but the one problem she no longer had was that of a man in her life. She didn't have it and didn't want it. Period. "Hang a left around that outcropping there," Julie announced firmly, looking dead straight ahead.

Although Julie and Brady had done their best to cover the horse's carcass with the canvas tarp, it was immediately obvious when they reached the spot that animals had gotten to the body.

Tanner hopped down out of the Jeep and scrutinized the remains. There was an undisguised scowl on his face. "Hell," she heard him say, "dammit all."

Julie, too, got out of the Jeep. "I guess it was predators," she said uneasily, aware of his anger as he stood there, stockstill, hands on his hips, and gazed long and hard at the dead animal.

"This is just great." He squatted down and shook his head. "You couldn't have left someone out here to stand guard?"

She eyed the crumpled tarp that lay off to one side. What was she supposed to do, apologize to this man a second time? Well, she'd be darned if she would.

"I could have," Julie said levelly, "but I didn't. It's a

shame, I agree, but I'm not going to cry over spilt milk, Mr. Tanner."

"Ben," he remarked, distracted.

"Okay then, Ben, I guess you made a long trip for nothing."

That got him. He jerked his head up and eyed her impatiently. "You called *me*, remember?"

"I remember," she said. "But this isn't exactly a laboratory where everything is sterile and neat."

"I'm aware of that. You could have guarded this carcass a little better, though. It's the only evidence we have."

"Evidence! That's my best mare and she cost me plenty! I want to know who killed her. If it's little green men, I need to know." Julie's temper flared in the heat. "This may be a kick to you, but it's my livelihood!"

He took off his dark glasses deliberately and eyed her without blinking. "And if the evidence was in one piece, maybe I'd have better luck finding out who did it."

Julie scuffed the toe of her boot in the dust. "Okay, okay. Maybe I should have had Hank camp out here and guard it. I just never thought..."

"I guess you didn't."

She narrowed her eyes, ready to retort, stung by this Tanner's unmistakable censure, but he was moving around, searching the area, carefully eyeing an overturned stone, a depression in the sandy soil, anything, everything.

Finally she had to ask. "See anything?"

He ignored her, then returned to the Jeep and took out a large black box that, upon opening, looked to hold the darnedest collection of paraphernalia Julie had ever seen. While she stood there studying its contents, Tanner—Ben, he'd said—went on back to the Jeep yet again and brought out a Geiger counter. He switched it on, held the box out in front of him, then made slow circles outward from the carcass for about twenty yards. Julie could hear the clicking sounds the box made, but there was no telltale increase. The area, she surmised, must have been free of any radioactivity. Thank the Lord.

When Tanner was done with the Geiger counter he scraped up some soil samples, packaged them in a plastic bag, took flesh samples from the horse, putting them in vials, labeling them with a pen. Very efficient, very methodical.

He put the material away, closed the big black box and turned to her, totally businesslike. "Are you certain the cuts on the horse's neck were done with a sharp instrument? Not sharp *teeth*?"

"Yes," Julie said, her back up again. "I know teeth marks when I see them."

He nodded, perhaps believing her. "How about footprints?"

"Sure, lots of horses. Mine, though."

"Tire marks?"

Julie shook her head. "Brady was here, too. We both looked around."

"Anything?"

"I didn't see anything but my mare."

"Okay, fine. There was only the mare's carcass then. So let me ask you this, Miss Hayden...Julie, what or *who* do you think did this?" His voice, though easy, challenged her.

"I haven't a clue. That's why you're here."

"Do you believe," he said deliberately, "that your mare's head was somehow surgically removed and then miraculously lifted straight up into the air and flown away?"

Julie took a moment to study the sardonic quirk on his lips. "Look," she said, "I don't believe in flying saucers or whatever you call them."

"UFOs."

"UFOs. Fine. On the other hand, Mr.—uh, Ben, I saw these weird mutilations in '83, and it's just as inexplicable now as it was then. I don't know any more than that. Do you?"

Ben held her gaze for an uncomfortably long time then finally he nodded, apparently agreeing with her statement of the problem.

"So," she finally said, breaking the uneasy moment, shifting her glance, "what now?"

"Now, I get these samples in order and sent back to Holloman."

"So we can go?"

"Of course. There's nothing more to see here," he replied pointedly, then folded up her tarp and tossed it in the back of his Jeep.

He made her downright edgy, Julie decided as she bounced along on the way home, and she was going to be glad to be rid of him. It was too bad, though, that predators had gotten to the mare. Maybe this Ben Tanner could have found some answers, after all.

"This way?" he asked.

"Oh, no, head through that cut over there."

"Thanks." He glanced at her, as if contemplating something, then swiveled his eyes back onto the rangeland. "If I recall," he said, "those mutilations a ways back all happened in the space of a few weeks, didn't they?"

"That's right."

"Interesting. Well, I was wondering, would you mind if I hung out here for a few days—in the bunkhouse, of course," he was quick to add, "just to see if another dead animal turns up?"

Julie pursed her lips and let out a sigh, not even bothering to hide it. She *could* tell him to get a room in Trading Post; the trouble was, Trading Post didn't have a single one to offer. On the other side of the coin, she mused, it was really very silly for her to be so distrustful of a logical request. She couldn't go on judging all men—especially the handsome ones—on the basis of her experience with Mark Hayden. And besides, Brady and Hank would never let anyone bother her.

"I guess you can stay in the bunkhouse," Julie replied unenthusiastically.

The miles stretched out ahead of them on the baking range, long dusty miles that went too slowly in the ensuing silence. Julie couldn't find a single thing to say to this man. She guessed she was out of practice conversing with people. The social graces weren't big on her priority list, although she could usually talk easily enough to people she knew. Maybe it was this man's abrasive way that kept her mouth shut and her head pounding with aggravation.

Julie took off her hat, wiped her brow over her throbbing temples and sought something to say, anything to break the awkward silence. She wondered if he were asking himself why she was so reluctant to let him stay a day or two at the ranch. Maybe this tall, handsome stranger sitting next to her thought she was weird, some kind of an eccentric.

For a moment her skin crawled with discomfort. Maybe she *was* eccentric. She'd chosen to live out in the middle of God's country all by herself, with only the company of two Indians to see her through. She'd erected a barricade around herself, a veritable fortress, that no man dared penetrate. And she'd done it, Julie knew in her heart, because she was insecure and anxious. To the outside world she appeared hardworking and competent. She'd even cultivated a too-quick tongue, but inside she often felt scared, afraid to go through life alone, yet more afraid to take a chance on another Mark Hayden. Not that anyone was asking.

She kept her eyes on the range ahead but was all too aware of Tanner sitting there so close she could almost count the whiskers growing on his chin and neck. Had he seen through her facade? Maybe he sensed that weakness in her, maybe she was as transparent as glass to him. She shifted in her seat, on edge, then clenched her jaw hard. *What do I care what he thinks?* She only wished he'd finish his work and get out of her life.

It wasn't enough that the bank was crawling up her back for a payment on her loan, that this Ben Tanner had stormed into her life, but when they drove up the rise that overlooked the ranch house, there was yet another problem. A dusty black Lincoln Continental was parked in front of her house. It had to be that reporter fellow Ken Lamont had warned her about.

"This is just great," she muttered.

"What?"

"Oh," Julie said, "that car down there, it's got to be that reporter."

"The one you had the shotgun for?" His lip curled ever so slightly in amusement.

"That's right," Julie said, irritated. "And if it *is* him, I ought to put some buckshot in the seat of his pants."

He laughed out loud then, his head tilting back, the strong cords in his sweat-streaked neck showing. "You would do just that, I bet," he said, grinning.

"You got that straight."

"I've got a better suggestion," Ben said, sobering. "Why not let me tell him he's not welcome? Save you the hassle."

A stab of confusion knifed through Julie. Not in a million years would she let this man, practically a total stranger, take over like that. Yet…yet there was this place inside her, that empty corner of her soul, that somehow ached to do just that. It was brought home to her that for an awfully long time now she'd had to cope with situations like this all by herself.

"Well," Ben was saying, "how about it? Want me to get rid of the guy?"

"I can manage," Julie remarked sharply, squaring her shoulders.

Her guess had been right, the flashy Lincoln did indeed belong to a reporter, a man named Gary Phillips from New York City. She found Phillips sitting outside in front of the bunkhouse, chatting with Brady and his son. It irked her doubly that Brady would give the man the time of day much less *talk* to him.

She shot Brady a scathing look, then turned to Phillips. "I'd appreciate it if you'd leave, Mr. Phillips," she said, placing her hands on her hips.

"It's Gary," he said rising, beaming, thrusting his hand out to her as if he hadn't heard a word she'd said. "Call me Gary. My *dad's* Mr. Phillips." He grinned from ear to ear like a Cheshire cat.

Julie bit her tongue to hold back any unladylike words that

threatened to emerge. What a little sleaze-bag, she thought, scrutinizing him. About five foot five, the dark-headed man had a pasty, lumpy-looking face that repelled her, but it was his eyes—they were bright and black and very small, close-set. Even a mother wouldn't trust those eyes, Julie thought.

"Gosh, this is great," Phillips was gushing, impervious to the fact that Julie wouldn't take his hand. "This is *great*. Brady here and Hank, too, have been filling me in on the history of this area. Wow! Did you know Brady's people, the...the..."

"Hopi Indians," Julie mumbled, exasperated.

"Yeah, them. Anyway, they've been in this place, this area, for hundreds of years. He was telling me about the drought this summer, and how the Indians pray to—"

"Say," Ben interrupted finally. "What's the name of your paper, Phillips?"

"Oh, yeah, I'm lead reporter for the *Nation*."

Ben grimaced.

"Yep, that's me," Phillips said. "I've covered every UFO event from coast to coast for ten years now."

"That's all very interesting," Julie said, "but I still want you off my—"

"A horse," Phillips said, undaunted, "it's head missing. Wow! I'll get a few pictures. Yeah, and you, Miss Hayden, maybe you could be standing alongside."

"Okay, Phillips," Ben said, stepping forward menacingly, "I think that's enough."

"And you are? I didn't get your name." Gary Phillips pulled a notebook out of his back trouser pocket and began scribbling. Suddenly, earnestly, he looked up at Ben with those shiny black eyes. "You are?"

"Ben Tanner."

"You're a rancher? Neighbor?"

"No."

"But you saw the UFO?" Phillips scribbled on doggedly.

"Look," Ben said, "you're missing the point, buddy. Miss Hayden here asked you to go."

"I can handle it." Julie butted in, hating the way Ben was taking over.

"Holy cow!" Phillips suddenly yelled, startling them. "*You're* the guy from Holloman!" He turned to Brady, who nodded, obviously enjoying himself.

"That's him, White Eyes, the UFO expert," Brady said.

Julie could smell the beer on Brady's breath and could have throttled him, but Phillips was practically slithering up Ben's pant leg. And Hank, who'd had a few, too, was slumping into a corner, chuckling. Julie felt like throttling them all.

"Holy cow," Phillips kept saying, "you *gotta* let me quote you, Tanner. Say, did you see a spaceship? You got any photos? How about burned grass? Man oh man, can't you just see the headlines? Why, the network news team'll be crawling all over here. Say, you gotta sign an exclusive with me, Miss Hayden. We could do a book, split the royalties..."

"*That* does it," Julie said, her cheeks stained with temper. "You get out of here, Phillips, and I mean *now*!" She started to turn on her heel, prepared to go fetch her shotgun, when she felt Ben clasp a hand firmly on her shoulder. He shook his head, smiled at her as if she were missing a joke and started to say something to Phillips.

But it was Brady who got in the first word. He stepped forward slowly, deliberately, and raised his eyes and arms heavenward. "There are no men from the skies here," he said, affecting the accent of a Hollywood Indian. "It is only a sacrifice to the Cloud People," he chanted, and Phillips rushed to pull a small cassette recorder out of his bag. "Ah," Brady said, "it is the Anasazi, the Ancient Ones, who do these mutilations."

Julie couldn't help herself; she stifled a smile the best she could. But it was all lost on Gary Phillips.

He scribbled furiously, his eyes bulged with greedy excitement, and he practically leaped out of his skin. "The who? Spell that for me?"

"The Ancient Ones," Brady repeated. "*They* are the takers of the heads."

"Oh, man! That's the takers of..." Phillips wrote tirelessly. "Great! Now, where do I go to interview these, ah, Anasazi, anyway?"

Brady came out of his trance and grinned, shrugging.

"You gotta tell me," Phillips said, breathless. "This is a scoop!"

Julie smiled wryly and tapped Phillips on the shoulder. "You've got a real problem," she said, affecting her own brand of gravity.

"It's no problem. Just point me in the direction."

"I would," Julie said, "but you see, the Anasazi disappeared over six hundred years ago."

CHAPTER FOUR

JULIE STIRRED THE TOMATOES and added a pinch of Italian seasoning and a wedge of butter for good measure. She hoped Ben liked stewed tomatoes, because that was what he was getting. There was no hotel in Trading Post, nor was there a restaurant that stayed open for dinner. She could have let him eat in the bunkhouse with Brady and Hank—she could have— but he wouldn't have any place to put all his paraphernalia.

Out of the corner of her eyes she watched him work in the kitchen at the scarred wooden table. He was busy labeling the samples he'd taken today. In the background her dad's old radio played softly from the living room, modern easy-listening stuff from a station up in Farmington. It was Barbra Streisand singing about moonlight. Heart-wrenching stuff, but it was soothing her headache. Julie hummed to herself and tasted the tomatoes with a wooden spoon. As good as Mom's.

"You know," Ben said, breaking her reverie, "Brady was pretty funny out there today. But he was kidding about that Anasazi business, wasn't he? He doesn't really believe in ghosts or spirits, does he?" Carefully, methodically, Ben went on dividing a sample into two vials, never looking up.

Julie leaned against the stove, folded her arms over her red plaid shirt and gazed at him. "Yes, he was joking," she said, "but lots of the Hopis do believe in that stuff. They have a real mystical outlook. And most of them believe they're direct descendants of the Anasazi."

"And what do the others think?" Ben wrote on one of the sticky labels he had scattered on the table, then stuck it carefully on a vial.

"Oh," Julie shrugged. "I guess they think like a lot of historians do, that the Anasazi died out completely."

"War?"

"Maybe," she replied, still watching him, his dark curling head bent to his work. "They could have died out from disease, famine, drought or war, I suppose. They say the Navajos were savages hundreds of years ago. Brady thinks the Navajo probably chased the Anasazi up into the high mesa where they built all those cliff houses."

"And what do you think?"

"Me? I haven't a clue. They were great road builders, we know that for a fact, even though they never had the wheel. Maybe they built a road and migrated south and died out somewhere along the line."

"Interesting."

She shrugged. "Everyone has his theories. I don't know if anyone will ever find out." She turned back to her stewed tomatoes, adding a touch of ground pepper. "You're a specialist," she called over her shoulder. "What do you think?"

"That spacemen took them up in their ships and flew off."

Julie's head swiveled around abruptly. "You're joking," she began, but then saw what was becoming a familiar quirk on his lips.

"Brady doesn't seem…how should I put it?" Ben raised a brow and glanced at her. "He doesn't seem very Indian to me."

"Oh, well," Julie replied. "You're right. He was educated off the reservation. He even went to college for a while."

"Hank, his son, too?"

She frowned. "Hank's a different story. He went to high school here, but he never finished. He doesn't know much about his heritage at all."

"Should he?"

"I don't know. Most Hopis have a real strong set of beliefs about things. They're taught to value spiritual life over material possessions. I guess that's why they've withstood the white man's influence better than other tribes. Hopis can't be

corrupted. But Brady and Hank don't stick to those rules."
What she didn't tell this supercilious, judgmental stranger in
her home was that Brady's wife had left him, that Brady hit
the bottle too much and that he was having a devil of a time
with Hank, who, not surprisingly, tended to emulate his father.
She also failed to mention how she worried about Hank, how
she wished she could reach him, how she felt so dreadfully
helpless where the young kid was concerned. But it was none
of Ben Tanner's business, was it? Brady and Hank were, after
all, practically her only family now.

"It's a shame," Ben remarked, as much to himself as her,
"that he's lost touch with his culture."

"Um," was all she would offer.

It made Julie as nervous as a cat to have this man sitting
in her kitchen. Oh, he wasn't doing anything to bother her—
not really—but just his presence was irritating, throwing her
routine out of synch just enough to be annoying. And then
every so often she'd get a hint of his maleness, his scent in
her private domain, the size of him filling the room, or she'd
feel his eyes on her back, those deep smoky eyes silently
watching her, appraising.

She'd decided after Gary Phillips had left that she was going to treat Ben Tanner politely. Distantly but politely. They'd
gotten off on the wrong foot, and most of it was her fault
because of her unfortunate mistake when he'd arrived. She'd
acted childishly; of course, he was to blame too, but she was
a mature woman and could rectify the situation.

It seemed that Ben had come to some kind of decision in
regard to her, as well. Not that a macho type like him would
admit his mistakes, but it was clear that he was trying to be
more accommodating.

"Well," she said, wiping her hands on her old apron,
"dinner'll be ready in about ten minutes. Are you almost done
there?"

"Oh—" he looked up "—I'm in your way."

"Not really. I thought I'd set the table, that's all."

"Almost through."

"You test this stuff yourself?" she inquired.

"No, no, I've got colleagues in the Air Force, *real* scientists, who run most of the tests for me."

"Then you're not a scientist?"

He shook his head, amused. "Hardly. I'm a retired pilot."

"Oh."

"I was an Air Force test pilot, and I saw a lot of stuff in the skies that I couldn't figure out," he explained. "I got curious."

"A test pilot," she said, repeating his words, a mental image flashing through her mind's eye of a Tom Cruise type in *Top Gun*, and she thought, *Ah-ha now I have his ticket, all right*. Ben Tanner was one of those fly-by-the-seat-of-his-pants hotshots, an all-American boy who'd gotten too old to fly but couldn't live without the thrill of it. Sure he was. And hadn't she pegged him right in the first place? Handsome as all get out, a certain calculating arrogance just beneath the surface of his calm. Oh yes, Julie'd bet the farm that in his heyday he'd been a true lady-killer, the slow-talking, smoldering type. And a real high-and-mighty know-it-all.

"I guess I should set the table now," she said, an unfriendly edge to her voice.

Dinner was not to be, though, not just then. She was just about ready to throw some croutons on top of the stew and toss it in the oven for a minute, when Hank came rapping at the back screen door. Coyote leaped up so fast from his place under the table that he nearly knocked Ben's samples over.

"What is it, Hank?" Julie asked, perturbed. To top it all off, Hank was reeking of beer. "Have you been out in the truck like this?" she began, angry.

"Well, I..." Hank said, slurring "...I saw something, Miss Julie. Really I did."

"This better be good," she said, folding her arms stiffly.

"I saw buzzards, Miss Julie. There was this dead animal down by Cottonwood Wash...."

There certainly wasn't enough daylight to see a darn thing, but Ben insisted they go anyway. And then when she and Ben got to the place twenty minutes later, there were buzzards sure enough, having a feast, but it was immediately obvious, even in the headlights of Ben's Jeep, that it was only the remains of a poor little doe weakened by the drought. *With* her head. There was nothing strange about it in the least.

Julie sighed and looked at her watch. "*That* was a waste of time," she said.

But Ben seemed not to notice her aggravation. He hopped out of the Jeep, flashlight in hand, and studied the scene for so long that Julie felt like telling him just where to get off. Then—the icing on the cake—he went and got that big black box of his and took samples of the torn flesh on the doe and of the surrounding soil.

She crossed her legs, uncrossed them, compressed her lips. Didn't he know anything? It was so pitifully obvious that the animal had died of natural causes that she wanted to laugh. Yet there he squatted, Mr. Determination, scooping up earth into vials with only the twin beams from the Jeep's headlights to guide him.

She sighed with boredom and watched him work for lack of anything else to do. Finally, after twenty minutes or so, he put away his kit and climbed back into the Jeep.

"I imagine," he said, switching on the motor, "that this will turn out to be a wild-goose chase."

"Um."

He turned the wheel, spun the Jeep around, kicking up dust with the tires. "I go on lots of goose chases," he said.

"I'll bet."

"Hope I didn't take too long."

"Dinner'll be ruined," Julie said as she hung on to the bar, but then she felt foolish and immature. "I suppose," she remarked, "you must be disappointed."

He nodded, fixed his eyes on the darkened range, and drove back in silence.

MORNING DAWNED cool and utterly cloudless. By noon it was another scorcher. Not in the least unusual this summer, but everything else about Julie's life seemed totally out of order, thrown into disarray.

It was, of course, Ben Tanner. First she'd fixed him breakfast, and then he'd insisted on earning his keep. It wasn't that she didn't need the help, either; it was more his constant proximity that bothered her.

She let him load the hay into the truck and drive it down to the fenced-in area where the horses grazed and where, thank heavens, there was a spring still running. It was hot, dirty work, the dust from the hay filling their nostrils as they heaved it down from the pickup.

After a minute Ben peeled his shirt off, inside out. She wanted to tell him that the chaff would stick to his bare skin and itch all day, although she didn't want him to think she'd noticed. But really, she couldn't help noticing—all that brown skin and black hair and sweat.

She bent to give Coyote a pat, an unnecessary pat, then straightened, looking away from him.

"Dang," Julie said, wiping her dripping brow, "I'd kill for a thunderstorm, one big cloudburst." She leaned on her pitchfork.

Ben stopped for a moment, too. "We haven't noticed the drought that much at Holloman," he said. "Oh, it's been hot, all right, but people are still filling their swimming pools."

"Must be nice," Julie said flippantly.

"Some of us just don't realise," he replied carefully, "what this does to the ranchers."

"Well, it's pretty bad. This drought might be my ruin."

"Loss of your stock?"

She glanced away from the sight of the sweat running down the hairs on his naked torso. "That," she said, "and a whole lot more. I really owe the bank, big-time." He was quiet, and she thought *What the hey, it's no secret*. "I took out a loan last year," she said, "a gamble, to buy that mare that got killed, among other things. There was always a chance of drought. There always *is* a chance." Julie sighed, reaching for the water bottle, aware of him watching her with interest.

"Oh, well," she said, poised to drink, "I can always sell out if I have to."

"Do you want to?"

"Heck, no. But there's this man—you've probably heard of him—Jack Murdock, that big-time Western novelist from up around the Durango area. He knew my Dad, and he always loved this land. Anyhow, he's made me a real good offer."

"And if you don't sell to him?"

Julie laughed. It came out too high-pitched. "The bank'll foreclose. I'll end up with ten cents on the dollar of what the ranch is worth."

"I'm sorry," he said quietly.

"Yeah, well, so am I," Julie replied, the tough girl. She shrugged. "Even my mom up in Farmington keeps telling me I ought to sell. She says the place will make me old before my time."

"Will it?"

"No. I love it here. I *did* love it here, before all the pressure this year, that is."

"Money problems will drive you nuts," he said, agreeing, and took up his pitchfork.

Julie leaned her head back against the vinyl seat while Ben drove to the ranch house. She'd let him drive this time, she knew, because she really was losing her strength, her will to go on. The heat only made it worse. It drained her; it was draining her finances, her determination, her life's blood. She was having dreams at night of rainstorms and puddles and mud. It was crazy. And she was starting to think about vacations, about selling out to Murdock and having money in the bank, about starting over somewhere. Farmington? No, but somewhere. First, that vacation, though, that much-needed time out from reality, that time to reexamine things and see her life in perspective. The trouble was she was stuck here, worried sick about losing everything, wanting to keep the place but balancing on a razor's edge. Vacation? There sure wasn't much hope of *that*.

They had tuna sandwiches and potato chips for lunch.

Hardly nouvelle cuisine, but filling enough. Julie drank a full quart of orange juice and then cleaned up the kitchen while Ben helped Hank rewire the electric drill that had needed fixing since Mark had thrown it against the barn wall seven years ago. There were lots of odds and ends around the ranch that needed fixing or replacing, Julie thought, while she put the plates up, things that had been broken or neglected—whatever—and Brady just never had the time.

Hank was impressed. He stopped by the house just to tell Julie that Mr. Tanner had gotten that old washer running again and wasn't that great. They could do their jeans in it, anyway. "He says he maybe can fix up the electric saw, too, and save us some time on the fence mending."

"That's nice," Julie said, turning to pinion him with a glance. "About last night, Hank."

"Yeah?"

"You know I've told you never to drink and drive. You know I mean it."

Hank's face fell. "I *wasn't* drinking, Miss Julie," he said, smooth, brown forehead creasing. "Honest."

She could have accused him of lying. She should have. But something inside Julie just didn't have the strength. It was the heat, she thought, and the uselessness of it. Why wouldn't it rain?

They bought groceries in Trading Post that afternoon from Mrs. Hickman, and Ben checked in with Ken Lamont, who offered to drive Ben's samples up to Farmington and Federal Express them to Holloman. Then they loaded the groceries into the truck, stopped at the post office and drove past the little branch bank where Thatch Fredericks was just coming out of the front door. He saw Julie's truck and waved to her, obviously wanting her to stop and talk. She kept driving, her eyes straight ahead.

"That man waved to you," Ben observed.

"Did he?"

"You saw him."

"So?"

"Isn't that rude? I mean, this being a small, friendly town."

"He's the bank president," she said in explanation.

Ben turned to look back at Fredericks but said nothing.

"It makes it worse, too, because he's really a nice guy. His wife and I went to school together. We were good friends," Julie babbled, and then she had no idea why she was telling him so much.

"Isn't there something you can do?"

"Not really," she said, studiously keeping her tone light. "Like I said before, I can sell out, maybe to Murdock. Who knows? It sure would make Mom happy, anyway, because all I ever hear is how worried she is."

"That's how families are," Ben said, and it struck Julie then, like a brick on her head, she hadn't even a clue as to whether or not he had a wife, kids, girlfriend.

"Are you married?" she blurted out.

He turned to glance at her. "I was," he said. "She passed away six years ago."

"Oh."

He said nothing. The air pulsed with his silence.

"I mean, I'm sorry. It hurts like mad to lose someone," she said, rushing her words.

"Yes."

"Kids?"

"A daughter, Laurie. She's starting college in Albuquerque."

My God, Julie thought, and stared at the road ahead. She hadn't any idea. He was just a man, a strange man that had come storming into her life yesterday, and all she'd done was crawl into her shell and wish he'd go away.

She turned her head and looked at him. Ben Tanner, widower, father, human being. And how openly he'd just told her all that. What if he asked her about her life? What would she say? How could she tell him about Mark Hayden without bursting into tears or dying of shame inside?

"Oh," she'd say, I was married, but the creep beat the tar out of me, and not just once, either, so I divorced him. I'm fine now, your average thirty-five-year-old divorcee who hates men. No, let me correct that—men are okay, I just don't trust them, not a single one of them. Could she say that?

Julie's gaze refocused on Ben's profile. He was no Mark Hayden. As handsome, there was no denying that, but a whole lot smarter, a lot more together. Did that make him any less dangerous, though?

She showered late that afternoon and let the cool water run down her shoulders and back for an indecently long time, considering the level of the well. It felt so good, though, a much-needed respite. Yet as the water trickled down her stomach and thighs, she couldn't rid herself of the image of Ben's torso and back, the lines of sweat on his gleaming, sun-browned skin, the muscles rippling and tensing as he'd lifted a bale of hay and tossed it into the truck.

He *was* beautifully built, perfectly proportioned, with long muscles in his arms and back and across his lean belly. He had long, nicely shaped legs, too. She imagined they'd be covered with that dark curling hair as well.

Julie shut the water off, began to plan dinner in her head, and determined not to think about Ben Tanner in any way other than as a person here to do a job. He'd be gone soon enough.

She made a macaroni salad and cut up steamed vegetables. Easy and light, and she didn't have to turn on the oven. She moved around the kitchen in a loose, gathered denim skirt and light blue tank top, fixing the meal, keeping her mind free of all but the task at hand. He'd be gone in a day or two, out of sight, out of mind.

"Hi," came his voice at the screen door, startling her.

"Come on in," Julie said, turning to the sink, as easy and contained as he was.

"Hey, Coyote," she heard Ben saying, and heard the dog's tail thumping against the chair leg. "Good boy, lie down now. Can I help you with anything? Julie, you need some help with dinner?"

"Oh, no," she said over her shoulder, "I've about got it.

There's cold beer in the fridge. Help yourself.'' She heard the door open and close, a can popping.

"Want one?"

"I have one. Thanks." There, now wasn't she under control? No more of that girlish fantasizing. She chopped up a head of cauliflower, her hands as steady as a rock. "Tell me something," she said after a time, steering her mind away from the reel of those smoky blue eyes on her back. "If you don't fly anymore, who pays you?"

"The Air Force still does," Ben said, and she heard him take a swallow then stifle a belch. "I retired from active duty but still get a check is what it boils down to. Kind of like moving laterally."

"You miss flying?"

"Sure. There was never a dull moment up there."

"I'll bet." She added broccoli to the steaming pot. "But your work now must take you all over, and it *is* different."

"I travel some. But not like before. I was stationed all over the place then, and now I have a home base, anyway."

"This may be a silly question," Julie said, still not turning, "but do you believe in UFOs?"

She heard his deep male laughter. "No way," he said. "Most of my colleagues do, but like I tell them, there's an explanation for everything under the sun."

"Really?" Now *there* was a statement.

"Everything."

A rugged individualist, Julie thought, a skeptic, a man who probably drove his other team members nutty with his egotistical, unbending attitude.

"So," she said, finally coming around to face him, "what's killing my animals?"

"One animal so far," he said, correcting her, and she noticed his head of clean, dark hair and his yellow dress shirt, slightly wrinkled, rolled up above those strong forearms.

"My one animal, so far," she said. He had khaki pants over strong thighs, and sat in the chair backward, facing her, his arms folded casually, beer can dangling loosely from fingers. His eyes rested on her. Julie cleared her throat. "What killed my mare?"

Ben smiled thinly. Had he noted her sudden discomposure? "I don't know what killed your mare, Julie," he said, "but I'll tell you one thing—it was human, from this earth and probably from close by. He, or she," he added, "knows the country better than you, I'd say, because he fooled you by leaving no tracks whatsoever."

"Interesting," she said, wondering. "So, can we find this...human?"

"Maybe."

"And maybe not," she said. "I can't afford to lose a single more horse or cow or sheep."

"I understand."

Julie drank from her beer, moving her gaze away from his intense one. "Well, so much for that," she said. "Dinner's about ready."

Once he got started, he talked easily, about exotic places in the Far East, about the Mediterranean, about the cool mists of England. There were no ghosts in Ben Tanner's closet, not a one. And her drab little life? She was too embarrassed to tell him that the farthest north she'd been was Laramie, Wyoming, and south—Dallas, Texas. Never to the east. Oh, she'd been to L.A. once; her dad had taken her to Disneyland. Big deal. Ben had seen the world, flown it, walked its strange and exotic lands, eaten its foods.

Julie took a forkful of macaroni and chewed on it pensively. "Has your daughter lived all those places, too?" she ventured.

"Some." He clasped his hands together and rested his elbows on the table. "Laurie's not a good traveler," he said. "She's a real homebody. I'll bet she never moves out of New Mexico. She loves it here."

"A woman of my own heart," Julie said and smiled.

"She'd like you."

She looked up suddenly, surprised, embarrassed but not sure why. "That's, ah, nice," she got out.

He talked about Laurie, and he mentioned Carol, his wife. The way Ben spoke about her, Julie got the feeling that Carol was still alive. She guessed he was really hung up on his wife. It must have been awful to lose a wife so young, and she supposed Ben wasn't over it yet. And it must have been hard on him, too, raising a daughter all by himself.

Yet even as those thoughts ran through her head, even as she listened to his quiet voice, Julie felt a sinking sensation in the pit of her stomach, as if there were a hole there, a void. She should have had kids. She'd wanted a child, but the time had never seemed right—or had that been her excuse, her way of distancing herself from Mark? Regardless, she sat there feeling sorrow fill that empty spot, and she knew she'd grown too still, too quiet, and that Ben was watching her, scrutinizing her as he spoke. He was thinking: Julie Hayden's an old maid, a frigid thirty-five-year-old spinster, dried up, full of regret that she doesn't even have a child.

"Laurie sounds lovely," Julie was saying, aware that there was a break in her voice.

"She's a good kid."

She felt a knot in her stomach, a fist tightening. It was anger and it was confusion. She came to her feet a little unsteadily and cleared the table, forcing him from her mind, ignoring his help, answering him in monosyllables. And all she could think was: why had he come into her painstakingly guarded world and disturbed it, cracked her peace of mind as if it were a glass house?

"That was a great dinner," he was saying. "Thanks."

"No problem."

"Can I help you do anything else?"

"No, everything's done." That she could get anything past the lump in her throat was a miracle. *Go away, Ben Tanner.*

Somehow they sat in her small living room and talked for a few minutes more. She hadn't the least idea about what. It was becoming painfully obvious, every time she looked up and found those blue eyes pinned on her, that she was desperately uncomfortable with him there. Yet he talked about his life, his child, his marriage, for godsakes, and how good it had been. He couldn't have been less interested in her, Julie Hayden, the old maid. She sat there, a sounding board, someone safe with whom he could wile away an evening while he waited for another animal to be slaughtered.

Julie's world was topsy-turvy, spinning out of her grasp. *He's probably exaggerating,* she told herself. *His marriage stank and his kid is a spoiled brat raised by a single parent.* Tanner had probably fought with his wife, maybe he had even hit her. Sure. It happened all the time and no one ever admitted it. Sure.

"I'll bet you're tired," he said, rising finally, filling the small space of her home to bursting. "Guess I'll turn in."

"I am tired," Julie said, endlessly glad he was going.

"I'll see you in the morning."

"Sure." She walked him to the screen door, at a safe distance, of course, and then, against her better judgment, watched as he moved through the shadows between the house and the bunkhouse, a tall, lean form beneath the brilliant points of desert starlight.

CHAPTER FIVE

IT STARTED OUT A PERFECT DAY. A breath of breeze stirred the curtains in Julie's bedroom, a cool morning breeze coming from the west, from the direction of Red Mesa. It was utterly silent in the house, with only the occasional sound of Coyote padding about and the smell of coffee brewing.

She liked it this way. Peaceful, quiet, a time to watch the dawn quicken over the rangeland, filling the world with light and color, a time to reflect on things without having to endure Brady's sarcasm or fret about Hank constantly swilling beer, driving her only vehicle half-drunk, a time to forget about money and banks and ugly little reporters from the cesspools of the city.

She poured herself a cup of coffee then stood at the kitchen window staring out at the dawn. Some of the cattle had wandered last night to the crest of a distant hill. With the pink glow of morning behind them, they were dark humps on the face of the land. The sight comforted her. Her cattle, her sheep, her brood mares—*her* land.

The peace stayed for nearly an hour, enfolding her, and then the phone rang. So much for her privacy.

"Julie, hope I didn't wake you up, but I know I have to get you before you're out on the range." It was Jack Murdock, the novelist.

"Hi, Mr. Murdock." Her heart sank—more problems, more worries.

"Now I realize you said you've got till August first to get your loan paid, but I just wanted to know if you've had time to reconsider my offer. I'd hate to see you lose money on that place. Your daddy worked so hard to build it up.''

"Gee, I really don't know yet. I haven't talked to Mr. Fredericks at the bank about it," Julie said.

"Well, you talk to him, but don't forget me when the time comes. I'll keep the Someday Ranch just like it is, only better. I'll even write a book about it," Jack said.

A book. How easy it was for these wealthy city dudes to see her spread in a romantic light. She remembered when her dad had made a bundle letting John Wayne film a movie on the place. Back then Westerns had been all the rage. Now it was cop films, spy stuff, science fiction. No one wanted to see the Old West, or the new for that matter. But Murdock had suggested Bud's place for the film, and she supposed he still saw it through rose-tinted glasses. He should see it from *her* perspective.

Julie was aware of the screen door opening with a creak behind her. It could only be Ben. She lowered her voice. "I'll sure let you know as soon as I've made definite plans, Mr. Murdock.''

"If you want me to talk to that fellow at the bank for you, it might buy you some time. I know how hard you're working, and I hate to see it all go down the drain. What's his name? I could give him a call.''

"Really, Mr. Murdock, there's no need. I'll take care of it," Julie said.

"And I can lend you some money to tide you over. We'll call it a down payment. You won't even have to pay me back until closing time. Just let me know and my lawyer will mail you the papers.''

"Thanks, but I really can't do that. I'm not even sure I'm going to sell the ranch at all.''

"Oh, you'll sell. Pretty girl like you running that big place all alone.''

Julie rolled her eyes. "I'll let you know," she said firmly and hung up. Then she didn't want to turn around. Ben was there, she'd heard him moving about in the kitchen, pouring himself coffee. He'd heard every word she'd said and probably had a damn good idea who it was and what he was offering. It was downright embarrassing to be in such miserable financial shape.

Of course, the longer she hid her expression from him the more humiliating it became—she had to face him eventually. Julie shrugged mentally, pulled up her barriers and turned around. She plastered a smile on her lips.

Ben was sitting at the kitchen table with his long legs stretched out in front of him, cupping a coffee mug in his hands. His own face wore a studiously impassive expression.

"Morning," she said. "Eggs for breakfast?"

"Sure, if that's what you're making."

She got herself busy frying eggs, making toast, searching for an unopened jar of peach jam her mother had made last Christmas. Ben sipped on his coffee, scratched Coyote's neck until the big yellow sissy groaned in pleasure, and watched her cook.

It was thoroughly unsettling, having him still there. She was only too aware of the way his hair waved over his ears and his brow, looking as if he'd just awakened. His beard was growing in already, a dark shadow covering his upper lip and chin and cheeks. And those darn smoky eyes of his, quick, intelligent, not missing a trick.

She spread jam on the toast and shot him a sidelong glance. He was still watching her, all right, his pensive gaze seeming to burn a hole right through her plaid shirt.

"More coffee?" Julie asked, feeling uneasy in the silence.

"Oh, I'll get it, thanks." But he didn't move, only sat there big and out of place in her kitchen, his brows drawn together in thought.

After breakfast Ben telephoned one of his colleagues at Holloman and found out that the samples Ken Lamont had sent from Farmington yesterday had not yet arrived. He phoned the deputy sheriff immediately, and Julie could detect a note of pure impatience in his tone as he spoke. Oh, he was being eminently reasonable, his voice slow and in control, but she'd been around him for nearly two days and she knew he was irritated.

"Okay, fine, you do that, Lamont." Then, "No, I'm sure there's nothing to worry about." He hung up and swore under his breath, his irate expression not fading until he caught Julie eyeing him.

He wanted to see that mare again, he told her then, and if she had time, could they cover some of the surrounding area? They had to have missed something out there, and the morning light was better.

She didn't have to go with him, Julie knew, and there was certainly plenty to do—herd the stock, check fences, haul hay and water—but then maybe they *had* missed something. It wouldn't hurt to look again.

He drove. By now she was actually getting used to his taking control, and besides, he wasn't a *bad* driver.

Well, at least she didn't have to keep chattering, not with Ben Tanner. There were long silences between them as he steered across the barren landscape, silences that didn't seem to bother him. Julie broke them every time with an inane statement or observation. She even talked about the weather. "It sure is hot," she said, then could have bitten her tongue.

"Yes, it sure is," Ben replied politely. "Must be ninety-five, at least."

"Maybe more. It's supposed to get to a hundred today, the radio said." Lord, wasn't there anything else to talk about?

He stopped his Jeep on a knoll and pointed to the high walls of rock that stretched across the entire western end of her ranch. "What's that?"

"Red Mesa."

"What's behind those walls?"

She squinted, looking at the familiar rock barrier. "The Navajo reservation, then Arizona."

"Is there a road or a trail that comes around or over Red Mesa?"

"No, it's impassable."

"Then that's that," he said.

Julie frowned. "You know, we haven't thought of a helicopter. I mean, what if whoever killed my mare used a helicopter?"

But Ben shook his head. "I'd have seen a depression in the ground or at least the disturbed dust from the blades."

"I guess you would have," she said. She pushed the brim of her hat up with a finger. "Why would someone do this to me? I just can't figure it."

"There's an explanation," he said, "and eventually I'll find it."

"Do you always solve your mysteries?"

"Almost always," he replied matter-of-factly.

He drove on. She sat on the plastic seat and bounced and sweated and wondered at his statement. Was he being arrogant? Or was he really that good at his work? She kept glancing over at him, but he stared straight ahead, his brow furrowed. He was even more handsome when buried in thought, she decided; that muscle worked in his jaw, the white lines around his eyes deepened. She liked that in a man, she was discovering, the look of total concentration, as if she were not there at all. And then she realized how much easier it was to be around this man when he was paying no attention to her, when she could watch him for minutes on end and he hadn't a clue.

Julie stared at him unnoticed. She wondered why he was letting his beard grow—away from the strict regulations of the military? Was he simply more relaxed here? Regardless, she had a sudden, inexplicable urge to reach out and touch those thick black scratchy hairs on his cheek. And how soft would his skin feel where his beard didn't grow? How smooth? Quickly she looked away, down at her hands. Was she kidding herself, was she really so terribly lonely and desperate that a strange man, *any* strange man, could begin to stir her imagination, to fill that void in her life?

Ben stopped again a little farther on. He turned and looked behind them, then jabbed his thumb in that direction. "Somebody's following us."

Julie peered out from under the brim of her hat. Sure enough, there was a line of dust, like smoke, moving toward them across the range. "Maybe Brady's looking for me."

"No, it's a car. I'm betting it's your pal, Gary Phillips."

"Oh, damn!" Julie said. "In his Lincoln Continental? Out here?"

"Looks like."

"What does he think he's going to find?"

"Want me to get rid of him?" Ben asked.

"No," she said flatly, "it's not your problem. I'll talk to Ken Lamont about him. He's on private property, after all."

Ben swung around to the south and headed back toward the ranch house. He deliberately picked the roughest route he could, smiling grimly. "I hope Phillips follows us. Maybe he'll break an axle or get a flat tire. Then maybe we'll be rid of him," he explained.

But the plume of dust stayed half a mile back nearly all the way to the house, where it finally disappeared, veering off toward the county road.

"Did you see that guy in his Continental?" Brady asked when they got back. "He went tearing by out to the road back there."

"Yeah, we saw him."

"He must be nuts. Reporters." Brady shook his head.

"Well, at least he's got air-conditioning," Ben said, wiping his forehead.

In the house they got sodas from the refrigerator and sat in chairs at the table.

"You're not finding out much of anything," Julie said.

"Nope."

"No ideas?"

"Not yet."

"Well, um, how long do you...I mean, how long can you stick around and wait? I mean, if nothing happens." Abruptly, ridiculously, she feared his answer. What in God's name had come over her? Two days ago she'd have paid him to get out of her hair. And now, suddenly, she was asking him how long he could stay.

He'd fixed her with his blue eyes and was holding her gaze for a startlingly uneasy moment. "I can stay as long as I need to," he finally said. "Is there a problem with that?"

"No," Julie managed, but her voice was nearly a whisper, as if she had no air left in her lungs. It had all gone with a big whoosh when she'd looked up and seen him staring at her.

She took a long drink of her soda and wished the floor would open up and swallow her. She shouldn't have asked him that. He was putting more meaning into it than she'd intended. And now the handsome, arrogant Ben Tanner was going to think he had a real edge on her and—

The screen door banged open abruptly, making Julie's heart leap. She spun around, spilling soda on the table, but it was only Brady, his hat pushed back, his brown face damp with sweat. "It's happened again," he said breathlessly. "Four of your sheep this time."

BEN STEERED around a clump of creosote bush and glanced sideways at Julie. It occurred to him to wonder what on earth he was doing out here in the middle of nowhere in the blistering heat with this tough lady and her Hopi Indian foreman, a perfectly intelligent man except that he affected Indian-style braids for some peculiar reason of his own.

Julie Hayden had been a real surprise. A pretty lady, slim and nicely shaped, nothing like he'd expected. She had lovely silver-blue eyes with dark lashes, eyes that stared through a man and judged him. Her chin was resolute, and he liked the way she carried herself, straight and sure. Her skin was very fair. He knew because he'd seen the soft, pale, untanned underside of her arm, smoothly translucent and traced with veins.

He recalled Ken Lamont briefly mentioning a divorce. So she'd been married once. When, he wondered, and for how long? Of course, he couldn't come right out and ask her. Another woman, perhaps, but not Julie. It was all too evident how leery she was of men—except for Brady and Hank, whom, Ben could already see, she considered utterly sexless individuals. In fact she treated them as if they were her children.

Did Julie have children? Could be. Maybe they were with the ex-husband, although Ben couldn't see her giving up a child for any reason whatsoever.

He gave her another look. She'd barricaded herself out on this ranch as if to hide from the world. She reminded him of a doe, slender and graceful, with big sad eyes, poised to run at any movement or sound. What had happened to make her so suspicious of men?

Still, he found himself admiring her. There were times when she seemed to let those walls down and she relaxed and then he saw a glimmering of the real Julie Hayden. She was full of competence and independence. She'd taken on quite a task, running the ranch by herself, holding on to it when her mom was apparently uninterested. And then there were the financial problems she'd spoken of. Lots of ranchers had money worries, but hers sounded serious. He wondered how she'd solve those problems—or *if* she'd solve them. And if she sold her ranch to that writer, what would she do then?

And why was he thinking so much about Julie Hayden's problems, anyway?

The Jeep bounced over a rock, and Julie grabbed at the bar on the dashboard.

"Sorry," Ben said, "I'm a little anxious to get there. How far is it now?"

"Brady?" she asked, turning toward the back seat.

"Couple of miles. At the base of Red Mesa," Brady replied.

Ben squinted and looked ahead to where the heat waves shimmered on the bleached-out earth. The wall of reddish rock rose, looking like a painted backdrop for a Western movie. It was too sharply delineated to be true, its color too deep, its shadows too precisely drawn, rising out of the paler flatness like a fortress.

Laurie would admire her, Ben decided. Julie was like his daughter in many ways. She was stubborn, fiercely independent yet femininely vulnerable. Paradoxical. A whole bundle of contradictory impulses wrapped up in a very nice shape.

It struck Ben then, as he was bumping over ruts and breathing in dust and sticking damply to the Jeep's plastic seat, that he was doing too damn much thinking about this woman. And, he admitted to himself grudgingly, he'd had a couple of moments when he'd felt like pulling her into his arms, silencing her with his mouth, feeling those womanly curves pressed up against him.

He'd thought about it more than once, like just a short while ago, before Brady had interrupted them in the kitchen. He'd been wondering what her mouth would taste like, how it would feel to nibble on that full, curving lower lip of hers.

Why? he asked himself. Why now, when he'd finally gotten his act together after being grounded, when he'd come to grips with his life, with this new work he was doing, with being both father and mother to Laurie? Why complicate things?

Was he lonely for a woman? Maybe he just needed to sleep with someone. The kids called it being horny. Was he horny? Now wouldn't that be a laugh at forty-one-years-old?

Ben shook himself mentally. He was here to do a job, not to get involved. It was the last thing he wanted. And he suspected a relationship was the last thing on Julie Hayden's mind, as well.

The four dirty white humps on the ground materialized out of a mirage. He stopped the Jeep and hopped out, everything forgotten but the spurt of excitement he felt. He was on the job.

Kneeling next to the first carcass, waving away the flies, he studied it carefully. A normal full-grown sheep, a ewe, lying on its side. Absolutely nothing interesting about it except that the head was not there, cut off behind the ears with an instrument so sharp that the incision was as clean as any surgeon could produce with the sharpest scalpel. And the cut was fresh, only hours old. Probably that morning.

He checked out the other three carcasses. Another ewe and two rams. Each had been decapitated with a sure hand, clean as a whistle. He checked the area with the Geiger counter, just to be safe, then took out his notebook and wrote a few lines—time, place, observations. He photographed the four bodies from several angles. He took samples and put them in vials that went back in the insulated box. Methodically, precisely, he collected every scrap of evidence he could. Even things that seemed utterly unrelated.

He forgot about the two people with him for a time, until he saw Brady circling the area, eyes on the ground.

"Find anything?" he called out.

"Maybe," Brady said.

Ben strode over to where Brady stood, still looking down at the ground. There, in the beige soil, was a faint smooth spot. "A footprint," he breathed.

Julie was at his shoulder. "What is it?"

"Footprints," Brady said. "There's another one over here."

"Strange," Ben said, following the faint imprints. "They're footprints, but..."

"Moccasins," Brady said.

Of course. The smooth, rounded shape. Soft leather moccasins. "An Indian?" he asked Brady.

The man shrugged. "Anybody can wear moccasins, white man."

"No kidding," Ben remarked, holding his own.

"*Could* be an Indian," Brady said levelly. "There's plenty around here who could do with some fresh meat. I wouldn't put it past some guys I know, in fact. The trouble is, whoever did this only took the heads and left the meat. Now, there's no Indians I know of who're dumb enough to be *that* confused."

"You've got a point," Ben said in agreement.

"It doesn't make any sense," Julie said, frowning.

"Can you follow the footprints, Brady?" Ben asked.

"You been watching too many John Wayne movies, *kemo sabe*," Brady muttered.

Ben saw Julie smother a smile but, frankly, the bitterness he saw in Brady was hard to take. In fact, Ben thought, rubbing his stubbly chin, the so-called plight of the Indian was always difficult for him to swallow. Hell, the U.S. government had gone out of its way to educate the Indians, see to it that none of them starved or lacked land or brand-spanking-new vehicles if they wanted them. Laurie always got mad at him, though, for being a hard-nose. Her theory was that the Indian had only been conquered a hundred years ago, and it was going to take a whole lot longer than that for them to fit into the white man's society.

"If I had my way," Laurie always said, "I'd give them their land back. *All* of it."

She had a point, Ben grudgingly admitted, unrealistic though it was.

"I've only found three footprints," Brady was saying, "but the ground's real rocky here. Sorry." But he didn't sound sorry.

"Damn," Ben said. "It's a lead, though. The first one. Martians don't leave moccasin prints."

He went back to the Jeep, took a long drink of water from the canteen they'd brought along and looked around, thinking hard, trying to make connections, put the scraps of information together. Nothing made any sense.

"Okay," he said finally. "We're going to walk in circles around these sheep. We'll cover every square inch and see if there are any more footprints. Maybe somebody parked a vehicle somewhere around here and walked to this spot."

"Sure," Julie said, "I guess it won't hurt."

They must have looked ridiculous, the three of them, if anybody had been there to see them. Walking slowly, in ever-widening circles, side by side, eyes pinned on the ground.

"Yo, *kemo sabe*," Brady said softly, stopping.

There was another impression in a spot of loose soil, a clear mark of a foot in a soft moccasin.

"Look," Julie said, pointing.

There in front of her was a cluster of ants milling around a dark drop on the ground.

"Blood," Ben said.

The sun pressed down on them as they trudged in bigger and bigger circles. Ben marked each print they found with fluorescent orange tape. They led toward the base of Red Mesa, but about a hundred yards from the wall itself the footprints petered out in a jumble of fallen rock and scree.

"Damn," Ben said, kicking at a rock.

"That's it," Brady agreed. "It's too rocky from here on. He could have gone anywhere."

"Well, we found out *something*," Julie said. "It's human."

"What we found out was that someone walked here fairly recently," Ben said sharply. "There may be no connection at all between the footprints and the dead animals."

They walked back to the Jeep. Ben poured some cool water over his head, drank the precious stuff in long gulps.

"You should wear a hat," he heard her say.

"Maybe," he said, but his mind was a million miles away, whirling with possibilities and questions. "Is there an Indian pueblo around here?" he asked. "A town?"

She shook her head gravely. "There's government land to the west and the Navajo reservation, like I told you, but that's maybe sixty miles away. Nobody's going to walk that far, not carrying four sheep heads."

"There must be a road, somewhere to the north or south."

"It's real far. County road five to the south, and a dirt track about twenty miles north that leads into Farmington."

He slumped against the Jeep, frustrated. He felt drained and angry. Something wasn't right. Something, a piece to the puzzle was missing. He'd find it, though. Sooner or later he'd find the piece and it would click into place and the picture would be clear.

"Look," Julie said, then pointed.

There was the churning cloud of dust, the glint of something bright in the sun.

"Phillips," Ben growled, "that persistent little creep."

"Think he's found the Anasazi yet?" Brady asked dryly.

"Okay, let's wrap it up folks," Ben said, ignoring him. "There's nothing more here." And he swung himself into the Jeep.

The shadows of Red Mesa stretched toward them as they left the area, sharp-edged, precise shadows that covered the range behind them, covered the four dead sheep and the curious moccasin prints. Ben glanced in the rearview mirror and had to ask himself: What else were those darkening shadows hiding?

THAT EVENING after dinner Ben sat quietly sipping coffee, frowning. He hated to be in such a bad mood around Julie, but he'd had such high hopes of clearing up this decades-old desert mystery once and for all. He detested failure, and he'd been onto something. He knew it.

"I found my dad's hat," Julie said, "if you want it."

"Oh…thanks. It might be a good idea." He tried to drag his thoughts away from the dead sheep and the footprints. "Sorry, I guess I'm preoccupied."

She sat on the couch with him, at the far end, gingerly, as if she were ready to leap up and run if he made a move. Why was she so careful around him? He searched his brain. Had he done anything, given her any reason to be so nervous? Aside from a few errant thoughts, he'd done nothing. She couldn't read his mind, could she?

"Um, I wonder…well, maybe we should have looked around some more out there today. Walked along the base of the mesa or something." She cleared her throat and smiled tentatively. "I think you got a little bit hot and bothered out there, Ben. You're not used to it."

"Guess I'm just a city slicker, after all," he said wryly.

"We can go back tomorrow and look around again," she suggested carefully.

"Don't you have anything better to do than look for little green men?" he asked.

She shrugged, looked down at the coffee mug in her hands, one delicate-boned finger tracing an imaginary line on the cup. "Not in this drought. There's not much to do right now but wait."

"For rain."

"Yes, for rain."

She was right. He didn't have to give up. He'd send this latest batch of samples off to Holloman and go back out there tomorrow. That person, that mysterious man who'd killed the sheep and then walked lightly, hardly leaving a sign over the hard stony ground, carrying their heads—had gone somewhere. Ben was being childish, brooding. Laurie would have said he was acting like a jerk, and she would have been right.

"Sorry for my mood," he said. "I get a little carried away sometimes."

"We all do, sometimes," she replied.

Her head was bent over her coffee. Her shiny, dark blond hair fell forward, hiding her face but exposing the pale white column of her neck. He was struck by an overpowering urge to run a finger along that fragile column.

"Well," Julie said, rising, "I better finish the dinner dishes."

He started to push himself up. "Here, I'll help."

But she was having none of it. "That's okay, I'll get them."

And then something inside him gave. "You do that every time," he said, not even aware of the accusing tone of his voice.

Julie turned abruptly. "I do what?"

"Refuse anyone's help. No, not just anyone's, *my* help." He hadn't the slightest idea where his anger had sprung from. He knew only that he was mad and that there was a hardening in his groin and that somehow the two were connected.

Julie had gone to the sink despite his outburst. She was

shrugging, dismissing him. He'd be damned if he understood women.

"Didn't you hear me?" He strode toward the kitchen, toward that stiff back.

"They're only dishes," she said, "what's the big deal? I can do them my—"

But he didn't give her a chance to finish. He exploded inside, never considering the ramifications, certainly not considering Julie's feelings, and took her roughly by the shoulders, spinning her around, crushing her lips to his.

Julie hung in his hard embrace as if she were too shocked to move. And all the while he kissed her thoroughly, his lips softening against hers when he realized she wasn't fighting him, his arms going around her back, pressing her to him, to his hardness as if he had every right, as if she wanted him to do so. He felt his breath mingling with hers and drank in the honey-sweet scent of her skin. The ache in his groin became a steady, persistent pain.

As abruptly as the passion had ignited within, it was suddenly over. Julie pulled away, breaking the connection, her expression turning from surprise and confusion to a defensive scowl.

He felt as if he'd been slapped. And then she said, "I think you better go now," and stood there with her hands on her hips, staring at him coolly.

He should have felt like a fool, or at least been the tiniest bit sorry, but instead that coil of anger in his gut grew hot all over again.

He'd be damned if he was going to apologize. She'd dismissed him at every turn, spurned his offers to help, barely even talked to him half the time. She'd needed that kiss, that show of force; she'd asked for it.

"Please go," Julie said again.

Ben shrugged, unaware of the faint smile on his lips, then walked across the old linoleum floor and pushed open the screen door. It gave its usual protesting squeak as he let it close with just the right bang behind him.

The night air was cool, caressing his hot face. The stars hung in the sky, and the moon rose full and silver, a round face looking down at him and chuckling at his human frailty. He walked a few steps toward the bunkhouse then stopped, turned and looked back at the low adobe house. There was a light on in her bedroom window.

The anger drained from him finally, and in its place came a chilling realization. What an arrogant, macho creep she must think him. And she was right. He'd sensed all along that Julie was somehow intimidated by men, and he'd sure reinforced that notion, hadn't he?

What, Ben wondered, would have happened had she *not* stopped him? But he steeled himself and told himself that it didn't matter. Nothing had happened. It was just as well, too, because he didn't need the hassles of romance in his life. Neither did she. They barely knew each other. All that had happened was a little flare-up of desire—a man and a woman thrown into proximity.

He began to stride toward the bunkhouse and wondered what she was thinking at that moment. She was a paradox, all right, a seething mass of contradictions, gentle and warm one minute, frightened and independent the next. And God knew what else.

He thought about Carol then. She'd been simpler, easier to read, straightforward. They'd had a rare understanding—except about his flying. Carol had always been terrified that he'd crash in one of those souped-up experimental jets he'd tested. Ironic, wasn't it, that Carol had died first. He thought of Laurie and how well she'd turned out. She was a good person, a beautiful person, and he felt real happy about that. But still, there were those occasional times when his memories were not enough, when he felt lonely for the simple touch of a woman's hand.

He thought about Julie again. She must be lonely at times, too, out here all by herself.

Unwanted regret filled him as he rubbed the whiskers on his jaw, opened the door to the bunkhouse and entered quietly.

CHAPTER SIX

COYOTE RAN IN CIRCLES around the remains of the four sheep, whining, his massive yellow neck quivering, his nose to the ground.

"Useless mutt," Brady grumbled.

The three of them watched the excited dog while he headed straight toward the base of Red Mesa. He circled, his bushy tail visible like a periscope above a rock pile, circled again and kept going.

"He's following a scent," Julie said. "Do you think…"

"Probably after a rabbit," Brady said.

"I wonder," Ben replied slowly.

"I think we should follow him," Julie said. "It can't hurt."

Ben shrugged, Brady rolled his eyes in derision, but Julie ignored their skepticism. She knew her dog. He might be an oafish mutt, but it was no rabbit he was after.

She was a few hundred yards along, following the dog, when she heard Ben calling to her to wait up. Both he and Brady were coming, both carrying their own canteens.

"I'm glad to see you decided to come along," she said flippantly. "I'd hate to solve the mystery and spoil your record."

Ben looked at her, his eyes shadowed under Bud's old hat, and shook his head. "We figured you shouldn't go off alone in this country."

She snorted. Brady wasn't worried about her. *He* knew she could take care of herself, so Ben was the gallant one. Well, he sure hadn't been gallant last night when he'd kissed her.

The memory of being crushed to Ben came rushing back

like a flash flood. She felt herself grow hot all over, and her skin prickled beneath her shirt. It had happened so suddenly, his unaccountable anger flaring up at her. And it *had* been rage on his face. Why, then, had he kissed her?

Ben was directly behind her, his big shadow falling on her shoulders. She was acutely aware of his nearness and could almost feel his warm breath on her neck. She had to forget him, forget that he'd been rock-hard against her. For godsakes, she had to forget that for a brief moment she'd given in to him, melting in those strong arms. *Forget it,* she told herself staunchly. *It never happened.*

The ground was rough, and the heat was sapping her, but she followed Coyote's waving yellow tail as he bounced ahead of her with unflagging energy. She let her mind go blank, forcing all thoughts aside as she followed the dog.

Eventually Ben took the lead. She allowed herself to feel relief, because he could no longer watch the stiff set of her shoulders or see how affected she was by his closeness. And then he stopped, several paces ahead of her. He was panting, standing there on the hard-baked earth with his hands on his hips, looking around. "Where'd that damn dog go?" he asked, breathing hard.

"Coyote," Julie called, "come!" Then she put two fingers to her lips and whistled. "Coyote!"

"Dog's probably lost," came Brady's voice from behind her.

Julie ignored him. "Come, Coyote! Here, boy!"

"He can't just have disappeared," Ben said, frowning, scratching his whiskered jaw as he studied the rampart of crumbling rock in front of them.

"Wouldn't think so," Brady said.

"Coyote!" Julie tried again impatiently, when suddenly he appeared twenty yards away from them, as if he'd emerged from the rock itself.

"Well, I'll be," Ben said.

It was Julie who was first to move. "It's gotta be a cave,

or something," she said, heading off toward Coyote. "We just can't see from here."

It was no cave. What they'd been looking at was an optical illusion. Directly behind a vertical bulge of rock was a cut into the wall itself, a narrow, weed-choked defile. Viewed from straight on, the cut was invisible, but once the three of them stood off the side, there it was, clear as day, a narrow fissure winding steeply up into the mesa wall. Coyote wagged his tail, barked, and took off up the path.

"Oh, man," Brady said, "I suppose we're going to climb *that*."

Julie shot him a look. "Stay here. I don't care. *I'm* going to see where it leads."

In the end all three of them began the climb. Coyote appeared high above them from time to time, then disappeared again, showing them that the trail—or whatever they were following—continued. It was rough going. The loose red rock kept sliding out from under their feet, causing dust and pebble avalanches behind them. Eventually Brady took the lead, mumbling something about clumsy White Eyes who ought to stay at home.

But Brady hadn't gone more than a few yards before he stopped and reached out to touch the rock wall that rose close beside the path. "Well, now," Julie heard him say, and when she caught up to him she could see why.

There was a smear on the rock, a dark stain. "Blood," she breathed.

Ben was at her shoulder. "Fresh, too," he said.

Brady had already gone on, making his way carefully along the boulder-strewn path. Shadows bathed the bottom of the narrow, steep-sided ravine in a pale violet light, and it was utterly quiet except for the rattle of dislodged stones under their feet.

"I never knew this was here," Julie said in wonderment, half to herself.

The end of the twisting trail came suddenly. One moment they were in dimness, swallowed by solid rock, and the next they stood in the open at the top of a descending scree field in strangely muted sunlight that made them all squint and shade their eyes.

Below them lay a valley, a long meandering valley that stretched as far as they could see, trailing off into a kind of blurry haze. The sky was white, subtle, as if obscured by mist.

"What—" began Brady and fell silent.

"Wow," was all Julie could get out.

Ben raised the binoculars he carried around his neck. "Amazing," he said, scanning the mile-wide valley, back and forth, again and again. "Amazing."

On either side of them the red striated walls of the mesa seemed to march away, rising precipitously for a good two thousand feet. And there below, on the floor of the valley, was an uneven line of cottonwood trees that also retreated from them, disappearing into the curving sweep of the clouded distance. A stream bed, Julie thought, feeding the arid land. Remarkable.

The three of them stood in silence for a time, still breathless, dumbstruck by this hidden and spectacular valley. It was finally Ben who spoke, shattering the awe they all felt.

He handed the binoculars to Julie. "Pretty valley."

"Strange. Brady—" she turned to him "—you remember a few years ago when there was a big forest fire near Flagstaff, Arizona, and the wind blew the smoke over New Mexico? Everything was hazy like this."

"Yeah, I remember."

"Is there a forest fire somewhere right now?"

"Beats me," Brady said.

"There must be," Ben put in.

"But why's the smoke only here in *this* valley?" she asked.

Ben shrugged. "An inversion, a walled-in valley. Simple."

"I guess." Julie shook off her doubts. "Well, do we go on or head back? It's your call, Ben." She lowered the glasses and met his eyes.

"We go on," he said. "Or at least I'll go on. You two can head back if you want. I'll meet up with you later."

"I better go or *kemo sabe* here will get lost," Brady declared.

Julie shrugged. "It's still early. I guess we ought to explore some more. Never know, we might just run into whoever killed my sheep. I wouldn't mind that." She caught Ben's gaze on her then, but before she could read his expression, he masked it with one of interest in the task at hand.

"You never know," he said.

Coyote found a path that led down the scree and onto the floor of the valley. It was a strange land they'd stumbled across, entirely different from the other side of the mountain, which was drier, more open, and cut into a crazy quilt of erosion. This side, this hidden place, was dotted with piñon and stunted juniper trees. As they descended they could see areas of shallow arroyos and those ever-present strange rock formation that jutted out of the cracked earth along the base of the red mesa walls, but the center of the valley, where the line of cottonwoods grew loftily, was gentler, more forgiving, green and softly misted by distance.

They made the streambed in an hour's time and stopped to rest. Coyote drank thirstily from the trickling water, planting his big yellow paws in the muddy bank, while Julie, Ben and Brady refilled the canteen and drank from it.

Julie glanced at Ben. "I wonder," she said, "if we should be drinking this water."

"We don't have much choice," he said, amused, raising the canteen to his mouth.

"We may be sorry," Julie said under her breath, and then noticed that Brady had moved on down the stream and was bent over, apparently studying something.

"What is it?" Ben came alongside her, but Julie only raised her shoulders. Then he, too, squatted down. "Is it another footprint?" he asked.

Brady shook his head slowly in puzzlement, then said something in Hopi. Finally he rose, eyes still glued on the print in the sand and let out a breath.

"Brady," Julie said, "don't be weird. What's with the footprint, anyway?"

He shrugged, as if shaking free of an unseen force. "It's nothing," he finally said, "just darn strange moccasins this dude was wearing, that's all." Then he laughed, but it wasn't an amused sound. Julie tilted her head, giving Ben an I-don't-know look.

But Brady was still searching the ground.

"Come on," Ben said impatiently.

"There're no more footprints," Brady said, his voice carefully neutral.

"So? The ground got hard or he stepped onto a grassy spot."

"No, the ground's soft, and he had to step somewhere right here. Unless he sprouted wings and flew," Brady said noncommittally.

Ben made a derisive sound and went to where Brady was standing. Julie saw him look, study the spot, walk around with his hands on his hips and scratch his jaw. "It got rubbed out, that's all," he finally said. "Let's go, Brady."

"Okay, *kemo sabe*," Brady said. "I'm sure you're right. Dude probably dragged a leafy branch behind him to cover his tracks. Hey, I've seen it in a million movies." And he turned and led the way downstream.

It was an easier hike along the floor of the valley, and the three of them, with Coyote ever in the lead, made good time as they walked deeper and deeper into this unfamiliar place. Julie was aware of Ben behind her now, as he would take her elbow from time to time and help her across a rock, over dead wood or around a clawing bunch of brush. He was only being polite, though. In reality he was unreachable, too caught up in his quest to notice his surroundings, to notice *her*. That was it, of course. And finally she couldn't help admitting the truth to herself. It stung that he'd touched her intimately last night and was totally ignoring her today. He was just another Mark, after all, wasn't he? Smarter, more together, but in the end exactly the same.

They rounded a bend in the stream, and Brady stopped short. "Look," he said, pointing.

There was a tall, crooked stick planted in the ground with stones piled at its base. Tied to the top of it was a bundle of wooden sticks, each decorated with colors and clusters of feathers that fluttered lazily in the hot breeze.

"Prayer sticks," Brady murmured.

Someone lived here then. Someone. She was sure Ben was going to say something sarcastic, but he didn't. He didn't say a word.

Brady continued to lead the way, moving along at a good clip, as if he were in a hurry to get somewhere. Sure, Julie thought, it was exciting, this discovery of such a huge valley, but what was the rush? She doubted he was trying to catch up with whomever had killed her animals. No, it was something else.

They stopped finally when Julie protested that there was a stone in her shoe. But even then Brady moved away from them, distancing himself, climbed a boulder and stood there, stoically staring off into the shrouded distance.

"What's with him?" Ben asked quietly.

"Got me," was all she said but, in truth, Brady's behavior was puzzling.

They refilled the canteens and sat for a minute, gazing around, craning their necks up toward the steep red walls that enclosed them. Julie took the binoculars and scanned the mesa.

"I still can hardly believe this valley's here. I wonder if Bud—my dad—knew about it," she said.

"Maybe," Ben offered. "It's hard to believe someone hasn't found that cut before. Of course," he said, "if we had a good topographical map along, we could probably pinpoint it."

"You're right, I'm sure," she said. "Or we might at least be able to see where it comes out. There's got to be a road or something up ahead. You know, another way in." She handed the glasses to Ben. "Brady," she called, looking in his direction, "what do you think? Should we try to find the entrance on up ahead? Brady?"

But he never answered.

Silence seemed to wrap them in an odd embrace then. Why weren't the birds chirping, the squirrels chattering up a storm? If was funny, Julie mused as she sat there resting, but she was so used to the sounds of the wilderness that she'd taken them for granted. And now, well, now she couldn't recall if there had been any sound at all in this peculiar place.

Ben was studying his surroundings keenly with the binoculars. She turned and was about to ask him if he'd noticed the lack of noise, but then she felt ridiculous. It was only the heat of the day; the animals were resting, that was all. She was being silly.

He seemed to sense her gaze on him and lowered the glasses. His eyes met hers for a moment before she glanced down at the streambed. "Look," he said, "it's a couple hours walk back out to the Jeep. I know you've got to be tired."

"I'm okay."

"Seriously," he said, "we don't know what lies ahead. We could come back tomorrow, bring some provisions and my gear, really explore this place from top to bottom." He was still watching her intently.

"I said I'm okay," Julie repeated, wondering at his sudden concern. "I'm just as curious as you are. I want to find out who killed my animals."

"We could find out tomorrow."

Julie shook her head. "I'd rather find out today."

They hiked on. Julie realized that the sun was beginning to move from its midday position, taking that hot lazy arc into the afternoon, and they *had* come miles already. Still, if they could find that man's path again, the guy with the moccasins who'd killed her valuable stock, it was worth every blistering step of the way.

By now they were all sweating. It was an odd heat, almost a humid one, which was amazing considering the dry spell, not to mention the fact that there was practically no humidity in the Southwest, especially in the summer. She glanced at the sun. It wasn't that typical blazing yellow orb of the desert sky. Not here. Instead it was a dull orange, hazy, no doubt from the fires that must have been burning in the west. She wished she had on shorts, something other than her jeans, but dreaming of cool cotton clothing wasn't going to help. She stopped often, splashing water on her face and neck, down the throat of her shirt. God, but it felt good.

Ben, too, soaked his head once in the cool trickling water and came up with a sigh. She found herself sitting on a rock staring unabashedly at him. No matter how much she hated to admit it, he *was* handsome. His dark hair was going every which way, half falling over a brow, curling around his ears, sticking up over his collar. He had a boyishly masculine look, a young look despite the sprinkling of gray that showed at his temples. And in his position, supporting himself with his arms over the water, she could see his long, tapered muscles straining at his T-shirt. He came up to rest on his haunches then but was still trading gazes with her, those blue eyes of his glinting with light reflected from the water.

She couldn't snatch her glance away, wouldn't be the first to do it. She'd show him that some good-looking man wasn't going to come into her life again and disrupt it.

Julie gave Ben an unmistakable look. It said, *You're nothing to me, mister. And neither was that kiss you laid on me.* She held his eyes for what seemed an eternity. If he didn't get it now, he never would.

It was Brady's voice that finally ended the moment. "Miss Julie," she heard, "Miss Julie." And she tore herself away from Ben Tanner and saw Brady, a few yards ahead. She was aware then of a strange inflection in his voice, an urgency. "Come here," he was calling, "come and take a look." He turned on his heel and pointed. "There. Look."

She followed the path of his hand into the hazy distance, up toward the side of the mesa. At first she didn't see, but then, yes, there was something there, some sort of…structure. Julie reached for the binoculars that Ben still held, then lifted them to her eyes. At first she couldn't quite believe what she was seeing. She refocused, blinking, settling her vision on the distant mesa. *It is,* she thought, wonder ringing through her like a bell. *It's really there.*

Quickly she handed the glasses to Ben and pointed silently, unable to voice her astonishment. He'd just have to see for himself.

"Wow," Ben said after a long, still moment. She could see him refocus just to be sure. "Holy…"

It was true then. He'd seen it, too. He handed back the binoculars, and she just had to look again. She lifted them. Yes, there it was, a miraculous structure built right into an overhanging wall of the dry red mesa, a jumble of geometric shapes that stood out clearly against the blurry red walls as if an artist had painted the scene then deliberately washed out the background. It was certainly a ruin, a cliff house—no, more, a palace, she thought, a big, beautiful palace!

"I *can't* believe it," Julie whispered, awed. "It's a cliff house, a real cliff house! We've discovered an Anasazi ruin!"

Ben took a breath. "You *sure* this isn't an already-discovered ruin? I mean…"

Julie spun around. She was unable to contain her excitement. "No way!" she breathed. "There're lots of them all over this corner of New Mexico, but none *here*. I mean, this is as huge as the one in Mesa Verde. Honestly, Ben, we'd know about this one. There'd be hot dog stands and super-highways—all that stuff!"

"I don't…"

"Oh, come on," Julie said, bubbling over, "let's go on. You'll see. I can't *believe* this!"

She turned back toward the cliff house but suddenly paused. There was Brady just standing there, rooted to the earth. What *was* the matter with him? "Brady, let's go," she said, still high as a kite. "Come on, don't you know what we've found? Where's your sense of adventure? Come on."

But he wouldn't move. Not even a muscle ticked in his jaw.

What was going on? Brady, the cynic, hadn't even one sarcastic remark? "Brady," she said, coming up behind him, "come on. Let's at least go take a look at the ruin."

After a long moment he finally moved, but it was only a slow, controlled twist of his head. His eyes, when they met hers, seemed to probe deeply into her brain, as if he were trying to tell her something, trying to warn her. "Miss Julie," he said in a hoarse whisper, in dead earnest, "it's Anasazi all right, but it's no ruin."

CHAPTER SEVEN

"NOW THERE'S a rational statement if I ever heard one," Ben said sarcastically.

But Brady had turned away, a closed expression on his face, and was continuing along the stream. Julie caught the look in Ben's eyes. It was one of pure arrogance. "I know better than you," it said. "I'm the expert here."

What was *with* those two? Ben followed Brady with his unyielding gaze then took a long swig from the canteen and handed it to her, while Coyote lapped noisily at the trickle in the rocky streambed. "So," he said, watching Julie drink, "do we follow Brady or head back now? It's going to be a long hike to that cliff house."

"I can handle it," she replied, wiping her mouth, "but are you sure *you* can?"

She'd expected some quick retort from him, some tough-guy comeback, but instead, surprisingly, he smiled at her knowingly. He wasn't going to take the bait.

They were heading west, as closely as Julie could figure. She kept glancing up at the distant cliff house as they approached it. She supposed she could have been wrong. Maybe it was a ruin that was already on the maps, an obscure one that few people visited. There was probably a road leading out of this valley farther on. And that was how the person who'd killed her horse and sheep had gotten to them. The only question left to answer was why.

"What's the nearest town on this side of Red Mesa?" Ben asked.

"Let's see. Shiprock, or maybe Sheep Springs. They're on the Navajo reservation."

"I wonder who lives here in this valley," Ben mused aloud.

"Maybe a Navajo clan," Julie said.

"*Somebody* is here," he replied, sounding awfully sure of himself.

It was still too quiet, Julie thought. Studiously quiet, as if the valley were holding its breath in the midday heat. There was an odd lack in this hidden place, something missing, as if nature withheld one of its elements from them.

She glanced at Ben, wanting to share her thoughts, but his expression was pensive. He appeared to be sorting data in his mind, computerlike. She shrugged, continuing on, trailing Brady, gazing at the distant cliff house that seemed oddly like a part of an unfinished portrait—too still, too perfect. What had Brady meant when he'd said it was no ruin?

With Coyote crisscrossing the streambed, nose to the ground, the three of them trudged forward, deeper and deeper into the valley, that inexplicable haze swallowing them. She glanced behind them in the direction from which they'd come and she could see nothing but purple haze. An eerie and persistent feeling began to haunt her that nothing here was quite as it should be. Still the trees and brush and rocks were normal. The cottonwoods lining the stream drooped dispiritedly but normally over the water. The high walls of the mesa were normal. Even the cliff house was perfectly ordinary, at least in this part of the country it was. And yet...

She kept expecting to come across a dirt road, or at least tire tracks, a sign fallen to the parched ground, a weathered fence post draped with rusty barbed wire, a bridge over the stream, some sheep droppings, a splintery telephone pole—anything.

But there was nothing like that, not a solitary sign of civilization at all.

After a time Ben stopped and wiped his forehead and neck with his bandanna. Julie took another drink from the canteen and then wiped her brow, too. Sweat trickled down between her breasts, dampening her bra. She turned away from Ben, pulled at the V on her shirt and blew cool air down her front. "It's hotter today," she said. "Isn't it *ever* going to rain?"

"Sure you don't want to stop and rest?" Ben asked, and she was positive there was a note of real concern in his voice.

Questioningly Julie looked at Brady, who was moving away from them, his eyes to the ground, intent on whatever he saw there. "No, thanks, I'm fine. Let's catch up to Brady."

But she wasn't exactly fine. She was starting to get a disquieting sensation in the pit of her stomach. All her instincts screamed at her that something was wrong.

What? The water trickled in the streambed, Coyote's tongue lolled out, the cottonwood leaves trembled in a hot breeze, the sky arced overhead, white with the smoke haze.

Maybe it was just the fact that it was going to take them so darn long to walk out to the Jeep. It would be dark. They had no food, and she was beginning to get hungry. Maybe they really should turn back now and come again tomorrow better prepared, with food and camping gear.

And then there was Hank. Oh sure, she or Brady had left overnight without informing him of their exact plans before, but she was worried about leaving him at the ranch alone for so long with both of them gone. He'd probably drive into Trading Post and have a few too many beers and get into trouble with Ken Lamont again. And if Hank got into too much trouble, Ken might just make good his threat to put the young man behind bars.

That was it, Julie decided, that was why she was feeling so uneasy, it was Hank. He'd been at the back of her mind all along. Maybe she'd better talk to Brady about it. But when she looked at him some distance ahead, there was something indefinable that kept her words bottled up inside her, so she and Ben and Brady kept walking deeper still into this uncanny place. And as she walked she felt, silly as it seemed, as if her ties to the outside world, the *real* world, were being cut off with each step she took.

"What time is it?" she finally asked Ben.

He looked at his watch, looked again as if confused, then tapped it with a finger. "Damn thing. It still says noon. My battery must have given out. I'd have sworn I just had it changed."

"It's long past noon," she said, "or at least I think it is."

"More like three or so." He tapped the crystal again and furrowed his brow.

"We've come a long ways," Julie said. But what she *wanted* to tell him was that they ought to turn back, but then Ben would think she was weak, and somehow Julie was afraid to give him that edge. Why was she feeling such sharp competition with him? What would happen, she wondered, if she did admit she was tired and hot and hungry? Was he going to take advantage of that? She turned and caught him looking at her with those appraising blue eyes of his. She straightened her back, deciding she'd go on, then glanced away.

Brady had stopped and was staring up at the cliff house, a hand shading his eyes. She and Ben caught up to him and they all stood there gazing up at the city wedged into an overhang in the rock face.

The sun had dipped in the afternoon sky and threw an ancient golden light on the hundreds of cubelike rooms that were piled one upon the other in orderly ranks. The same sun, thought Julie, that was the giver of life to all the Southwest Indians, the entity that had been and still was the focal point of so many of the mystical ceremonies of the Hopi, the Tewa, the Zuni, the Pueblo tribes. The huge structure was bathed in that peculiar gilded light, but the black empty windows of the aged pueblo stared out across the valley like blind eyes. A chill gripped Julie despite the heat, and she felt Coyote pressed hard against her leg as if he, too, needed reassurance.

"That's quite a sight," Ben was saying, "quite a sight." Then unaccountably his voice seemed to fade and for a few moments Julie felt as if she'd been instantly transported through space to another time, another era, long, long ago. The heat of the day enshrouded her as if she were being wrapped in warm, soft blankets. It was centuries ago. The land was alive, vibrantly so, the Ancient Ones milling about in this old time, brushing past her and disappearing into the hot, quiet shadows of afternoon. She took a quavering breath, afraid yet not afraid, as faces from the distant past seemed to float before her eyes. She could see those ancient people standing by the stream, kneeling and grinding their corn. She could smell the sweat from their flesh, feel their fires, look into their black fathomless eyes. She could even hear the far-off, muted sound of drums, pounding in exotic rhythm, pounding with a message, pounding...

"Hey" came a voice at her ear, "Julie. You all right? Julie?"

It was Ben's voice. She drew in a ragged breath and struggled back through the years. There was Ben, sure, and Coyote practically pushing her over. Up ahead was Brady.

"I knew we should have stopped and rested," Ben said. "You're ready to drop in this heat."

"I'm all right now," Julie managed to say. It was over. That bizarre unearthly experience had passed and was gone. "Honest," she said, "I'm okay." She wondered then if she could tell Ben what had just happened. Would he scoff and laugh?

"Did you hear anything just then?" she ventured. "Sort of a hollow booming?"

He looked at her strangely. "The wind came along, a few gusts. Why?"

"Oh, nothing. I just thought...well, never mind, let's keep going."

But Brady was staring at her and for a brief moment his eyes pinioned hers, the same black fathomless eyes she'd just seen in her fantasy. She blinked. It was just Brady. "Let's go," she said staunchly. "We've come too far to quit now."

"Whatever you say," Ben said, giving her a slight bow of his head. "Lead the way."

Brady had already started walking again. Was it Julie's imagination or had he dropped his usual shambling gait to move more quietly, tirelessly, his shoulders square and erect. Did she really know Brady at all? she wondered in momentary panic.

She started on, Coyote walking very closely at her side. The hairs on his back bristled. She looked around, but there was nothing to disturb him, nothing but dust and rabbitbrush and tired cottonwood trees under the towering red rock walls enclosing them. She had to force herself to remember that she was merely walking in a place she'd never been before, that the cliff house, like thousands of similar ruins, had been abandoned for over six hundred years. The Ancient Ones were dead, gone, vanished.

The sun sank lower, the valley floor and the cliff dwellings abruptly cast in deep shadow as the cliffs cut off the sun. Now the pueblo appeared entirely different, not so empty and innocent, but dark and forbidding. Coyote growled deeply in his throat. The air itself had become heavy, close, holding a warning. "Turn back," it said. Somehow Julie expected to see the sky darken and storm clouds boil up, and she was positive she heard distant thunder—or was it drums? But the dome above them was still perfectly cloudless.

It must have been five o'clock, maybe later, Julie guessed, yet time had lost its meaning. She glanced up at the cliff house every so often, and once it seemed to have grown more distant, while another time it practically loomed over them. It was the murky air, she decided, and the awful, unearthly heat that was distorting everything, muddling her thoughts, confusing her.

Julie wasn't certain when she first saw it. All she knew was that she'd looked up once more toward the darkening cliff house and there it was, a wisp of smoke, lifting from the ancient pueblo, a question mark on the still air. She froze, frightened more by her instant acceptance of the significance of that rising smoke than by anything else.

Ben had seen it, too, and was staring up silently at the steep cliff, as well.

"My God," Julie whispered, "that smoke..."

She could feel Ben standing close, directly behind her, and then heard his low laugh. "Look," he said, his tone rational, cocksure, "you're making too much of it, Julie. I'd bet you anything that someone's living in this valley, the person who killed your animals, and he's just using the old cliff house as a hideout. Who knows, there could even be an isolated tribe of Navajo or Pueblo Indians living here."

"I guess..." Julie began doubtfully.

"I don't know," Brady interrupted, speaking for the first time in hours. "I think you may be in for a surprise."

He was going to say something else, but Coyote started barking just then, barking furiously, and Julie's heart gave a startled leap. Then the bushes around them seemed to rustle and shiver and split apart, and suddenly they were staring into the faces of six Indians in full hunting gear, brandishing six wooden lances at their throats.

WHEN JULIE'S HEARTBEAT finally slowed, she became cognizant of Ben, who was holding Coyote's collar, yelling, "No! Stay, boy," and of Brady standing there stock-still, his mouth open in mute shock. And all the while those six Indians stared back at them, as unmoving as they were, their lances still pointed menacingly in their direction.

It was Ben who took command of the crazy situation. "Okay, guys," he said to the Indians while he restrained the dog, "joke's over. You can put those spears down."

They did nothing, only stood there like statues, their young, sun-bronzed faces expressionless, those sharp-tipped lances still pointed straight at the three of them. The only thing Julie could see that made the strangers at all human was the trickle of sweat running down the temple of one of them. Inanely she wondered why he didn't wipe it away.

It was Brady who finally moved, stepping forward slightly, eyeing them in fascination. He cleared his throat. "Do you speak English?" he tried, and Julie noticed a break in his voice. *Of course they speak English,* she thought. Brady was just overcome by his surprise at finding them here.

But not a one of them moved a muscle, not even a quiver of an eyelid.

And then Ben tried. "Come on, boys, give us a break. It's been a long day."

"They don't speak English," Brady said with a singular certainty.

"So, try Spanish," Ben put in, and he shook his head, smiling, obviously taking this as some big joke.

Brady tried and failed. Then he spoke in an Indian dialect with which Julie was not familiar—Hopi? Navajo?

"Tell them to put down those lances," she said, finding her voice. "This isn't funny."

"I'm *trying*," Brady replied.

"I've got an idea," Ben said, his tone dripping sarcasm. "Tell them we're friends."

"Ben," Julie admonished, "cut it out. For godsakes, can't you see this is no joke?"

"Frankly..." he began, then shut up.

Brady kept trying, obviously using bits and pieces of many local Indian dialects. Finally Julie saw one of the mens' eyes flicker, and Brady seemed to relax, trying more of the unfamiliar dialect, searching for words in a language he hadn't used in years, repeating phrases over and over, pointing, making signs with his hands.

It was all too crazy. Here they were, Julie thought, in the middle of New Mexico, for Lord's sake, trying to communicate with these men as if they were beings from another planet. She wanted to laugh, she *would* have laughed, except every time she looked at Brady the humor of the situation drained right out of her. Brady, who saw the world as one big bad joke, was not in the least amused. He was taking this absolutely seriously. And Brady, for all his faults, was not a fool.

Brady tried to communicate with the men for some time in a kind of guttural dialect of Hopi. Often he used sign language. Sometimes the Indians appeared to understand him. At other times they grunted among themselves as if in distrust.

"Tell them we're friends," Julie said, nodding to Brady.

"I did."

"Tell them *again*," she said. "And to please put down those weapons."

She heard Ben sigh. "Look," he said, stepping forward, handing Coyote over to her, "it's getting late. I don't know what their problem is, but either they march us to their village and put us in a big boiling pot, or they can damn well take us somewhere and feed us, and we can clear up this whole mess."

Brady turned to him. His expression was devoid of humor. "They'd probably *like* to boil you. Maybe stake you out in the sun, *kemo sabe*."

"As long as they feed me first," Ben replied dryly.

"Stop it," Julie said, "both of you. This is serious." She looked at Brady in earnest. "What is it, some kind of ceremony we've stumbled onto? I mean, is it a private thing? We can go..."

But Brady shook his head. "It's no ceremony, Miss Julie." He gave a short strained laugh. "Maybe I'm not getting this right, but they say...at least they're using an old word for...Anasazi."

"Oh, right," Ben said.

"I mean it," Brady replied. "They're telling me they're Anasazi."

"And I'm a Martian."

But Julie wasn't listening. Instead she was thinking what a mad charade they'd come across. She stared at the men through wide eyes. Anasazi. Certainly they were kidding. She stared at them more intently. They were smallish, five feet five or so, well built, and sported long hair braided with feathers and leather strips. But their clothes...they wore honest-to-goodness breechcloths of tanned leather, hide moccasins—*moccasins!*—and turquoise jewelry on leather thongs. They sure looked like real, old-fashioned Indians, all right. But then that just couldn't be now, could it?

At some point Brady must have finally gotten it through to

them that they were friends, because the Indians lowered their weapons as they continued to converse in short, barely comprehensible phrases with Brady.

"This is incredible," Julie said, turning to Ben, but he'd sat down on a rock, knees splayed, looking somewhere between bored and impatient. "That's what gets me about you," Julie said coolly. "You think you've got it all figured out. Well, Ben Tanner, I have a feeling you're *not* going to find this one so easy to explain."

He held her eyes for a long moment, his handsome, sunburned face utterly closed to her. "We'll see, won't we," he said in a slow, lazy voice, and she knew at that instant that somehow, for some inexplicable reason she'd accepted with a certitude that shocked her even while her mind fought for equilibrium, that these men were truly Anasazi.

Ben moved his gaze from Julie's face to Brady. "Okay," he said, rising, "we came here to find out who's messing with Julie's livestock. I don't care if these boys here are men from the moon, let's just get on with it. If they live nearby, tell them we want to see their village, talk to someone in charge. Can you handle that, Brady?"

"You want to go to their village?" Brady asked, then grinned. "Okay, *kemo sabe*." He swiveled his head slowly and meaningfully, then craned his neck upward toward the cliff house. "I just hope you can climb."

Three of the Indians led, and three followed cautiously, as they all made their way to the base of the cliff. Julie felt their distrust as if it were a living entity, their distrust and, strangely, a fear of the three strangers who'd invaded their valley. She kept fighting for balance, for some kind of tie to reality, yet everything was elusive that sticky hot afternoon. And she *was* hot, and dusty and hungry, but she hardly felt the discomfort. Ever since she'd come into this strange, secret place, she'd been unable to shake the feeling of displacement, as if she were Alice in Wonderland, and at every turn there was a new, utterly strange discovery to be made. Discoveries that couldn't be true but were right there in front of her eyes.

It was disturbing to accept the evidence of her senses when her mind had been trained that such evidence couldn't exist—disturbing but a little exciting and intriguing, too.

Alice in Wonderland.

"Do you think Brady's gone off the deep end?" Ben asked as they followed the Indians.

"No," she said.

"You believe these are really Anasazi Indians?" he asked, not trying to hide his incredulity.

"I don't know. They're something, something different, Ben. Can't you see that?"

"There's some explanation," he said. "Come on, Julie, wake up. This isn't a fairyland. It's reality. The Anasazi are gone. Period. They disappeared two hundred years before Columbus discovered America."

They reached the bottom of the cliff. Julie craned her head up to the pueblo, and she could see people up there, hear voices, smell the smoke of their fires. And the drumming started again, hollow and low and rhythmical, coming from up above. She saw Ben shoot a look upward; this time he heard it, too. Was it a warning, a welcome or simply a way of communicating?

One of the Indians called out, and someone lowered ladders to the ground—heavy, sturdy ladders made of saplings tied together with leather straps. No nails, no rope, no sawed boards. Impossible, Julie thought, but there it was.

It must have been a hundred-yard climb up those ladders. Ben led, with Julie and Brady following, while Coyote was hauled up in a basket. She was afraid to look down, so she just kept watching Ben's boot heels. Every so often he'd stop and glance down at her, checking, throwing her a big white reassuring smile. And then at the top he was there, reaching to grasp her hands, pulling her up quickly and effortlessly, so that she was suddenly brought up against his chest.

"All right?" he asked, breathing hard from exertion. And when she nodded, breathless herself, he reached out and pushed her damp hair out of her eyes. His gesture was tender and gently caring, surprising her, confusing her.

"I'm fine," Julie managed to say, then stepped away from the intense discomfort she felt whenever he was too near. She imagined rather than saw his patronizing smile.

"So," Brady said, panting himself, "you want to see the medicine chief?" He shot Ben a hard look.

"Medicine chief?" Ben repeated.

"That's as well as I can translate it for you, *kemo sabe*. Take it or leave it."

"Please," Julie said, "let's bury the hatchet for the time being. No pun intended, either."

"Truce," Ben said to Brady.

"Okay, White Eyes, truce."

Julie looked around in amazement. They stood on a wide ledge of stone. Behind them, against the cliff, was a semicircular jumble of houses built of finely fitted sandstone blocks. Square windows and T-shaped doorways pierced the walls. The whole complex looked familiar to her because she'd seen the ruins at Mesa Verde and Chaco Canyon, and she'd seen a thousand photographs just like this in books about the Southwest. But this pueblo was different; this pueblo was alive, a living, breathing town, a place inhabited by real Indians. None of the walls were crumbling, none of the pottery shattered or the baskets torn. And everywhere there were people, the small brown Indians who lived in the pueblo. People. Real live people. She couldn't make her mind fit around the reality even as she saw a toddler run to his mother crying, scared by the bizarre strangers who'd appeared in his home.

A crowd gathered around them as their six companions talked and pointed at Brady. Brown faces stared, a little frightened, disbelieving and wary. But she noticed a very curious thing—the Indians were staring at Brady, only at Brady. It was as if she and Ben didn't exist. And, although she couldn't see who was playing them, all the while there was the boom of drums—a rhythm that was like the unseen heartbeat of the pueblo.

She stood stock-still, holding Coyote with one hand, and she felt Ben move closer to her. She had an irrepressible urge to reach out and hold his hand.

Then the throng parted and a man came toward them, a tall gaunt-faced man who was beginning to stoop with age. He had a distinct aura of dignity and power that struck Julie instantly.

"The medicine chief," she heard Ben say and, uncharacteristically, he wasn't in the least sarcastic.

The man made an impressive figure, wearing a wide, flat necklace of beads, a headdress of feathers and a face painted in stripes of black and white. He spoke and Brady answered as best he could, pointing and repeating phrases, gesturing.

"He's certainly got that air of authority," Ben said at her ear. "Impressive."

Julie nodded. "Oh, Ben," she said then, "look around you. It's so...so *real.*"

"So's a Hollywood movie set."

"Stop it. Can't you drop that hard-core macho stuff for one second?"

"If I have a reason to," Ben whispered, and grinned at her, his face so magnetic she wanted to run.

"You're an arrogant one, Tanner," she said. "But someday someone's going to bring you down off that high horse."

He looked at her for an unending moment, imprisoning her, then said, "Who? You, Julie?"

She felt her pulse quicken, and her skin tingled against the terrible hot air. She wanted to back away, but she couldn't; he'd know then. He'd know she was scared. "No, not me," she managed to say, "I'm not interested in that job." But there hadn't been true conviction in her voice. She glanced away, casually dismissing him, her heart beating far too quickly.

The medicine chief had stopped talking and was judging Brady with wise old eyes, sad and disturbingly knowing. He was not frightened by their arrival, not startled, not even skeptical. And he, too, seemed not to notice Julie or Ben. When his eyes turned in her direction they looked through her as if she were invisible. She shivered inadvertently.

Eventually he spoke as if giving orders to the crowd gathered around. It was so frustrating not to be able to talk, to communicate, to understand. What was he telling them?

She studied the people who listened to the elder so intently. Women, children, teenagers, filled the spaces in front of the stone houses, stood on flat rooftops, staring curiously, suspiciously, at Brady and ignoring her and Ben. The children had liquid black eyes and bangs across their foreheads, the women had jewelry of beads or polished stone and finely cured buckskin dresses that were fastened at one shoulder, leaving the other brown shoulder bare. They wore their hair coiled in thick buns over each ear like the butterfly style of traditional Hopi women. The men wore necklaces, too, and fringed breechcloths and hide moccasins. There was the scent of piñon smoke in the air and meat cooking.

"Okay," Brady said, turning to Julie and Ben. "I can't understand a lot of what he said, but this is the general gist of it. He calls himself Tayosha. He says that his people here in the valley are the only ones left. He says they are Anasazi, but he's using that other word. These people speak a real odd sort of dialect of Hopi. I can barely understand them, but a few words are similar." Brady pushed his hat back and rubbed his forehead with his wrist. He looked from Julie to Ben and back, and she could see he'd been profoundly affected by meeting these people.

"Brady," Julie said, "did he say anything else? Anything at all?"

Brady whistled through his teeth softly. "He said plenty. I can't understand most of it, though."

"Go on," Ben said.

"Well, there's this business about the spirit world on the far side of the mesa."

"What spirit world?" Julie frowned.

"Ah, Tayosha says something like it's an evil place, this spirit world, and only lost souls of the dead live there."

"Interesting," Ben said. "What was he getting at?"

Brady had a lopsided grin on his face. "That *you're* from that world."

"Um," Ben said, "I take it that's bad medicine."

Brady nodded. "Real bad."

It struck Julie then, suddenly. "My God, are we in danger here?"

"I don't think so," Brady was quick to tell her. "You see, you're already ghosts. You don't exist in this world."

"Ghosts?"

"Sure. You're from the spirit world, you're not real."

It was Ben who said, "Let me guess. They think you're a regular guy, one of them."

"Well," Brady said, "at least *I* look familiar to them. You know."

Ben eyed Tayosha speculatively. "It all sounds fine and good," he said, "*if* you believe they're a lost tribe of Anasazi. I don't happen to be in the market for that one, myself."

"That's your problem," Brady said defensively. "If you don't like it, then leave. They'll be plenty relieved to see you go."

"I'm sure of that. Trouble is, Brady, it was you folks who called for my services. You're stuck with me."

"Do you two *have* to argue constantly?" Julie asked. "Can't we just get some food and water and talk this out like rational people?" She looked at Tayosha then back to Brady. "Will he put us up for the night? Can you ask him that?"

In the end, although Tayosha was apparently not too happy about it, he agreed, nodding toward one of the men who'd brought them there in the first place.

"Tell him thank you," Julie said to Brady.

"I don't think he can hear that," Brady replied levelly, "from you."

They followed the man through a maze of houses, up ladders, across courtyards, down and around. Everywhere they walked, people stared at Brady, some timid, some curious, some plain frightened. Julie wanted to reach out to them, to the women and children especially, and say, "I'm not a spirit. I'm flesh and blood like you. I just live a few miles away. I won't hurt you." But of course they'd never understand.

Their guide left them in front of a three-room house. A woman came silently in her soft moccasins and left in front of the T-shaped doorway a beautifully decorated pottery jar and two large baskets woven in intricate designs.

Brady said something to her, thank-you, Julie supposed, and she smiled warmly at the woman, trying to communicate friendship. The woman gave her an utterly blank glance, not seeing her, ducked her head and left.

After a time Brady took to himself, wandering to a corner of the courtyard where he squatted down onto his haunches and gazed around. Julie tried not to disturb him; there were sorrow and wonderment in his dark eyes, an intensity of feeling she could only guess at. She let it alone.

"Is he okay?" Ben asked her, tilting his head in Brady's direction.

"I think so," she replied. Then, "Well, maybe not. Brady's not real in touch with his people," she said. "This has to be a devil of a homecoming."

"Especially if he believes they're Anasazi," Ben said with more care than usual.

Julie looked at him curiously. "What if they *are* Anasazi?"

"Don't tell me you've swallowed that story, too."

"I haven't swallowed anything," she said. "But if they aren't, then tell me what they are."

The black and red and white patterned jar the woman had left was filled with water; one of the baskets was filled with flat corn tortillas, the other with a bean and venison stew. The basket was so closely woven that it was completely waterproof, Julie noticed as she sat down to eat. She wondered fleetingly if she could take such a beautiful basket home with her, but no, certainly not. It must be really valuable, priceless to the woman to whom it belonged. After all, she couldn't go out to the store and buy another one.

They ate hungrily. "Not bad," Ben said.

Brady did eat but slowly, savoring every mouthful as he wandered off again.

Julie wondered if the water was pure, but they had no choice, so she drank from the gourd dipper. It was cool and fresh with a vaguely muddy taste. She drank again, then held the dipper up, realizing that someone, some woman in the pueblo, had carried that water from the stream all that way up those ladders, and the knowledge humbled her immeasurably.

Women were building fires all around them, on rooftops and in front of their dwellings. The sun had long since sunk behind Red Mesa, and the western sky was pale and washed with a dusty pink. Julie and Ben sat with their backs against the warm stone in front of their house, watching the activity around them.

"So," Ben said after a time, "you suppose the heads of your animals are around here?" He looked straight ahead while he filled another tortilla with a bean gruel. "Animal totems are common among primitive people," he went on. "They believe that they can take on the strengths of the animals they kill."

His voice was filled with surety, and Julie envied him his logic, the simplicity with which he saw the world. She herself was torn between belief and distrust of her own senses, between possibility and reason. And Brady...well, Brady simply believed.

"I suppose Tayosha's a good suspect," she said.

"A *prime* suspect," Ben put in.

"But I don't feel angry at him," Julie said. "You know what I mean?"

"Yes."

"And I can't exactly go up and accuse him."

"No, you can't."

"Ben," she said after a pause, "it really does look as if these people have lived here, this way, well, forever."

"Impossible."

"Nothing's impossible."

"You know," he said, still gazing out across the valley floor, "sometimes I envy people their simple acceptance."

"My acceptance isn't—" she began.

"I said that badly. I meant that life is a whole lot easier if a person can take certain things on faith."

"I'm surprised you realize that," she said quietly.

"Yeah, well, Laurie would be, too. She thinks I'm an old codger who's too cynical. Maybe she's right."

She watched Ben's face in the flickering glow of firelight. His beard was growing thicker and darker, covering his lean jaws and upper lip. She recalled, abruptly and without warning, the feel of his breath, quick and warm on her face, and his lips and the rough caress of his beard against her skin. She could still feel the phantom touch of his hands grasping hers to help her off the top of the ladder and the warm spot where he'd kept his hand when they'd been brought to this house. She was glad he was there, and she was torn between hoping his skepticism was right and praying it wasn't. She wanted badly to lean on him and believe his reassuring logic.

Julie turned and pressed her face into Coyote's rough fur. She wanted to believe him, but she couldn't. Within her was the same certitude that had come to Brady—these were truly the lost children of the Anasazi.

CHAPTER EIGHT

BEN TOSSED a few dead juniper stumps into the fire pit. He struck a match and held it to the twigs he'd used as kindling, then blew gently on the tiny flame until it caught. The twigs hissed and cracked, little sparks leaped into the night sky like fairy dust.

He sat on his haunches in the baked dirt courtyard in front of the house they'd been given and glanced around. On the next stone terrace down he could just make out the dark head of a woman suckling an infant by the warmth of her fire. Men talked nearby in an alien, throaty tongue, and older children raced freely along the ledges of the terraces, laughing, playing a game that resembled tag. The night air echoed with subdued chatter and smelled of piñon smoke and cornmeal cooking, of the ancient stone surrounding him and of human bodies, aromatic, earthy, not at all unpleasant. But then, he thought wryly, these people hadn't been dousing themselves in perfumes and deodorant for centuries.

What was he thinking! Had Brady, with all his hogwash about the Anasazi, been getting to him, too?

The full moon lighted up the entire valley, and when Ben looked down from his lofty perch, he saw that there was a mist lying low on the ground, obscuring the stream and the trees along it and crawling in ghostly fingers up the sides of the mesa. A mist—but there couldn't be mist in zero humidity in a goddamn drought! Hell no, it was just smoke from some forest fire combined with a serious inversion. Sure, that's what it was.

He gazed at Julie who was sitting quietly stroking Coyote's

fur over and over, staring into the growing flames. She looked hypnotized, as if she were about ten light years away from him. He felt left out and a little jealous of her preoccupation, childishly resentful.

He pivoted around. "Still hungry?" he tried.

"No, I'm fine now," she replied languidly, her gaze fixed on the embers.

Wasn't she even worried about Hank back at the Someday Ranch, probably drunk? And there was Brady, sitting cross-legged, apart from them, lost in unfathomable musings. Brady could be forgiven this transgression over logic, but Julie—what excuse did she have for her peculiar behavior? Was he the only sane one among them?

Ben rose impatiently and strode to the perimeter of their courtyard. He jammed his hands in his pockets, idly rubbing a line in the hard-packed soil with a boot tip. There was an explanation here and he was going to find it. These were no Anasazi—he wanted to laugh at the very notion. Probably they were a tribe of hippies, Indians, but hippies nonetheless, who'd reverted to their roots and weren't about to give the White Eyes the satisfaction of a straight answer. And here Julie was, thinking these Indians had somehow spanned the mists of time—survived in this hidden valley for seven hundred years for godsakes—undiscovered. Anasazi. Sure.

A woman's voice singing softly to a child lifted into the night. Maybe he was being obstinate about this place; he sure was in the minority when it came to accepting Tayosha's line. But that was his job. He wasn't about to let his brain turn to mush just because of some Indians who'd decided to live like their ancestors. That Tayosha character was probably laughing himself to death. Well, in the morning, Ben was going to find some answers, come hell or high water. By noon he'd know the who and why of the animal mutilations, and he'd find out just exactly who this tribe of Indians was and where the hell they'd come from.

Ben and Julie slept inside the stone dwelling on tightly woven straw mats furnished by the same silent woman who'd brought the food. Brady chose the outside, close to the fire. Under the stars of his ancestors, Ben thought derisively. It was a three-room house, low and squat, with no furnishings to speak of. There was a basket here and there, a jar of water, but the place had obviously been deserted for some time. Had the former occupant died? Was the number of inhabitants in this cliff pueblo dwindling? Maybe the kids had become bored and gone back to civilization. He thought about Brady's boy for a minute. He could just see Hank living here without his ghetto blaster, his beer and pickup truck and tight-fitting blue jeans. The young people in this valley were at least living without the corruption that Ben saw so much of lately. But then you'd think these kids here would miss stereo systems and VCRs, refrigerators stacked with Cokes and fast-food burgers. And what about education? It must drive some of them nuts here. It would drive *him* nuts.

He lay on his mat in the room next to Julie's, hands clasped behind his head, thinking, questioning, hypothesizing. Again and again in his mind he kept recalling the problem Brady had communicating with these Indians, his Anasazi. If they'd concocted their own language, wouldn't they have used a few more modern words or at least understood Brady? It made no sense.

But this was night. Come morning he was going to do some exploring and get his answers. Heck, he'd play Tayosha's game, get Brady to ask the medicine chief for a few guides and head off to the far end of the valley. There'd be a road, he knew, probably a town. And when Ben got there he'd have his answers, all right. *Someone* knew of the existence of this clan.

It must have been well past midnight when Ben became aware of the lack of sound. The high cliff pueblo was unearthly quiet, asleep. Not even a dog barked or a cat. He hadn't seen any cats, had he? It was then that he noticed there *was* a sound, a faint sound, a soft soughing now and again. It was a woman's breathing as she slept.

He envisioned Julie as she'd been when they'd first returned, a sleeping robe wrapped around her shoulders, her eyes sleepy and dream-filled, their heavy dark lashes falling like miniature fans against her soft skin. He'd gone into her room and against her mild protest seen to it that she was okay, and she'd lay down quietly, snuggling into her robe for warmth against the chill of the desert night. She'd slept almost instantly.

Ben sat up and scrubbed a hand through his hair restively. He'd never sleep tonight. He stood and went out into the main room that opened onto the courtyard. The fire had died completely, and Brady slept nearby, at peace. Coyote, too, had wandered outside. He lifted a tired head, gazed at Ben, groaned and went straight back to sleep.

Julie. Was she still all right? Maybe she was awake now, as restless as Ben in this strange place. It wouldn't hurt to check on her.

He moved as silently as a cat toward her room. He knew somewhere in a corner of his brain that he wasn't really checking to see if she was okay. He wanted to look at her, to see the soft rise and fall of her breast in sleep, to know that her hair was spread like gold beneath her, exactly as he imagined it would be. He wanted to know her secrets.

He found himself standing over her like a Peeping Tom, standing there immobile, his heart beating against his ribs. It was dark in that cool cubicle of stone, but he could make her out all right because the moon was so darn bright, lying on her side, a hand under her head, the robe slipped from her shoulders.

She'd taken off her clothing. He could discern a white bra strap against her pale skin, a rounded woman's shoulder, a long pale column of neck. His heart thudded, and he could hear a thunder in his ears as if a storm were breaking. A vise-like desperation seized him while he stood there transfixed, wanting her. And then he recalled with clarity the feel of her body pressed to his, the way she'd felt in his arms that instant she'd almost yielded to him.

His breathing grew ragged. He knew he couldn't stay there

undecided; he'd go mad. But she didn't want him, she'd made that much plain as day. It was only lust burning in his belly, a cruel twist of fate that he desired this woman and she couldn't care less about him. The irony of the situation struck him full force, and if he hadn't been so shaken he would have laughed.

Ben stole out of the room before he did something they would both regret. He stretched back down on his own mat and locked his jaw in frustration. Why her? Why was this happening now? Was it simply sex, or was it Julie herself? She was so independent, but it was the hidden softness beneath her competent exterior that enticed him so powerfully. There was a mystery in Julie's life, something he couldn't get a handle on, yet it was there, like an unhealed wound, a vulnerability, a pain.

It took till dawn before Ben finally sank into a fitful sleep, into that half-awake, half-sleeping state where thoughts were vaguely controlled. He had a notion just as the sun tipped the far rim of the mesa—he wondered if his solitary life was so very satisfying after all.

TAYOSHA SEEMED CONTENT to get rid of Ben and Brady. He provided guides for their walk up the valley, food and leather pouches of water.

Julie, however, opted to stay behind.

"I don't like it," Ben said, turning to her, frowning as he gathered his things.

"I can take care of myself," she declared.

He rolled his eyes.

"Come on, Ben, these Indians are the most peaceful people I've ever met. You've got to admit that much."

They did appear genuinely harmless. He nodded grudgingly.

"It's kind of like a vacation for me," she added, smiling. "Well, sort of. I can do my own exploring right here. Maybe I'll learn how to make a basket." She glanced at Brady who, like Ben, was scowling. "I'm fine. Honest. And I'm sure

Hank's fine, too. We've both been gone before without telling him. He'll think the three of us camped out to watch for another try at my animals.''

"Hank'll be okay," Brady said, but there wasn't much conviction in his voice.

"All right," Ben said, "but the mutt stays with you. And don't go off anywhere by yourself," he said, and then watched as she saluted him facetiously. "*Please* don't go off alone," he said. "We'll see you tonight, tomorrow morning at the latest."

He really was reluctant to leave her. He couldn't be positive these Indians were totally harmless. But then, he thought as he climbed down to the valley floor, she was probably just as safe here as anywhere, and a hell of a lot safer than in a big city like Denver or Chicago or New York. And she *was* a big girl, after all.

Ben, Brady and two guides headed west along the streambed on a well-trodden trail. The two guides spoke to Brady, but ignored Ben so faultlessly that he was impressed. They did not acknowledge his existence by a gesture or a look or a word. He was simply not there.

Already the sun was pressing down on them from the merciless white sky, and he took off his shirt, tying it around his waist. Sweat trickled down his neck, and the waistband of his jeans grew damp.

It wasn't long before they came across a series of irrigated, terraced fields that had been planted in semicircles to hold precious moisture. Ben stopped and studied the vast irrigation systems of these Indians, the check dams, catch basins and ditches. He noticed the corn plants, their bases hollowed to hold water and filled with pebbles to prevent evaporation. There were squash plants, too, carefully tended by women already at work that morning. But everything had a tired, dusty patina, and the ditches and check dams held not a drop of moisture. The drought.

He remembered an article he'd scanned in magazines that told of the technologically advanced irrigation systems used by the Anasazi that enabled them to live in such a dry climate. These guys must have read the same articles.

As they hiked he saw flocks of wild turkeys, which had been domesticated, and there had been dogs in the pueblo, but he never caught sight of a horse or cow or sheep. Not even a chicken. It struck him that the Anasazi had vanished long before the Spanish arrived to introduce those domesticated animals to the continent. This was crazy, a crazy, elaborate game being played on him, a hoax. And if it weren't a game, then the whole thing was as bizarre as it could get. He itched to get to the far end of the hidden valley to find the missing piece to his puzzle.

After a time Ben accepted the lack of telephone poles and roads and houses. He decided the Indians here had deliberately chosen to live without the accoutrements of civilization. But there *would* be a way out, a way other than that cut he, Julie and Brady had discovered.

Something else struck Ben that morning. It occurred to him that he hadn't seen a jet stream in two days. This corner of New Mexico was on the corridor to Los Angeles, and there should be a substantial amount of air traffic. He craned his neck, squinted and searched the white sky. Nothing—not a cloud or a bird or a plane. Just the sun, bigger than he'd ever seen it before, and the hazy paleness overhead. Well, he'd watch for a while; surely a half hour wouldn't go by without a jet crossing the continent thirty thousand feet above.

Then he forgot about it, because they came across another pole holding a cluster of prayer sticks.

"It looks more like it should have a skull perched on top," he muttered to Brady.

"These are a more powerful way of contacting the gods," Brady replied straight-faced, and Ben shut up.

It was two hours later that he recalled his search for jet streams, but he still hadn't seen one. He gave up and guessed he'd just missed them.

All told they hiked a good fifteen miles that day. The land at this western end of the valley was similar to the eastern end, the direction in which Julie's ranch lay. Twisted juniper trees dotted the hillsides, and red striated rock rose to the lofty summit of the mesa, which faded into blurry rose from the smoke. It was arid, and the day was as hot as all the rest. Only the trickle in the streambed supported life.

Ben scanned every inch of the land with the binoculars, fully expecting to find some sign of modern society before they came across that road or town or a Bureau of Indian Affairs trading post that he believed in his heart must be there. Surely there was going to be a discarded beer or Coke can left by hikers along the route.

He saw nothing. There wasn't even a cigarette filter bleached white by the sun or a bit of shiny foil.

They stopped seldom, only to refill their water bags or gnaw on a strip of deer jerky the men carried. Ben wondered just how long this valley stretched, fifteen, twenty miles, farther? As the sun dipped toward the far hazy rim of the mesa, he could see no break in the wall, the pass that he'd expected to find, the one that would lead to the outside world. Tayosha's spirit world, he thought disdainfully.

"Ask them how much further," Ben asked Brady as he tapped his watch. It still didn't work.

"They say not too long," Brady came back and told him.

Well, now, Ben mused, that was impossible. He could see in the muted distance that they'd have to hike around that mountain up ahead. From where he stood, it looked like a solid wall of red rock, but he knew there had to be a cut leading out, probably onto the eastern edge of the vast Navajo Indian reservation.

They marched on toward the huge blood-orange sun that now sat on the rim of the mesa. And then, Ben noticed, they began to hike in a more northerly direction, the sun lying on his left shoulder. They walked on doggedly, and Ben was sure they were making an arc, a semicircle, as they followed the base of the mesa. Before he knew it, they'd made a half circle, the sun was at his back, and they were heading east again. To his left and right were the perpendicular walls of the mesa, always there, with never a break in them. Had they, could they have reached the head of the valley and never come across a way out?

Fact and logic struggled in Ben's mind uncomfortably. He'd literally walked from one end of this valley to the other, and he couldn't deny it. There was no way out.

He sat on a rock, feeling hot and drained and bewildered, and stared into Brady's knowing eyes. "Well, *kemo sabe*," Brady said, signaling for the others to stop, "are you satisfied now?"

For once in his life Ben had no retort handy.

"Well?" Brady said.

"Look," Ben said, whistling between his teeth. "I don't know what to make of this yet. There's got to be some explanation."

"The explanation," Brady said, "is staring you in the face."

Ben shook his head. "The whole thing's impossible. This tribe *can't* have been holed up in this valley for hundreds of years."

"Why not?" Brady said, then turned and left him sitting there with a perplexed expression on his face.

They had to make camp that night on the return trek. For one thing the guides were reluctant to travel after dark, something about the souls of the lost who roamed the mesas. But Ben didn't care what their reasoning was, he was too tired to go on anyway.

Brady and the two men built a fire. Dinner was simple and filling: jerky, flat corn bread resembling tortillas, a rabbit one of the men shot with his bow and arrow. Maybe, Ben thought, the bow and arrows were for his benefit—the Indians probably had pistols and hunting rifles stashed somewhere back at the cliff dwelling.

Despite the close quarters, the two Indians were careful not to touch Ben or even to get too near him. They never looked directly at him, and Brady had to give him his food and water. It was really weird but, what the hell, Ben thought, if these guys wanted to play games, it was okay with him. He supposed they were getting some kind of a perverted kick out of it.

He noticed that funny mist again, the one that lay in the hollows and curled in tendrils around the gnarled mesquite when it grew dark. It looked like the dry ice they used in cheap horror movies to make a scene creepy, but he supposed there was some singular combination of temperature, smoke and barometric pressure that caused it. When he got out of this valley, he'd definitely check on current forest fire locations. Yeah, sure, the Forest Service would know.

"Hey, Brady," Ben said as he watched one of the men prepare the rabbit, "ask him if I can see that knife he's using." Ben was betting it was steel, but much to his surprise, when Brady handed it to him, he saw that the handle was bone and the blade obsidian. It was sharp, though, plenty sharp enough to cut off an animal's head. "Ask them about Tayosha," Ben said. "Find out if their medicine chief ever ventures into the, ah, evil spirit world." *This* was too much.

It took a while, Ben saw, for Brady to get them talking about Tayosha. Obviously these men feared and respected the man, but in the end, talk they did.

Brady turned to Ben, his dark Indian eyes glowing red in the firelight. "It seems," Brady said, "that Tayosha is the only one who ever goes into the spirit world, and only because his medicine is strong enough to protect him."

"Oh, really," Ben put in, but only half-heartedly scoffing this time. "So what about the animal heads? What did they say?"

"If I've got this right," Brady said, "it seems that Tayosha goes to the outside world only when there's a drought. He brings back heads, all right—" Brady looked at Ben meaningfully "—as sacrifices to the Cloud People and the Sun Father. Then it rains." Brady shrugged. "These guys are really in awe of Tayosha, I'll tell you. They say it's only because of his great power that they've survived."

"Ask them if there was a drought some years back. What

did Julie say, in '83? Ask if Tayosha brought back some animal heads then,'' Ben said.

"I'm not so sure 1983 means a lot to them,'' Brady said dryly.

"Okay, say eighty moons or so.''

Brady spoke, the Indians answered.

"Yes,'' Brady retorted. "There was a drought. They were boys, but they remember. Tayosha brought magical animal heads to sacrifice and then it rained.''

"Brady,'' Ben said after a time, "show them my pocket knife.'' He pulled it out and handed it to him, then had another thought, taking off his wristwatch, too. He studied their reactions carefully as the two short, dark-skinned Indians took the items from Brady and touched them as if they were forbidden objects of worship. Their awe and fear seemed so genuine that Ben felt a surge of wonder course through him. Maybe they really *were* a lost tribe of the Anasazi, he thought briefly, but as soon as the notion brushed his consciousness, Ben dismissed it as the mental ravings of a romantic idiot.

Long after the moon rose over the mesa, illuminating the eerie rock formations around them, Ben kept at Brady to glean more and more information from the men. The guttural dialect they used fell on his ear disturbingly as they told of their life in that valley, how they had been there for tens of thousands of moons, how many, many years ago the fierce head pounders—the Navajo, Brady explained—chased them into this valley where they took refuge. They told of their perception of the evil world outside, that it was a spirit ground where mens' souls were sucked from them, leaving them demented.

"They got *that* right,'' Brady said in sharp irony.

Ben smiled. "Okay, so ask them if there are any stories passed down about men in shining armor on horses—you know, the Spanish conquistadors.''

Brady spoke to the others for some time then looked at Ben. "They don't know what I'm talking about. They don't have any words for those things.''

Ben snorted. "Hell, Brady, the Spanish conquered this area over four hundred years ago!"

"Hey, *kemo sabe*, I know that."

The camp quieted eventually, and Brady and the others drifted off to sleep by the fire. But Ben felt fully awake for the second night in a row. Noiselessly he put more wood on the fire, sat, then crossed his legs and rested his chin on his folded hands. He hadn't seen any roads today nor any sign of civilization, and he sure hadn't seen anything like glass or plastic or paper or wire. Nothing from modern society. Certainly no candy wrappers or any kind of litter. It just made no sense. He was used to dealing with evidence, not the lack of it.

He gazed into the flames and felt an urgent need to get back to the cliff dwelling, to tell Julie everything he'd seen and heard. She'd be relieved to find out that Tayosha was definitely behind the mutilations of her livestock. He felt himself smiling. You bet she'd be relieved to know at last, and maybe they'd have a chuckle together about all those stories of little green men in flying saucers. The guys at Holloman were going to get a chuckle, too. Ben Tanner had solved the decades-old mystery. It sure was a strange solution.

Julie. Was she sleeping right now in that cool dark cubicle with Coyote at her side? He wondered. And he asked himself whether she was maybe awake, wondering where *he* was. That would be interesting, Ben thought, and he might just ask her tomorrow. He could hear himself saying, "Hey, Julie, I couldn't sleep last night because I kept thinking about you. Was it the same for you?" Sure he'd ask her that, as soon as he swallowed this Anasazi business—which was going to be never.

He lay down and pulled his sleeping robe around him. Just before he drifted off, it occurred to him that the full moon was still shining down. *Wait a minute.* The same moon had been out last night and the night before and the one before that, too. The same moon had laughed at him back at Julie's several days ago, and a full moon for a week was an impossibility.

But then he yawned and rolled over and guessed he'd noticed it wrong.

THEY MADE IT TO the base of the cliff dwelling by noon the following day. Ben had been anxious to get back, worried about Julie, wondering if she was worried about him, and so he'd pressed the pace, declining rest stops, even the food that was offered him.

But she wasn't at the pueblo.

"Take it easy there," Brady said, touching his arm while Ben cast around the little stone house anxiously. "She's down washing her clothes in the stream."

"How did you know that?" Ben demanded.

"Because I saw her there when we were on the ladders." Brady grinned.

"Thanks for telling me." Ben turned to go.

"No problem. I'da told you sooner, White Eyes, but I didn't know you cared so much," Brady called after him.

She was there, all right, kneeling by the streambed, her jeans and shirt spread out on rocks to dry. She was wearing a soft beige dress made of tanned deer hide, and her blond hair was twisted into pinwheels above each ear. She looked absolutely—he searched for the word—lovely, like an Indian princess with golden hair. As he came up quietly behind her, he couldn't help but notice that, like the other women washing their clothes in yucca suds, one nicely curved shoulder was bare, gleaming in the sunlight.

It was Coyote who gave him away. The dog flew up from his place at Julie's side and raced to Ben, tail wagging, torso twisting. Julie spun around abruptly, then she smiled, relaxing. "You're back," she said.

"Yep." That was it, couldn't he find anything else to say?

"So, did you find your road?" She remained in her kneeling position, her buckskin dress riding above her rounded white knees, well up her thighs.

"No. There was nothing. It seems to be a closed valley."
He found a smile creeping onto his lips. "I see you've gone,
ah, native."

Quickly Julie looked down at her attire. He'd have sworn
she blushed. "Oh, this dress, it was just there when I woke
up."

"I see." He fixed her with his blue eyes. "So you're communicating?" He nodded at the other women nearby.

She shook her head sadly. "Not a word. They pretend I'm
not here." She gave a rueful smile and looked up at him with
soulful blue eyes. "It's been sort of lonely."

It came over him like a wave of hot lava. He wanted to
hold her and comfort her, enfold her in his arms and unpin
her hair until it flowed over his hands. He felt an overwhelming rush of protectiveness—this woman should never be
lonely, never again in her life.

And he wanted her physically, right then and there, on the
sandy bank of the stream, under the blazing lemon yellow
sun. The urge was powerful and utterly primitive. He felt as
if he were one of the Ancient Ones himself, standing over his
woman, ready to mate, to fill her body with his.

She was still looking up at him with those transparent ice-
blue eyes, looking right into him. She knelt by the water, her
wet shirt in her hands, and knew everything he was feeling.
Their gazes met and refused to part. His breath seemed to halt
in his chest, and his veins swelled and pounded like drums in
his ears. She knew everything, every secret of his soul.

He fought it. There was that watchful corner of his mind
that held back, that was ashamed of such weakness. It told
him to forget it, that he was acting like a romantic schoolboy
who couldn't keep his britches buttoned, that he wasn't going
to start anything with Julie or any other woman, for that matter. He had enough in his life already, what with his job and
his daughter and his fond memories of Carol.

Ben let a slow breath out of his lungs and willed his desire
to fade. "You know," he said, forcing control into his tone,

"all the evidence points to these people really being a lost tribe. I don't know if they're Anasazi, but it's damn strange."

Julie seemed to be gathering her wits as well. "I know," she said.

"And we were right, it was Tayosha who killed your animals," Ben said.

"I thought it probably was."

"And you're not mad?"

"Not really. He wasn't doing it against me, personally, now was he?"

"Not at all." He thought for a moment. "But God knows, if it doesn't rain soon he may go after some more of your stock."

She nodded, as if agreeing with him, as if she were finding it as difficult as he was to break the spell that had just been conjured up between them. Ben found himself squatting down alongside her, looking into the thin, trickling stream of water.

"It's funny," Julie said, "but in this valley it seems like everything outside is unreal. I can't remember it very well. I can hardly remember my own phone number or...or Ken Lamont's face."

"Um." Ben trailed his fingers in the water. "I can remember Laurie, but Carol, my wife...I can barely recall her face sometimes. Scary. I guess we've been real preoccupied."

"You loved your wife very much, didn't you?" Julie asked out of the blue.

Ben stared into the water. "Yes. She was a good person. I still have trouble sometimes accepting the fact that she's gone. I still see things and think, 'Wow, I'd like to tell Carol about that.'"

"You don't want to forget her," Julie said.

He looked up, surprised at the grave tone of her voice. "No, I don't. And I never will."

Julie didn't say anything else. She busied herself wringing out her clothes. Eventually she folded the damp garments neatly and rose. Ben looked up at her.

"It's a special place, isn't it?" Julie asked softly.

"I'll give it that much," he agreed.

"You know," she said, "I feel…and don't you dare laugh at me, but I feel as if I'm closer to myself here. My real self. I feel as if I've been so preoccupied with the ranch and money and all that stuff that I lost touch somewhere."

"Um," Ben said, strangely understanding just what she was getting at.

"Oh, Ben," she said in a whisper, "you do believe, don't you? You know now that this place is magic."

He never answered her. There were no answers. Instead he found himself silently following the path of her gaze, up to the ancient dwelling above them whose geometric angularity was softened just a bit by the inexplicable haze that hung like gauze in the air.

CHAPTER NINE

THE MEDICINE CHIEF'S FACE was painted in black and white zigzags. It loomed over Julie as he made strange motions with his hands, motions she knew were magical, and she was afraid.

She cast about in panic. Someone had to stop this man before he hurt her, but there was no one there, only the darkness, like a long tunnel reaching away into the distance. The medicine chief smiled and his lips moved. He was saying something that she couldn't understand no matter how hard she tried. Then his face dissolved in flashing splinters of black and white and there was noise and a commotion, and she jerked awake to a sense of overwhelming confusion.

"Goddammit, get your filthy hands off me!" she heard someone scream in a raucous voice. "You sons of—"

There was more noise, the crash of something being knocked over, feet scuffling, angry mutterings, the thud of human body against human body.

"Touch me again and I'll have my lawyer on you so fast your head'll spin!"

Julie shook her head and tried to clear it. That voice. Who was it? Not Brady, not Ben.

A dark shadow appeared in the doorway of her room. "Julie?"

"What's going on?" she asked groggily.

"Got me, but I want you to stay put until I find out."

"Ben..."

"Stay put!"

By then Julie was sitting up, peering into the darkness. She heard a sound, a match being struck, and she could see Ben in the other room, then his bearded face lighted crazily by the flair of the match.

"Who's the goddarn head honcho around here, anyway!" that vaguely familiar voice yelled.

Ben swore, his fingers burnt, and he lighted another match, cupping it in his hands as he headed outside. She could just make out his naked torso against the dark line of his jeans, which were still open at the top button.

"Gimme that!" came another shout, close by now. "That's a twelve-hundred-dollar Nikon camera!"

That did it. She wasn't staying put, not with all this commotion. And where was Brady?

Hurriedly she pulled the buckskin dress over her head and adjusted it as she felt her way to the outer room where firelight from outside flickered against the wall in a restless tattoo. Unaccountably she felt apprehensive, as if something awful had happened with the coming of this stranger.

"Well, I'll be," she heard Ben say, "our pal, Gary Phillips, is here."

Her heart sank. "Oh no," Julie said, moving close to Ben. "What're we going to do? It's bad enough they won't accept us…"

"The first thing we're going to do," he said, his eyes meeting hers with reassurance, "is go down there and find out just exactly what's going on."

On the terrace below them, Julie could see that a huge fire was being built in the central plaza—no doubt for the unwelcome occasion of Phillips's arrival. Shadowed figures milled around it, angry voices and muffled shouts rose from the confusion. Sleepy people emerged from houses all around her to stare and whisper. Somewhere a baby wailed and was silenced abruptly.

"Come on," Ben said, "we better get on down there."

She hurried after him, careful not to trip in the darkness. Few of the Indians followed, though. Most huddled by their low, T-shaped doorways, whispering and frightened.

The fire was hot and bright, dancing on sweaty faces. Brady detached himself from the undulating darkness and moved to Julie's side. "It's that reporter," he said quietly.

"I know, I heard him."

"Who the hell are you?" came Phillips's voice again. "Can't you jackasses understand a word I'm saying? What's going on here?"

Ben strode directly toward the voice, pushing through the Indian men who behaved as if he didn't exist. "Okay, Phillips," he said, "cut it out. Shut your mouth for a minute, will you?"

"What the hell? Oh, it's you. Tanner, right? Who're these—"

"*Shut up*, Phillips," Ben said. "These Indians don't understand English."

"Oh, for godsakes!" Phillips scoffed.

"Come on, Miss Julie," Brady said, taking her arm. "I think our brave White Eyes may need a little help."

Tayosha stood implacably by the fire. His face was haggard, untouched by paint, his hair hung down his back. Several young men held Gary Phillips's arms while the reporter struggled, his face pasty white and greasy with sweat and fear.

"Okay, Phillips," Ben said, "I really do suggest you button it up."

"Just tell them to let me go, Tanner."

"Sorry, no can do. I don't speak their language, and they don't speak mine."

"Bull!"

"And what's more, I don't know why they're acknowledging you. They sure as heck haven't even looked at us."

"You're nuts, man. Now just tell these gorillas here to let me go and give me back my camera!"

"I told you, to them I don't exist. I can't tell them anything."

"But I can." Brady moved closer.

"Well, for godsakes, tell 'em *something*," Phillips hissed.

Brady assessed the panting reporter for a long time. "Do

you think I should tell them that you're harmless, Mr. Phillips? I sure hate to lie.''

"You're just as crazy as they are," the reporter snarled.

"Maybe so." Brady cocked his head. "What'd you do, Phillips, to get them so ticked off?"

"Nothing. Nothing! I just took a few pictures, that's all. I found this place that you guys have been keeping secret..."

Brady laughed. "We haven't kept it secret. We never knew it was here."

Tayosha stepped forward then and said something to Brady, pointing in the direction of Phillips. He was angry and upset Julie could see, and she didn't blame him.

Brady replied, repeating a word over and over again, *Ikwatsi*, the Hopi word for friend.

Tayosha spoke again. Phillips looked from the medicine chief to Brady and back again, his face oily with sweat, his small black eyes glittering with fear and unquenched curiosity.

"Who in hell are these guys?" Gary said out of the corner of his mouth to Ben. "Is this some kinda joke or something?"

"It's no joke, Phillips. This appears to be a real primitive tribe. They're still in the Stone Age for all I can gather."

"Come *on*! Get outta here, Tanner. I'd just as soon believe in UFOs."

Ben shrugged. "Believe what you want."

Julie saw the wheels going around in the reporter's head. Realization and greed shone from his eyes. Apprehension crawled up her back.

She tugged on Ben's arm. "We've got to get him out of here."

"I don't think I'm in control of this situation, Julie," he said quietly.

Brady turned to face them. "Well," he said dryly, "it seems that your photographic efforts created quite a stir."

"Just a few pictures," Gary mumbled. "What's the big deal?"

"Your flash. You were trying to steal the Sun Father's power. Bad thing to do, White Eyes."

Gary gave a derisive snort of laughter. "Steal the Sun Father's power? What kinda garbage is that?"

"Not garbage," Brady said. "Not to them."

"Tell 'em I'm sorry, then."

"It won't matter. You're not really here."

"Oh? Then where am I?"

"Nowhere. You don't exist." Brady shrugged.

"Well, if I don't exist, how'd I steal the Sun Father's power, huh, tell me *that*?"

"It's your camera."

"So get me my camera, then. Talk to that guy, that chief, will ya?"

Brady tried. Julie watched as he bent his head to Tayosha and spoke, making signs as well, for some time. Eventually Tayosha, no doubt not knowing what else to do, nodded to the men holding Phillips. They released him gladly, then stepped back and stared at their hands in wonder. Julie hadn't a clue what they thought they'd been holding, but whatever it was obviously frightened them. They moved into the shadowed throng that stared for guidance only at Tayosha.

"Whew," Phillips was saying, "these folks are some kind of weird. So, what now, pal?" He looked at Brady.

"I'm no pal of yours," Brady said. "And be real careful around here, Mr. Phillips. They could still decide to stake you out in the sun for the ants to eat."

Gary's bright eyes shifted in alarm. "Ah, yer kidding."

"Maybe and maybe not," Brady said cryptically. "Come on, you better stay with us tonight, or what's left of the night, anyway."

They climbed back up to their house in the flickering darkness. Phillips followed Julie closely; she could hear him huffing and puffing behind her. Surrounding him like a noxious cloud was the sharp body odor of fright.

"Hey, Miz Hayden," he said. "This is some circus you got going for you here."

"It isn't a circus," she answered coldly. "It's a pueblo. This is their home."

He whistled. "Some home."

"They'd probably think the same of New York," she said.

Brady found a sleeping robe for Phillips to wrap himself in, and slowly the pueblo settled back into quiet.

"This place gives me the heebie-jeebies," Julie heard Phillips whisper into the dark.

"Shut up, Phillips," Ben said once again, and then there was silence.

But Julie lay there, surrounded by the unfamiliar smells and soft night sounds of the pueblo, and her heart caught to think of the far-reaching implications of Phillips's arrival. No longer was the tribe safe from its spirit world. After hundreds of long, peaceful years, the descendants of the Ancient Ones had been discovered.

BY MIDDAY Julie despised Gary Phillips just as vehemently as Ben and Brady did. The first thing he'd done that morning was to ask where in hell the bathroom was. Once that matter was explained to him, to his utter stupefaction, he complained about everything from the food to his dirty, sweaty clothes, from the heat to the lack of running water.

But worse, once he saw that no harm would come to him from the tribe, he commenced to scurry around like a beetle, unhindered, blatantly picking up whatever he wanted, leaving behind his penknife, his watch and pens for the bowls and baskets and jewelry he was snatching up. He babbled constantly, even though the people looked straight through him as he grinned, picked up the turquoise-and-leather bracelet and put down in its place a twenty-nine-cent pencil.

Oh yes, Julie was finding it easy to detest him, yet oddly he fascinated her, as if he were a relic that had escaped the sewers of a dirty, frantic metropolis.

He did look bizarre, she thought, scampering up and down ladders and stairs and over roofs, dressed in sweat-stained city clothes that were by now covered with dust—pleated white linen trousers and a black dress shirt shot with silver. She almost wanted to laugh, but when she thought of the reporter's motives in being there, she grew cold all over. Ben and Brady had gone down to the valley floor once again, Ben wanting to look over the fields, to study them. Julie knew that the clear evidence of this tribe being ancient was still not quite enough to convince Ben. She wondered what it was going to take. Even so, she was content enough to stay behind and watch the women at their chores. It was truly a marvel how they ground their corn, sewed, made full use of their limited resources. There were baking stones in front of each family's house. The woman of the next-door family spat on the stone to see if it was hot enough, then she brushed the flat surface with a bunch of corn husks tied together and dipped into a small bowl of melted animal fat, or so Julie guessed from the aroma when it hit the hot stone. Then the woman spread the corn batter with a sure, practiced motion over the surface, waited for it to cook, peeled it off and laid it with the pile of others in a shallow basket.

It was fascinating to watch the women bustle about busily, carrying baskets on their heads up ladders, negotiating maze after maze of terraces. Julie watched for a time from her own spot then ventured out among them, moving freely anywhere she wanted, as if she really were no more than a wisp of shadow passing.

It hurt that they feared her, hurt even more that they ignored her. Their fears she could perhaps put to rest in time, but this sense of isolation was overwhelming.

Nevertheless, she wandered around her level of the cliff dwelling and took in everything she saw, wanting to remember each detail, to have it to savor when she returned home. She could see inside several of the dwellings, making out storage pots and baskets in special rooms containing dried corn, piñon nuts, berries, unfamiliar roots and seeds. Something that looked like salt was stored in a small, furry pouch, a prairie dog or a squirrel skin, Julie guessed. Dried meat hung on wooden racks. Pots held beans and squash and dried fruits.

And all from one single valley. Was it possible that she lived such a short distance away and could barely keep alive a few sheep, cattle and horses? And how about her vegetable garden? It was pitiful. Was she lazy, then? Or maybe she was so dependent on modern conveniences, like lavish irrigation, that she'd forgotten how to survive. Perhaps, Julie thought, the survival mechanism was in everybody; it was just that modern man had repressed it.

She plumped herself down on a sandstone wall and thought about her own survival. Why did she need money? Couldn't she learn from this experience, take home with her the knowledge that could perhaps free her? And another notion seized her. She could have been brought—steered—to this magic place by some kind of unseen hand, by fate or whatever. It was possible. This valley was teaching her that anything was possible.

In front of her at a neighboring house was an older, bent woman working with two white slivers—bone needles. She threaded one with a long thin sinew and began to mend a robe like the ones that had been given to the outsiders for sleeping. And all the while she talked and laughed with a woman who appeared to be her daughter. Gossiping, Julie thought.

Her daughter finished cooking some corn cakes, put the basket inside the house and came out once again with a basket of dried corn. She took it to a metate, a stone trough with a slab of flat stone used to grind corn into meal. Julie had seen old metates in museums and in books about the Anasazi, so she knew exactly what it was. She couldn't even comprehend the hours and hours it must take these women to grind enough corn to feed the entire pueblo of hundreds of people.

The younger woman drew the stone back and forth patiently, tirelessly, bent over on her knees. She gossiped all the while, perfectly content in her work. Not impatient, like Julie would have been. There was so much to learn here, so much to take back....

Julie hardly heard the approaching footsteps, and when she

did, her heart fell. She'd forgotten him for a time, forgotten how he was scurrying about robbing the poor Indians blind.

"Hey! Here you are," Phillips said, popping up to her like a jack-in-the-box. "Say, where are the others? Ben and Brady?"

"In the valley." Julie looked down at her hands, willing herself to keep her temper.

"Oh. Hey, will ya look at the stuff I got? Of course, I left them all something of mine."

"So do pack rats," Julie said.

"Oh, yeah, that's pretty funny, pack rats. Well, anyhow, I wish I had a truck to get all this stuff out. Say, maybe if you guys could help…"

He was dancing with frenetic energy, beaming with the joy of acquisition. "Ya know, Indians are big these days. Real big. All the galleries carry this stuff. It's big money, *big* money. I'm gonna rake in the dough, make a fortune on this stuff. See? See this? A bowl. Gorgeous, isn't it? And these beads? And the bracelet. Ivory, I bet. Inlaid with turquoise. Worth a mint."

Julie stood slowly. "Aren't you ashamed of yourself?"

"Ashamed? Why? I'm giving them stuff. Hey, I'm no chiseler. They'll love my watch and my knife. So what if the watch stopped. So, it needs a new battery. So, for five bucks they can get a battery, big deal."

"That's disgusting."

But he didn't even listen. "I gotta get that Tayosha to sign an exclusive," he said, pulsing with energy. "Think of the story! The artifacts! Why, we could run ten thousand tourists a week through here! A motel, a pool, snack stands, curio shop, a big parking lot. An elevator up here. Say, ten bucks a ride up, entrance fee."

"Oh God!" Julie cried. "Stop it! That's obscene!"

"What?" He was genuinely puzzled. "I didn't say anything dirty."

Julie turned her back and left him there.

Ben and Brady were just returning from the valley when

she got to the central plaza. Coyote bounded playfully toward her in greeting, then ran off to sniff at an Indian dog, who slunk away, terrified.

"Wow," Ben said, "they've got an incredible system down there. I'd swear nothing would grow, but they've got—"

"Ben," she said, interrupting him. "Ben!"

He stopped and studied her. "Something wrong?"

"Yes, something is wrong. It's Phillips. Do you know what he's been doing all morning? And he's talking about hotels and parking lots and…and an elevator!"

"It's just a bunch of hot air."

"Ben, do you realize what that would mean? They'd be exposed to the world. It would…it would destroy them. You can't let him do it."

Ben wiped the sweat from the back of his neck. "Look," he said, "you're getting all worked up over nothing. The guy's a nobody. He doesn't even have a clue what he's found here. He never will."

Julie cocked her head. "Oh, really? You sound as if you've got it all figured out."

"Not by a long shot," Ben countered. "But I do know one thing, and that's how we can prove or disprove the validity of these people being Anasazi."

Julie eyed him carefully.

"Have you read about the new method of telling how closely certain people are related?"

"No," she said, not liking the direction he was taking.

"Scientists use DNA," he went on undaunted, "to link certain peoples, their common heritage. Now if this tribe is related in the recent past to, say, the Hopis, we can pinpoint it. But if their DNA varies to any degree from the other Native Americans, we'll know that, too. It's amazing work they're doing now, Julie, and—"

"DNA," she breathed, "I'm not hearing this." Anger roiled inside her. "You're as bad as Phillips. No, you're worse, you're smarter and should know better."

"Look, Julie, I was only—"

"Oh, go stuff it, Tanner," she said and stalked off.

But Ben caught up with her before she left the central plaza and put a detaining hand on her arm. "Hey, wait up. I'm sorry. Slow down there, will you?"

She stopped and turned slowly to face him. She was furious at his callousness, at his inability to realize what was at stake here.

"Don't you get it, Ben? These people have to be left alone or they'll be destroyed. Do you want to be responsible for that? Or would you rather teach them how to fly jets? Or better yet, show them how to build the bomb!"

She was breathing hard she was so angry, so desperate to make him understand. She felt tears prick under her eyelids as she faced him, deathly afraid she wouldn't be able to convince him.

Ben stood over her, his black brows drawn together. Then slowly his face relaxed. "Aw, hell, Julie, I said I was sorry." A crooked smile tilted the corner of his mouth. "And I don't apologize too easily." Then he put his hands on her shoulders and his eyes bored into hers. "Okay," he finally said, "okay. You're right. We have a responsibility here."

But she hardly heard his words. She stood there breathless, feeling his hands hard on her shoulders, feeling his eyes burn into hers, watching his mouth, his beautiful mouth from which she couldn't tear her gaze. She hadn't been so close to a man since Mark. No one had touched her in all this time, all these long, lonely years. And Mark's love had turned to violence and ugliness in the end. Abrupt fear spurted hotly inside her. She couldn't let herself care, go soft like this, because it made her vulnerable. Blood pounded in her ears and she had to force herself to concentrate on what he said.

"Okay, I concede that much. We have to talk about it. We have to consider carefully what the impact of exposure would be on these people. But damn it, Julie, it's a big decision for two people to make. I can't play God and neither can you."

She held his gaze, sensing the warmth of his hands and

smelling the clean male odor of him, feeling her confusion and her ragged breathing. Suddenly she could not bear his closeness another moment and twisted away.

It was Ben who solved the problem of Phillips and the things he'd stolen. With about as much finesse as a bull in a china shop, he grabbed Phillips by his shirt and told him: "Either put back every last item you ripped off or I'm going to throw you over the edge of the cliff."

"You wouldn't."

"I would, and I'm big enough to do it." Ben started to pull him toward the drop-off in front of the house.

"Okay, okay," Phillips yelled. "Lemme go! I'll put it all back!"

Julie had been inside but had come out to see what was going on. Phillips had given in with only a few choice curses, a coward at heart. She supposed Ben knew that. She hated even the threat of violence, and she wondered if Ben had really been serious. She decided that with Gary Phillips no amount of reason would work. Ben probably knew that, too.

It was then that Julie felt an odd sensation—the self-conscious, edgy feeling that someone was staring at her. It was especially peculiar because everyone had carefully avoided looking at her for days. She glanced around. There was a pretty young girl on the terrace above, a coffee-colored girl with delicate hands and feet and glossy black hair wound around her ears. For the briefest moment Julie's eyes met hers before the girl snatched her gaze away, her expression went blank and she busied herself at a task. But it had been something, a tiny sign of recognition, a first step.

"Brady," Julie said, nodding toward the petite girl who was bending over, her strings of shiny beads swaying with her movements, "do you know who that is?"

"That's Mika," he said, "Tayosha's eldest daughter. Why?"

"I think," Julie said thoughtfully, "that she just looked at me."

The rest of the afternoon was spent quietly, without incident, because Phillips had gone off to disperse his ill-gotten booty. But at dinnertime he reappeared, his fake Rolex on his wrist again, talking a blue streak, the uncomfortable confrontation with Ben that afternoon evidently forgotten. "Boy oh boy, this is even better than UFOs. I'll get an exclusive story in the dailies, the *Chicago Tribune*, the *L.A. Times*, the *Washington Post*. I'll run the stuff under my byline with picture credits. Geez, wish I had some more film. Copyrighted, sure, I'll get it copyrighted. Maybe a paperback. It'd take me a week to write it up. I know a publisher who'd die to get his hands on the story."

"Shut up, Phillips," Ben said in a bored tone.

"You can't do that," Julie said angrily. "I won't let you."

"A movie, sort of an *Indiana Jones and the Temple of Doom* adventure. I'd be signed on as technical adviser," he continued unperturbed.

She gave up. He'd never listen, not Phillips. She knew his type, a little like Mark but worse. He had the thrusting need to be noticed that was often mistakenly called ego. Not that he was stupid, just blind, absolutely blind to everything but money and recognition. He probably had to buy women. God, she wished he'd never shown up at her ranch that day!

Later, as the cooking fires died down in the hot darkness, Ben took her aside. "Don't worry about Phillips," he said. "Brady and I will talk some sense into him."

"I hope so," Julie said fervently.

"You really care a lot, don't you?" he said, and his voice held a gentleness she'd never heard in it before.

"Yes, I care a lot. I feel responsible. It's my fault you're all here. I should have just ignored the dead horse."

"You didn't know, Julie. Don't blame yourself."

"I can't help it."

He touched her face then, laid his big hand against her hot cheek until she felt herself melt inside, and every ounce of her being wanted to sag against him, to feel his strength and hardness and the rough black beard on his face. "Take it easy," he said. "Get a good night's sleep, okay?"

She tried a crooked smile. "Okay."

She lay in her sleeping robe in the smoke-scented night listening to the three men breathe in the other room, listening and thinking and alternating between hope and regret. Early in the morning hours she heard one of the men rise and go outside to relieve himself, but before he returned she finally fell into a deep, dream-tossed sleep.

THE CALAMITY was discovered in the morning. Julie was jerked awake to the sound of Brady's voice, talking in an agonized tone to Ben. "The little rat kidnapped her, he just took her! Sometime in the night!" Brady was saying.

"You sure? Maybe she's just off with a boyfriend," Ben said, ever the voice of reason.

"No, Tayosha told me. The whole place is in an uproar. Goddammit, Tanner, this is our fault!"

Julie appeared in the doorway, ducking her head out of habit. "Who? What?"

Brady whirled on her, his face pale, his eyes glittering. She'd never seen him like this, not even when Hank had gotten into trouble. "Phillips kidnapped Mika. They're both gone."

She felt her blood freeze in her veins. "No," she whispered, "oh, no."

"Look, maybe we can go after them, catch up. We know where he's headed," Ben suggested. "The path through the mesa."

"He's been gone for hours," Brady said.

Ben cursed.

"And he stole a kachina, too, a real valuable one," Brady said, his voice quavering.

"Oh my God," Julie said.

"I'd like to get my hands on the sleaze-bag," Ben said tightly. "I think we should go after him right now. He can't be that far ahead."

Then Julie realized that a wail was filling the air, a high

keening, and the noise of gourd rattles and many voices were approaching their house.

Tayosha appeared, dressed in his finery, his face painted in black and white again, followed by a big crowd. Women wailed and men muttered.

"Bray-dee!" Tayosha called out. The members of the crowd held wooden prayer sticks decorated with eagle feathers, which they waved, a froth of feathers upon a moaning, hissing sea of faces.

The three strangers stepped outside their house. Julie's heart strummed hard against her ribs. She was scared, miserable, angry, guilty.

The medicine chief talked, his face taut, while the throng swayed and murmured and lamented. Brady listened, his expression stoic, his eyes fixed on Tayosha. Beside her, Julie sensed that Ben was impatient. She heard him curse under his breath. His fists clenched. She put a hand on his arm to restrain him.

"He says," Brady translated, "that his daughter, Mika, is gone because we have brought the shadow of evil with us."

Julie felt tears spring into her eyes. "What have we done?" she whispered. "What have we done by coming here?"

Tayosha spoke again, gravely, then he and his whole retinue turned and moved away, carrying the sounds of their grief with them. Julie let out a breath that she felt she'd been holding for hours. Ben held her arm, steadying her, and she was thankful.

"Oh God," she cried, tormented, "what about Mika?"

Brady's face was as hard as stone. "Mika has entered the spirit world on the other side of the rock wall that is the boundary of the earth," he said. "Her fate is sealed. To the tribe she is already dead."

CHAPTER TEN

JULIE CLIMBED into the front seat of the Jeep and caught her breath. "I was *sure* we'd catch up to him," she said, still breathing hard. "I mean, we practically ran the whole way out of the valley."

Ben shoved the key in the ignition, pumped the gas pedal and waited for the engine to turn over. "We'll find him, Julie. Worrying yourself sick isn't going to help."

"How are we going to find him?" Brady put in from the back.

"I'll figure something out," Ben said with conviction.

Julie sat in miserable silence as they raced across the rangeland, heading toward the Someday Ranch. The idea that they'd brought Phillips to the valley, however inadvertently, dug at her with sharp talons. They *had* to find Mika—no matter how long it took—and take her back to her people. How could Phillips have done such a vicious thing?

At first Julie hadn't noticed it, she'd been too consumed by her worry over Mika, but it struck her abruptly with force: everything, every scrub oak and juniper, rock and crevice on this side of the mesa seemed—she searched her mind—different. The shadows were clear and precise, the air diamond-sharp. The striated layers of rock on Red Mesa were perfectly delineated, the blue cloudless sky was utterly pellucid, the horizon endless. What about those forest fires she had thought blazed to the west? Why wasn't it smoky here?

The vinyl seat creaked beneath her, and the sound of the engine groaned disturbingly in her ears. Where had the quiet of the valley gone? A sense of not belonging to either world gripped her, and she had to fight for equilibrium. Three days, she thought as the ranch house came into sight. They'd only been gone three days. Yet everything had changed.

"Well, I'll be damned," Ben said out of the blue. "If this isn't crazy!" He was looking at his watch, then back at his driving then at his watch again. He held his wrist up and shook it. "What time does it say?"

Julie craned her neck and focused on the watch face as the Jeep bounced. "It's 1:35."

"It didn't work yesterday or the day before," Ben said. "I guess it needs another new battery." He shrugged, dismissing the oddity.

Hank was there at the ranch. He must have heard the Jeep approach because Julie saw the bunkhouse door open, and the young man sauntered across the yard toward them. He kept his narrow face carefully bland, but his brows were drawn together and a dozen questions hovered unspoken on his lips. At least he appeared completely sober.

"Nice of you guys to show up," he drawled. "I was ready to phone up ol' Ken Lamont, but I figured that moron couldn't do any more than I could."

"Relax," Brady said as he climbed out, "everything's okay. We'll explain."

"Oh, sure, great, you tell me to relax after you leave me sitting here for three whole days." His lips twisted in derision as he followed the three of them into the house.

Julie stood in the middle of her living room feeling helpless and lost, as if everything in her life had changed dramatically. She saw her home through new eyes: the worn linoleum, the painted walls, the plaid of the living room couch. The colors were so bright, the surfaces so smooth. She ran her hand over the Formica counter and felt its cool, utterly slick surface. She turned the faucet on and was surprised at the crystal clearness of the water.

Smells struck her like bludgeons: gasoline, furniture polish, soap and detergent, coffee that had been left on the stove. Plastic and glass, stainless steel and a cotton dish towel—

every item in her house that she'd taken for granted—were all sources of rediscovery. How on earth had mankind traveled so incredibly far from its origins?

She only half listened to Hank as he asked Brady questions, while she tried to reconcile this life with that other one inside the valley. She felt displaced, as a foreigner must feel on emigrating. It was disconcerting.

And then she jerked out of her musing and remembered the reason they were there. Mika. Julie kept envisioning the girl's pretty oval face and huge limpid eyes as their gaze had met briefly that one time. If Phillips harmed her, harmed one little hair on her head…

"And the irrigation pump," Hank was saying to her, "it quit working on Friday afternoon, and I had to drive to Farmington to get the part, because I know Jake's Hardware closes on Saturday."

Hank fixed the pump, Julie's mind registered. Wonder of wonders.

"And the bank called, too, just before I left for Farmington. That guy, Fredericks, asked me when you were going to stop by. I didn't know what to tell him, so I gave him a line of garbage."

"That's okay, Hank," Ben said, "sounds like you did fine."

"Oh, yeah." Hank leaned one shoulder against the wall negligently. He was uncharacteristically talkative, perhaps a sign of relief. "Murdock called too. He wanted to know when you were going to be home so he could maybe drive on down from Durango and visit or something."

"Oh," Julie said, "I'll have to call him and tell him not to come."

"I can do it for you," Ben offered carefully.

"No, no, I'll do it," Julie said, "but later." She turned to Ben and Brady. "What're we going to do? Mika…"

"And," Hank went on, "that guy, that guy from the city, had a flat tire out on the west range this afternoon, and wait'll you hear this one—he drove on the rim all the way to the house here 'cause he couldn't find the jack. What a nerd.''

It was Ben who first reacted. "Some guy had a flat?"

"Yeah, you remember him, that short little reporter with the rat face."

All three of them stiffened.

"Phillips?" Julie whispered.

"Yeah, Phillips. That's him. I even had to help him change the tire."

"Was he alone?" Brady asked in a grave voice.

"Well now, Pop, that was the weirdest thing. He had some young girl with him. She was all huddled up in the back seat. I could hardly see her through the smoked glass, but I kept wondering. I mean, where'd that guy pick up a young girl around these parts?"

"Was she," Julie asked slowly, "all right?"

"Don't rightly know, Miss Julie. I could hardly see her. I was thinking about calling the cops, though, just to check, but then Phillips took off like the devil himself was chasing him, and then that guy Murdock called and I guess I kind of got busy." Hank shrugged. Then, "You mind telling me what's going on here?"

Ben ignored the question. He stood in front of Brady's son and pinned Hank with a hard gaze. "Try to think," Ben said, "did Phillips say anything at all? *Anything* about where he might have been heading?"

"This sounds serious," Hank said flippantly.

"It is," his father said. "Now, think."

"Well…he did say he was in a real hurry. He was sweating like a pig, too, and his clothes were real grungy."

"Think," Julie urged, coming to stand behind Ben's shoulder.

The young man straightened slowly. "He asked how far it was to the interstate. I told him it depended on whether he was going north or south."

"And?" Ben said.

"He was headed south. Maybe Albuquerque."

"Did he actually *say* Albuquerque?"

"I guess not. But where else would he be going? His car had a sticker on the bumper from some car rental agency in Albuquerque, and the airport's there."

"Oh, God," Julie said, feeling her whole body slump. "He's flying her to New York. I know he is. He'll parade her around like she was a sideshow freak!"

But it was Ben who said, "Just hold your horses. I'm betting he isn't going to get on a plane. Not quite yet."

While Julie wondered at Ben's statement and watched as he strode purposefully to the telephone, Hank stared from one to the other of them, bursting with questions but trying to appear unconcerned.

What was Ben doing? He was flipping through the phone book, his dark brows forming a rigid bar over his eyes. Then he dialed a couple of numbers, talked for a while, frowned both times, and sank into a chair with his head hanging. Whatever he'd been trying had obviously not worked.

"Come on, Pop," Hank finally said, "what's the big secret here? I mean, you guys leave me all alone to do everything, then you come back all of a sudden and won't even tell me where you've been. I ain't no kid."

"I'm *not*," Julie corrected automatically.

Ben glanced up at Brady then. "You may as well tell him," he said, and Julie nodded slowly.

"But," she put in, "this is a secret, Hank. You can never talk about it outside of this house, with anyone but us. You have to promise."

"What the hell?"

"Swear it," Julie said.

"Okay, I swear, I'll keep it forever," he said sarcastically.

And so the story emerged of how they'd stumbled across the hidden entrance to the valley, and how they'd found living there a tribe of Indians who called themselves Anasazi.

"Anasazi!" Hank said scornfully, but a look from his father sobered him.

And they told him about Tayosha's daughter, Mika, and

how Phillips had taken her and a valuable kachina doll and escaped the valley.

"That girl in the car?" Hank straightened sharply. "That young girl in the car was kidnapped?" He frowned, and the scar that split his eyebrow made him appear faintly diabolical.

Julie, Ben and Brady nodded.

"And I let him just drive out of here?"

"It wasn't your fault," Ben said in a level voice. "You had no way of knowing."

"But, I…I knew she looked kind of scared. I even thought about calling that idiot, Lamont. Why didn't I *stop* that rat-faced creep?" he asked, more animated than Julie had seen him in ages.

"You couldn't have known," Julie said softly. "None of us realized."

"Miss Julie," Hank said with new determination. "I gotta take the truck. I'll find that guy. I can do it."

"You're going nowhere," Ben interrupted. "At least not until we have a lead on Phillips. You got that, Hank?" And something in his tone of voice, that air of authority, silenced the young man.

Ben explained just who he'd been calling earlier. "I contacted a friend at Holloman," he said. "He put me on to someone at Los Alamos. There's a carbon dating lab there."

Julie cocked her head. "I don't get it. How is someone at a lab at Los Alamos going to help us?"

"Okay," Ben said, letting out a breath, "I admit I'm grabbing at straws, but everyone who reads, Phillips included, knows that Los Alamos was where the atomic bomb was first developed. They also know that there's a world-renowned government laboratory there—including a carbon dating center."

"So?" Julie said.

"So," Ben went on, "Phillips nabbed the girl, as flesh and blood evidence, but he also ripped off that kachina. Now, if Phillips is going to get proof that the artifact is ancient, *An-*

asazi ancient, then he's going to have to get it carbon-dated, isn't he?''

"He could do that in New York," Brady said.

But Ben shook his head. "He could, but I'm betting he won't. He's got the most efficient center right here in New Mexico. If he were to fly Mika and the artifact all the way to New York, and they proved to be fakes, then what's his editor going to do?''

"Probably fire him," Julie said slowly.

"Exactly. The guy's a reporter. Reporters verify their facts. His reputation is at stake.''

"Ben," Julie said, "how can we be certain? What if—''

"We'll know," Ben interrupted, "because when Phillips walks into that reception area at the lab in Los Alamos, we're going to get a call from the man I talked to earlier.''

"And if he doesn't call?" Brady asked.

"Then we'll rethink it.''

"You're always damn sure of yourself, aren't you, White Eyes?''

"I better be this time, hadn't I?" Ben said gravely.

The problem kept rearing its ugly head all afternoon, hanging over everybody with leaden apprehension: where had Phillips gone with Mika? Was he already at the airport, boarding a flight for New York with that poor girl in tow? The suspense was awful. Julie couldn't bear the waiting, the helplessness of not knowing. She felt keyed-up and fatigued at the same time. She paced, she tried to tidy up the living room, she stared at the phone, willing it to ring, she drank too much coffee.

At five o'clock, when they'd just about given up hope that Phillips would arrive in Los Alamos, the phone rang shrilly. Ben snatched it up. "Who is this?" he demanded. There was a pause. Then, "For crying out loud, man, go write a book or something and leave the lady alone. If she wants to talk to you, she'll call. Yeah. So long.'' He hung up and then seemed to realize what he'd just done and cast Julie a sheepish look.

At 6:20 it rang again. This time Julie grabbed it. "Hello?

Yes, yes, Mr. Tanner is right here.'' Excitedly she handed Ben the phone.

The computerlike logic with which Ben's mind worked never ceased to amaze Julie. Oh, she might have thought about Los Alamos eventually—a week after Phillips had left New Mexico with Mika and Tayosha's kachina, but Ben just knew. It was as if he'd crawled into that quagmire that was Phillips's brain and had come out with the answers. But then, Julie thought as she gathered her things to leave, Ben was like that—accurate, determined, rational. Was that why he fascinated her?

Hank insisted on going, arguing that it was his fault that Phillips had gotten away in the first place. ''I changed his tire, for godsakes, and he didn't even help!'' So that meant that Brady had to stay behind. If it had even been a week ago, Julie would have worried. He'd have gone straight to the bunkhouse and popped open his first beer of the day, no matter the hour. But Brady had somehow undergone a change. He was speaking with more authority, making decisions. He even walked and moved with purpose, with...pride, she decided. That was it, contact with the Anasazi had awakened in her foreman a sense of belonging, a pride in his race that had long since been dormant.

They took Ben's Jeep. They could have taken her pickup, but Ben was insistent that he could make better time on the cross-country back roads in his four-wheel-drive. She had no inclination to argue; with Ben Tanner one did not argue and win.

It was uncanny, Julie decided, to be able to drive away from the ranch yet again without those feelings of guilt and worry she usually experienced. What she had told Ben back at the stream yesterday was true: she was feeling somehow closer to herself, to the things that counted. She'd gotten tremendous satisfaction from eating the wholesome foods of the earth—a lot more satisfaction than she'd ever felt writing a check for groceries, especially a rubber check. Or washing out her clothes. She'd done that all by herself in the trickling water, with her own hands, using the time-honored yucca suds that disappeared harmlessly back into the ground. The Indians had everything they needed without the superfluity, the overwhelming, wasteful consumption of modern society. They had little in the way of material goods, but it was enough. In the way of spiritual peace they were wealthy beyond imagination. Not one of Tayosha's tribesmen would ever feel the alienation of a modern human being; each person was a vital part of the social fabric. Security was built into every belief and ceremony, every simple, everyday task. And each person believed without reservation that the universe was magic and that the gods would watch over him if he lived his life properly.

They could not accept a strange race that lived beyond their valley, because it would destroy them; therefore they did not.

Incredible. And yet there were those, Gary Phillips for one, who could pass right by the marvels of the Indians and see nothing but the money to be made.

Ben had mentioned DNA testing to try and place the Indians of the valley ethnically. Was he just another Phillips, the same book with a more pleasant jacket?

What she did know was that she was strongly attracted to Ben. It had begun, she guessed, from the first moment she'd seen him at her door and he'd had the guts to push aside her gun; his proximity had kept her on edge ever since then. She wanted him to stay, but another part of her wanted him out of her life. He unsettled her, he fascinated her. She hated his arrogance, yet she could listen to him talk forever. She wanted him—with mindless desperation at times—to touch her hand, to pull her into his arms. Yet she was afraid, afraid he'd hurt her. Emotionally she was terrified she'd fall in love with him.

Oh God, she didn't know *what* she wanted. And even if she did know, Ben was still hung up on his wife's memory. How could Julie fight that one even if she wanted to?

She sighed, then turned her head and glanced at Hank, who sat in the back, his dark brows drawn together, looking out the plastic window. His determination to rescue the young girl, who he felt, without justification, that he'd wronged, was an unfamiliar, ill-fitting garment. How odd that this crazy situation had given not only Brady but Hank, too, a purpose.

And Ben. What was his role in this? Was it his lot to expose this lost culture to modern society? Ben must know, with that towering intellect of his, that to expose these innocents to the world would destroy them utterly.

Hank dozed off in the back as dusk fell. Ben drove fast, but they hadn't reached the main highway yet, where traffic would increase. The infrequent vehicles on the road flicked their high beams off in unconscious salute to the Jeep's passage as it raced by, heading south.

"My God," Julie said once, "I hope we catch up with him in Los Alamos. What if…"

Ben shook his dark head. "No 'what ifs,' Julie. We can't afford them. If he's not still there, I'll follow him to New York if I have to," he said with savage intensity. "I won't let him get away with this."

She could have loved him then for his absolute confidence, his quick, sure knowledge of right and wrong, his ability to throw aside caution and rush toward a goal.

And then she wondered about Carol again, the woman who was always going to stand between Ben and another love. How had his wife dealt with this difficult, mercurial man? Carol hadn't liked his flying, he'd told Julie, but she'd let him do it, hadn't she? She'd known, as Julie was learning, that Ben had to fly free. His wife must have loved him very much, Julie decided.

"I wonder how Mika is?" she finally asked. "It must be terrifying for her. She won't understand anything that's going on."

"No," he said grimly. "It'll be pretty bad for her." He paused then and went on. "That girl's just about the same age as Laurie. When I think…"

"I know."

"Sometimes, Julie, I despair of our human race. There's evil in the world, true evil. Look at a man like Phillips. And we have no way of dealing with pure evil. Oh sure, we put people in jail for breaking the law, but there are people who never break a law. They're just plain bad.''

"Oh, Ben, there's good in people, too. So much good. Aren't you forgetting that?''

He turned and his teeth flashed white in a smile, then his eyes were back on the road. "That's what I like about you so damn much. You're a romantic, an incurable romantic. You're just waiting around to believe the best in everyone.''

"And you're a cynic. You have to *prove* everything. You think facts are the same as the truth," she replied staunchly.

"Aren't they?'' he asked, bemused.

"No. The truth is here—'' she put her hand on her heart "—and facts are up here.'' She pointed to her head.

"So you believe they're totally unrelated.''

"Sometimes.''

"Illusion and reality.'' He flashed her another grin. "Well, I guess that's what I deal in, isn't it?''

Cuba passed by, a blur in the night, then San Ysidro and the tiny Jemez Indian reservation. She shut her eyes tightly and prayed that Mika was still in New Mexico.

"Oh, I hope—''

"I know,'' came Ben's voice.

Julie felt his hand come to rest on her knee then, and she melted. One moment Ben was cynical and tough, the next, gentle and understanding. And she wondered how she had ever thought him arrogant. He was simply sure of himself, that was all.

His hand rested there, warm and reassuring for a long moment and finally he removed it, obviously uncertain himself, and rested it on the steering wheel. But his touch was still there, phantomlike, the nerves under her skin still leaping.

What if she let go, let her heart fly free again? What if she could always feel the sweet hot rush of blood through her veins?

And what if, Julie thought suddenly, what if she opened herself up to this man and he turned right around and betrayed her?

They had to turn north after San Ysidro; it was only forty miles or so to Los Alamos. The road ascended and descended, carving its way through the red, mesquite-dotted hills. Julie's hands were balled into fists in her lap. "What if he's left Los Alamos already?"

"He has to wait for the results of the carbon dating. He'll still be there."

She only nodded. This time, she sure hoped he was right.

The dark fled on either side of them, sliced by the Jeep's headlights.

"Julie," Ben said.

"Yes?"

"I…ah…" His voice was tentative, so unlike his normal assurance she was surprised. "I'd like to ask you something."

"Sure."

"Look, I know you have some money problems, with your ranch and all." He took a big breath. "I hope you don't take this as an insult, but I could help you out. Lend you some money to pay off your loan. Not charity, you understand, a loan."

Her first reaction was acute embarrassment. "Oh, Ben…" The confusion swept through her. "I couldn't."

"Why not?" he asked contentiously.

"I couldn't. I'd never be able to pay you back."

"Sure you would."

"It's awfully generous of you—"

"I only said a loan."

"*More* than generous. Thank you for the thought, Ben, but I'll deal with it somehow."

"Yeah, how?"

She looked down. "It's not your problem. I would never ask you to help, to get involved."

"You didn't ask. I offered."

"I appreciate it, really I do, but—"

"Julie, you could lose your ranch," he said quietly, implacably.

Her chest tightened, and she shook her head as if to deny

his words. "No," she whispered, "I can't. Especially not now."

"What do you mean, you can't? Sorry to bring up ugly facts once again, but you sure as hell can."

"No, I'll fix it. Somehow."

"Well, the money's available if you change your mind," he said gruffly. "Let me know."

"Ben…"

"Forget it. Sorry I offered. It doesn't matter."

"I'm not sorry," she said softly, and wanted to reach out and touch him but thought better of it. "Thanks," she said instead. Then her cheeks grew hot in the ensuing silence, and she was glad the darkness hid her face. Her heart gave a joyful leap. He cared about her then; he must. He cared enough to help her save the ranch. She was astonished at how glad that knowledge made her. He cared.

They made Los Alamos by ten-thirty, winding down out of the hills and crossing a deep gorge that rimmed the town. It was a compact place, Los Alamos, dotted with discordant structures—government laboratories and power plants and electrical high-tension pylons and barracks.

Hank stirred in the back seat. "We're here?" he asked groggily.

"Yeah, we're here," Ben said, pulling into a gas station.

"What do we do now?"

"If Phillips is here, he's staying in a motel. I'm going to get a list of places from the phone book. There can't be too many."

"So, how do we know which one he's at?" Hank asked.

"That car of his. We can't miss it."

While Hank filled the Jeep with gas, and Julie went to the ladies room, Ben located a phone book and began copying down addresses. When she got back, he held up his notebook and shook it triumphantly. "There are ten motels here. It'll be easy."

They began on the west side of town, where they'd come in on Route 4, driving through Los Alamos on the main street, turning off to investigate a couple of motor hotels on the main drag. No Continental, no Phillips. Ben even went in and asked the night clerks if there was a Gary Phillips registered. There wasn't.

They reached the edge of town and a lonely water treatment plant and had to turn back, finally locating the turnoff to the big laboratory and the museum, where they found motel row, with its neon signs and turquoise swimming pools, the billboards announcing king-size waterbeds, cable TV, continental breakfasts and children under twelve free.

"He's *got* to be here," Julie said, staring out the window. "Oh Lord, what must Mika think of these lights and noises and people?"

"It must be like being in hell," Hank said. "God, I'm gonna kill that Phillips!"

"No, you're not," Ben said, "because I'm gonna do it first."

"Neither one of you is going to kill anybody. We'll get Mika and Tayosha's kachina, and we'll leave," she said firmly.

They drove up and down parking lots for twenty minutes. No Phillips. *He isn't here,* Julie cried to herself. He'd left. He'd taken Mika and gone to the airport at Albuquerque and boarded a flight to New York.

The sixth motel they came to was a big one with a bright green-and-yellow sign out front. It had four long wings with the doors of its rooms leading straight out onto the parking lot.

"It's a good bet," Ben said. "He won't want to parade Mika through a lobby."

Slowly Ben drove along each row of cars while Julie and Hank searched for the Continental. It was vacation time, and the motel was full of campers and station wagons from Wisconsin and California and Kentucky. Los Alamos was a big tourist attraction. It had been a private boys' school far out in the country until it had been taken over by Oppenheimer and his cadre of scientists to develop the atomic bomb that eventually ended World War II. People came from all over to see it.

"Find it?" Ben asked.

"No," Hank replied.

Ben drove around the unlighted rear of the last wing. His headlights swung around in an arc then illuminated the last row of vehicles.

"Pontiac, Ford, Chevy," Hank chanted to himself. "Camper, Honda, wait a minute!"

Julie's heart stopped; she strained to see in the darkness.

"No, damn, it's a Caddy," Hank said disappointed.

A moment later she saw it. A dusty black Lincoln Continental with its unmistakable rear end. She couldn't find her voice for a second, and Ben drove right past it.

"Stop!" she whispered harshly. "It's there!"

"Well, I'll be damned," Ben said tightly. "We got him!"

"What do we do now?" Julie asked, suddenly frightened.

"We get into his room," Hank said resolutely.

"How?"

But Ben was out of the Jeep already, heading toward the green metal door that was directly in front of the Lincoln.

"Wait," Hank said, "hold on there," and he jumped out and hurried after Ben.

Julie followed more slowly, scared, worried about Mika, worried what Ben and Hank might do to Gary Phillips.

But it was too late. Ben was already rapping on the door loudly. "Sorry," he called out. "Sorry, sir, but it's the night clerk. There's a problem with your car, sir."

CHAPTER ELEVEN

NOTHING HAPPENED. Ben knocked again. "Mr. Phillips, sir…"

"Yeah, what?" came a muffled voice through the door, and Ben felt triumph surge through him.

"Excuse me, Mr. Phillips," he said in his best humble voice, "but we have a problem with your car."

He heard the reporter fumbling with the doorknob, and he could taste victory, hot and metallic in his mouth.

The door cracked open, the room was still dark. Good, Phillips wouldn't recognize him. Ben's heart pounded in anticipation. Just another second and he'd have him.

"Yeah? What in hell…" Phillips was saying.

"Sir, your car. If you could just come out here and move it."

There were mumbled curses, the rattle of the safety chain being removed from its slot. Without hesitation, Ben threw his weight against the door, shoving it open, bursting into the dark room, grabbing at Phillips and propelling him, squirming and flailing, across the floor and onto the bed. The reporter's breath drove out of his lungs in a strangled gasp.

Ben was vaguely aware of Julie and Hank rushing into the room behind him. Julie was saying something in a breathless voice, but adrenaline and fury flooded him in a kind of madness, and all he could think was that rat could have taken Laurie.

"The lights!" Julie was crying. "Hank, get the lights!"

Abrupt whiteness glared in the room, blinding Ben. He was

panting, kneeling over Phillips, who was trying to drag air into his lungs in tortured wheezes.

Ben's eyes adjusted to the brightness, and it was then that he saw Mika, huddled in a corner, a forlorn bundle of brown skin, tangled hair and buckskin.

Gary contorted under him, finally recovering his breath, but temper flared scarlet in Ben's head, and he wrenched the man's arm behind his back, barely registering Phillips's sharp cry of pain.

"Ben, no," Julie was saying, and then he felt hands on him, attempting to pull him off Phillips, small hands that dragged at him futilely.

He wanted to shake off the irritating hindrance, but there was something so insistent in the voice, something that was tugging him back from the brink. Slowly reason crept into his brain, banishing the blood red madness.

"Ben, please!" She was almost sobbing, pulling at the fabric of his shirtsleeve with all her strength.

He became suddenly aware that he was kneeling on the rumpled, pajama-clad body of Phillips. The reporter was unmoving, moaning, his face pressed into bedclothes, his hand pulled up behind him nearly to his shoulder blade. Ben let out a harsh breath and released his hold slightly. Phillips moaned again.

"Lock the door, Hank," Ben said, surprised at how rough his voice sounded. He turned his head to find Hank. The kid was standing there, staring at Mika in the corner, a dumbfounded look on his face. "Hank! Lock that door," he commanded.

Finally Ben stood and glared at Phillips, who was rolling over, groaning, cradling his arm. His pajama top was torn, revealing a pasty-white, hairless chest. Ben was aware of his own chest still heaving.

"Oh, Ben," Julie said, shaky, "I thought you were going to kill him."

"I should have," was all he could find to say. He whistled

between his teeth and noticed Hank crouching now next to Mika. "How is she?"

"Okay, I think."

"You can't do this," Gary Phillips was muttering. "Break in here! I'll call the cops! You're crazy! Almost busted my arm."

Ben felt the madness percolate in him again. "Call the cops. Go ahead. And I'll tell them you kidnapped this girl. Kidnapping and theft. That'd be ten to twenty years, Phillips."

"You can't do this," Phillips repeated.

"I just did," Ben said. "We're taking Mika with us. And the kachina. We're taking them back, Phillips."

Gary glared at him, his bright black eyes glittering with venom. He uttered a foul word and was silent.

Ben would have loved to call the police on Phillips. He wished he could, but then he'd have to explain where Mika came from—the valley, the strange, primitive tribe that he couldn't quite call Anasazi in his own mind. But if they were, if they truly were, then he'd have to betray the valley's secret, and he wasn't at all sure what to do about that.

He saw Julie then, really saw her, staring at him as if he were a stranger, and Hank, kneeling by the young girl, trying to talk to her, trying his few words of Hopi. His arm was around the girl's shoulder, and she was looking at the young man with her liquid black eyes, trying to understand him. Her chin trembled and tears spilled onto her cheeks.

"What a nightmare she must have gone through," Julie whispered.

"You'll pay," Ben said to Phillips. "You'll pay for this, you lowlife."

"I was doing my job, that's all," the reporter said with false bravado.

"You better not have touched her, Phillips."

Gary twisted his mouth. "An ignorant little native like that?"

Suddenly Ben was aware of a muffled curse, and Hank

hurtled across the room at Phillips. Ben and Julie threw themselves on him just as his hands were tightening on the reporter's throat. "No," Ben said, "he's not worth it, Hank! Stop it!"

"You're crazy, all of you!" Phillips cried, his voice raspy. "You're nuts! I didn't touch the stupid chick!"

Hank's chest heaved, his fists were clenched. He shook from repressed anger. His whole being was taut, his eyes snapping. And it occurred to Ben that this couldn't be the same young man who reportedly idled his life away uselessly.

"Okay, Hank, take it easy," he said. "He's not worth it. We're leaving. We're going right now. We'll never see him again."

"Wait a minute," Gary said, recovering from his fright in record time. "Wait a minute. We can make a deal. Negotiate."

"No deals, Phillips."

Phillips got a sly look in his beady eyes. "The kachina. Did you know it was dated at 1295 A.D.? That's *old*, Tanner, real old. It's worth a flaming fortune." He thrust his face up to Ben's. "They're real Anasazi. Think of it! A six-hundred-year-old kachina doll, the real thing."

"It belongs to the Indians," Julie said, her blue eyes sparkling like ice.

"Okay." Phillips shrugged his shoulders and held out his hands. "So I'll make a deal with them. Fifty-fifty split, after taxes."

"You make me sick!" Julie said.

"Okay, okay, sixty-forty. I'm an easy man."

"No deal, Phillips," Ben repeated tightly. "Money can't repay that poor kid for what you put her through. Her tribe considers her dead, because you took her out of the valley, did you know that?"

"But I can make her *rich*, guys," Gary said with obtuse sincerity. "Rich! Exclusive interviews with—with Barbara Walters, even! Radio, TV spots, a book, a movie! She'll have every Tom, Dick and Harry bustin' down her door with offers. I'm doing her a *favor*, guys!''

Ben shook his head in disgust. "Do yourself a favor. Drive on down to Albuquerque and get on the first plane back to New York. And don't come back. Don't *ever* show your face in New Mexico again."

"Oh yeah, big guy, and are you gonna make me?"

Contemptuously Ben turned his back on him. "Help Mika out to the car," he said to Hank, trying to keep his anger in check. And to Julie, "Find the kachina. Let's get the hell out of here."

Julie began to cast around the room.

"Where is it, Phillips?" Ben said. "Now."

"The closet," he mumbled.

"Get it, Julie," Ben said. "We're out of here. This place stinks."

Within moments, the kachina safely tucked under her arm, Julie was opening the door, the fresh night air washing in on them. Hank helped Mika to her feet and began to lead her out. The girl moved woodenly, stiff with fear. It could have been Laurie, Ben thought darkly.

He glanced one last time at Phillips. "If I were you," he said, "I wouldn't breathe a word about this. They'd lock you up in a nut house and throw away the key. So long, pal."

Ben drove back through Los Alamos and onto the highway. The four of them were utterly silent for a time, shaken. It was late, the roads practically deserted, and he made good time, but his mind whirled with unanswered questions. He had time to think as he drove, time to digest Phillips's information about the kachina.

Six hundred years old. Impossible. Used continuously by Tayosha's family for six hundred years. Utterly impossible.

"Ben," came Julie's voice from next to him, interrupting his thoughts. "I was afraid of you for a while there. You were so violent. I thought…"

"I'm sorry. I don't normally do things like that. Hell, I

never do things like that. It was that character, Phillips. The man's a sociopath.''

"I hate it when people are violent," she said softly but vehemently. "I can't stand it."

"Hey, it's over. You'll never see me like that again." And then he realized that he was thinking in terms of the future. Julie and the future. And she was so studiously quiet that she must have realized it, too.

Hank's voice came from the back seat; he was trying to talk to Mika. Ben heard her murmur something and whimper, and Hank replied haltingly.

Julie turned in her seat. "Is she all right, Hank?"

"I don't know, I really don't. She just keeps saying something that I don't understand. Damn!"

"She doesn't know what's happening to her. What a frightening experience. I'll be awful glad when we get her home."

"Miss Julie, what did Ben mean back there in the motel when he said her tribe considers her dead?" His voice was low and intense.

Julie sighed. "He meant, Hank, that we were warned before we left the pueblo that any member of their tribe who leaves the valley is thought of as dead. This is the spirit world here. Only their valley is the real world."

"Goddammit!" Hank said. "So what's going to happen to her? What if her tribe won't take her back?"

"We have to try," Ben said. "This probably has never happened before in their whole history. When her father sees her all in one piece and unhurt, he's sure to take her back."

"But what if he won't? Listen, if they won't take her back, I'll keep her. I'll take care of her. Sure, she can stay with me on the ranch!"

Julie shook her head sadly. "She could never live in our world, Hank."

"Why not? I'll teach her English. Sure, I could do that." His young voice was so full of hope that Ben felt sorry for him. Mika couldn't ever make up six hundred years, not in one lifetime.

The miles sped by. Julie told Ben that Mika had fallen asleep on Hank's shoulder. Poor kid was probably exhausted.

It must have been halfway back to Trading Post when suddenly the Jeep swerved. A surge of adrenaline shot through Ben, he'd damn near fallen asleep.

"God," Julie breathed, clutching the bar in front of her. "Are you all right?"

He wasn't. He was drained. It was the aftermath of all the pent-up anger he'd unloaded on Phillips—it could sap a man.

"*I'm* going to drive," Julie announced. "No arguing."

"But you must be tired, too."

"No, I'm fine, really. But you're not."

He rubbed a hand over his eyes and had to refocus for a minute to see where the white line on the road was. "Yeah, I'm pretty tired. That fracas back there must've taken it out of me." It galled him to admit weakness, but he really was afraid he'd crack the Jeep up if he kept driving. He hated to fall apart in front of Julie, but sometimes there was no negotiating with your physical condition.

She drove the rest of the way while Ben dozed. Every once in a while he'd jerk awake and talk to her and try to stay alert, but then his eyes would close and he'd nod off for a few more minutes. Once he opened his eyes, shifted positions and glanced at her. She was wonderful. He couldn't help but admire her profile, the strong chin and pretty nose with its slightly upturned end. A car passed, and its headlights picked out the gleam of her cheek and forehead, the curving length of her eyelashes, the long graceful line of her neck.

She drove competently, just as she did everything. She didn't complain or whine or belittle, she accepted the situation and did what had to be done. A romantic, yes, but one with strength and ability and beauty.

He dozed and jerked awake again. "You okay?" he asked.

"Sure, go back to sleep."

"I wasn't asleep."

A slow smile curved her lips. "Okay, so you weren't. Do whatever it was you were doing, then."

Gentle teasing, a closeness he hadn't felt for years. Someone he could trust utterly, someone with whom he could share the adventure of life.

It struck Ben abruptly. Was he talking about...love? Whoa there. *Love?* But he barely knew her. A week or so. You couldn't get to know a person in a week. It must have been something else he was feeling. Maybe a closeness to this woman. Yet this closeness he felt was dangerously near to love.

There were things about Julie he didn't know. He recalled just tonight when she'd cringed from the violence in Phillips's motel room. There'd been something in her voice then, an edge, a real horror of what Ben had almost done. Yes, an edge to her voice, as if she'd had experience with violence, personal experience. Her father? No, she spoke of him with reverence. Who then? A boyfriend? Her husband? He looked over at her again. She'd never said a word about her marriage; she'd steered away from the subject, from anything personal, from her past.

Ben closed his eyes and took a deep breath. Anger rose in him all over again, anger at the man who'd hurt Julie, whoever it was. What kind of a rotten coward had she fallen in with? He'd like to meet the guy, he'd like to—

"Almost there," Julie said, turning off the highway at Trading Post.

She was wonderful. Wounded somewhere along the line, too careful with her feelings, but a perfect companion in a crisis. Ben admitted to himself that he felt a hell of a lot more than platonic admiration for her, though. It might be love, he wasn't sure. And Julie would have to give it a chance before he would know.

BEN STOOD AT THE CREST of the hill and caught his breath. What Julie had been saying about the atmosphere in the ancient valley struck him profoundly while he gazed down. The morning light was unearthly, the distance obscured by that bluish-purple haze, the edges of the tall mesa walls that surrounded him blurred. Reds were more pink in here, browns were softened, green was tinted by gray. He saw the hues of the valley, and he couldn't deny what he saw, yet how was it possible?

He could hear the others approaching from behind along the narrow cut that was the entrance—the only entrance—to this magic place. Brady and Hank helped Mika along, and Julie followed them with Coyote on her heels.

Ben wiped the sweat from his brow. "I hope we aren't making things harder for Mika by coming back in here like an army," he said.

"I know," Julie agreed, "but I wanted to come along. I feel as if, well, this might be the last time, Ben. We're intruders here."

"I only hope they want Mika," he said pointedly.

This time it took them only two hours to make the trek to the base of the cliff dwelling. They might have made it quicker if Mika hadn't been plodding along lethargically—the walking dead, Ben thought. He itched to know what was really going on in her head, and he might have been able to find out through Brady, but Mika wasn't talking to anyone. She moved like an automaton, Hank ever at her arm, leading her. Hank had grown protective of her, trying to make her eat something last night when they'd gotten to the ranch, sleeping in the living room at her feet, urging her to take some food that morning. And Hank seemed to be the only person to whom Mika responded at all.

"Tayosha's not going to like this," Brady said as he craned his neck upward.

"She's his *daughter*," Julie put in.

"Yeah, but she's dead to the tribe. They're not even going to look at her."

Ben saw the pained expression on Julie's face, wished there was something reassuring he could tell her, then began the long ascent up the ladder.

Tayosha did greet Brady, and seemed to acknowledge Hank

but, as always, he gazed straight through Ben and Julie, and never even turned in the direction of Mika.

Julie was rattled. She kept at Brady to explain to Tayosha that they'd brought his daughter back and that she was safe and unharmed, but he seemed not to hear Brady at all.

"Dammit," Julie said, "he can't *do* this to her. Brady..."

"Look," Ben said, taking her arm and drawing her aside, "you're not helping things. We better make ourselves scarce and give the old fellow time to work this out."

"And if he doesn't?"

Ben let out a breath. "We'll worry about that later."

Everything was much as before when they made their way to the house that had been theirs for those three days. The Indians of the pueblo went about their business as if these strangers didn't exist. No one made eye contact, no one even stopped his or her work for a moment. If someone was thinking about Mika or her fate, there wasn't a sign of it. When the five of them got to the tiny house, there were already a jar of water there, however, and a pot of warm corn porridge and flat tortillas. Ben wondered why they were feeding the nonexistent ones, but then maybe the food was for Brady and Hank.

"So we just sit here and wait?" Hank said, pressing Mika down to a sitting position. "And wait for what? Why are they treating her like this?"

"I've told you a dozen times," Brady said angrily, "she went into the other world. To them she died."

"So why doesn't her father die when he goes out there?" Hank scoffed as he sat down next to Mika, his arm going around her shoulder. "Tell me *that*."

"Tayosha's medicine is powerful. He's protected by the gods," Brady said.

"That's bull and you know it. I think you're as nuts as the rest of them."

For a minute Ben thought Brady might strike the boy, but instead he seemed to let his anger flow from him. He shrugged finally. "I feel sorry for you, son," he said. "There's a wealth of knowledge staring you in the face here, and I'm afraid you're too bottled up inside to see it.''

"*You* can see it, though?" Hank shot back boldly.

"That's right." Brady smiled thinly. "For the first time in my life I can finally see."

The hours seemed to crawl by that day, and Ben felt edgy, stuck there, knowing that they were all unwelcome, growing more certain by the minute that they could sit there waiting for years and Tayosha would still not acknowledge Mika.

Julie was pacing the earthen courtyard, anxiously back and forth. He watched her from where he sat leaning against the wall, his hands hanging loosely over his knees. If the situation weren't so insane, he would have liked the way she set her shoulders so squarely, the sure, swift strides of her strong, shapely legs, the slight tilt of her chin, the way her golden hair swung on her shoulders. There was that competence to Julie, the feeling a man got that she knew just where she was headed; good or bad, she was prepared to cope. She had a sharp mind, but a woman's mind, one that at times was alien to him, yet he felt safe talking to her, felt as if Julie understood him and accepted him whether or not she was always in agreement. Yeah, he liked watching her, all right. It was just too damn bad that they were in such a tenuous position here. He figured he'd better talk to Julie and Brady pretty soon and let them know that he was starting to think they might as well leave for home.

"Look," Julie said, and he saw that she'd stopped her pacing and was staring up at the cliffs high above them. "That looks like...Tayosha. What's he doing?"

Sure enough it was Tayosha, far above, making his way to the very top of the sheer cliff. He appeared to be clad in his finest, a feathered robe trailing behind him as he climbed like a mountain goat up the side of the mesa.

"Where's he going?" Hank asked. "He'll kill himself up there. The guy's screwy."

It was Brady who answered. "I suspect he's gone to consult the gods."

"So where does that leave us?" Ben asked.

"Sitting here," Brady said, "and waiting."

"Great." Ben sighed in exasperation. It was going to get dark soon, too dark to walk back out. Mika was already weak as it was, Hank was sitting there growing more frustrated by the moment. Julie was as nervous as a cat, and he, himself, was getting fed up. Here they'd rescued the girl, half killed themselves to rush her back to her people, and now it looked as if they were just supposed to wait there, rotting, while Tayosha went to the summit of the mesa to pray. And Mika— Mika was simply dying.

CHAPTER TWELVE

HANK STOPPED his angry pacing and faced them. "I've got to get Mika out of here. She's gotta eat or she's gonna die."

"You're going nowhere." Brady put a restraining hand on the young man's shoulder. "You'll do what you have to."

"Why?"

"Because it's their way. We go by their rules, like it or not. Their customs have worked for them for a thousand years. I think," Brady said meaningfully, "that you'd do well to learn from these people. Your own set of rules haven't worked so well for you, son. Now have they?"

"And they've worked good for you, right, Pop?" The boy's eyes flashed in challenge.

"I'm learning," Brady said, surprisingly undaunted by his son's sarcasm. "At least, by coming to this valley, I know now what I've been missing."

Julie hurt for both of them, for their arguing and for Hank's inability to see the beauty of the Indians' ways. But she understood his frustration, too. Maybe they shouldn't have told Hank the secret or brought him with them. Maybe it had only made things worse.

A dense orange glow settled over the cliff dwelling as cooking fires were lighted in the growing dusk. The air grew heavier, laden with the odor of broiling meat and burning juniper. Those sounds of children's laughter that Julie had grown used to were not to be heard that night, though, and she guessed it was because the shadowy strangers from the other world had returned. Worse, they had come back with yet another spirit, Mika's.

The girl stoically accepted her fate, although to Julie she looked paler and thinner than before. Brady was trying to explain to his son that soon Mika would disappear, that she would wander off to die somewhere because she knew it was her duty. And there was Hank, railing against Mika's fate, fierce in his determination to help her.

Mika finally closed her eyes and seemed to rest. It crossed Julie's mind, utterly out of place, she knew, that Hank and Mika made a good-looking young couple. Hank sat with the girl's head resting on his shoulder, his smooth, narrow face set, his eyes restive under the rakish slant of his split eyebrow. But he was quiet now, as if afraid to disturb what little peace she'd found, and in that quiet Julie sensed an inner struggle to find meaning in all that had happened. If there was such a thing as love at first sight, Hank was a victim of it, and with that love had come all the pain in the world.

No one saw Tayosha appear. One moment Julie was gazing out across the expanse of the valley, musing over the mist that had again spread along the floor like groping tentacles, the next moment Tayosha was there in the courtyard, an aura of power surrounding him like a shroud, an almost visible halo of unearthly light. Her blood halted in her veins.

He spoke to Brady for some time; then, without a waver of intent, he disappeared again, seeming to float away as he descended the terrace to the next level below. Julie had to shake herself.

"Wow," she said, turning to Ben.

"He's something," Ben allowed.

"And," Brady said, stepping forward into the circle of firelight, "he's smart. He might have found a way to bring Mika back to life."

"Well, it's about time," Hank said angrily. "Who's the old guy trying to kid?"

"He's not kidding anyone," his father said. "This is dead serious stuff. Try to give it some respect."

"Okay, okay," Hank muttered.

"What did Tayosha say?" Julie asked. "I mean, how's he going to bring her back?"

"He spoke to the gods when he was on top of the mesa." Brady shrugged. "I guess there's this ancient ritual the gods told him about."

"Um," Ben said, "convenient."

"But it's not foolproof. Tayosha says that if he fails, there's great danger to his daughter."

"Danger?"

Brady nodded. "If he blows it, then Mika's soul will wander in the evil spirit world for eternity."

"What do you want to bet," Ben said under his breath, "that Tayosha pulls it off?"

"Hey, *kemo sabe*," Brady put in, "why don't you stow it for a while?"

"I only meant," Ben said, a smile tilting a lip, "that Tayosha's a pretty wise old codger."

Mika wore a tanned beige dress whose fringe reached her ankles, and around her thin throat and down her chest hung beads and long, intricately woven leather necklaces of turquoise and polished red stone. From her ears dangled turquoise, and her eyes sparkled from a blue dye on the lids; her lips were blood red. That night a keening old woman who looked straight through her had led her away to an empty house where she'd found the clothing waiting. Julie had wanted to go along—and it was all they could do to keep Hank still—but Brady had warned them both not to interfere. They all wondered just what this ritual given Tayosha by the gods entailed. Was it physical? Did they, themselves, dare view the ceremony?

"Hey," Brady said, "you may as well watch. Did you forget? You White Eyes don't exist."

Coyote was tied securely inside the house, and Julie let Ben lead her down to the central courtyard where the Indians were gathering and a huge fire had been built. They stayed cautiously out of the way, not wanting to interfere, finding a spot near a wall where they could watch the events of the night unfold.

"Tayosha will bring her back," Julie said in a hushed voice. "I know he will."

Ben put his hand on her knee as they sat in their corner. "Sure, he's got it all planned," he said. "Don't worry."

She felt his shoulder against her and his hand, warm and strong, on her leg, and she felt a little safer, a little less rocked by the noise, the crowd, the drums and poor Mika's situation.

The women of the pueblo came first and gathered in a circle around the fire. Their necks and arms glittered with jewelry, and they wore their finest dresses, covered with designs and feathers and quill beads. The men formed an outer circle.

The rhythm of the drums quickened, insistent, compelling, at one with the beat of Julie's heart. The sound was all around her, reverberating off the ageless stone walls and inside her head, filling it, pulsating. She felt Ben's hand tighten on her knee, turned to look at him and tried to smile, but it wouldn't come, and her heart kept pounding, leaping in time to the hollow boom of the drums. She could feel Ben's pulse where he touched her, throbbing with the drums, too. She closed her eyes and felt herself slip deeper under the spell of the night.

The haunting wail of flutes began. The men started a slow, cadenced dance. They swayed, their lips moving in a primeval chant, their feet stamping. The women began to sway as well, their hips grinding in slow circles, turning themselves away from the firelight, then swinging back again in an arc, all in unison.

And then Mika was there in the center of the circle, a jewel among the other dancers. Still no one looked at her. She was a spirit, and Julie wondered what the dancing and chanting meant. Could they really bring the girl back to the land of the living?

She felt Ben's knee move against hers, warm, firm, a source of reality in the place of disturbing enchantment. And over there, next to Hank, beyond the circle of men, was Brady, yet another thread to the real world.

Julie finally saw Tayosha. He was standing, arms raised, just behind the circle of men on the far side of the terrace. The light from the fire flickered redly over him in undulating waves.

Ben nudged her gently, nodding in Tayosha's direction.

"I see him," Julie whispered.

The medicine chief was clad in the attire of a king. A many-layered robe flowed from his shoulders, and around his waist was a belt from which dangled bits of fur and bones and leather pouches. He was wearing a necklace of brilliantly colored stones and feathers, and in one raised hand was a kind of rattle that hissed and sang in harmony to the drumbeats.

But it was his face that stunned Julie. He was painted grotesquely. White and black striped his nose, cheeks and neck, while one eye was circled in blood red. He was no longer mortal, Julie thought, but a spirit—or a god, perhaps—come down from the top of the mesa, from the world beyond the valley, to lead these innocents in the pagan ritual. Surely he had the power to bring his daughter back to life.

Julie held her breath.

Slowly Tayosha began to move in a wide circle behind the men. He chanted, raised his arms. His eyes flashed. And all the while Mika kept turning toward him, her face utterly impassive, but Julie was certain the young woman's eyes glistened with tears. Of faith? Of fear?

The ritual went on and on, tirelessly, into the shadowed night. Julie watched when a purifying potion, an emetic of bark and roots, was boiled in a clay pot over the fire then passed from one person to the next until all but Tayosha and Mika had consumed it. Shortly, one by one, each became sick, as if cleansing himself, then went back to swaying and chanting and rattling bone bracelets.

She searched the crowd of faces for Brady and Hank. Yes, there they were, still standing motionless, watching the ceremony. Brady looked on with a kind of reverence, while Hank's face registered wonder. Julie could practically see him itching to be with Mika during her ordeal. He must have been going through hell—a hell, she thought, that she was becoming too familiar with herself.

It was incredible to Julie how long she and Ben sat there by the wall motionless, their bodies touching in so many places, their breathing heavy in expectancy. She watched Mika, waiting for a sign that life was being returned to her, and she wondered how Mika would know. A sign from Tayosha? She was a brave young woman, her faith in the healing powers of her father unshakable. It was difficult for Julie to put herself in Mika's place, to comprehend the tremendous courage it must have taken for Mika to face her own death and to have accepted the injustice of it. Now there she was, hour after endless hour, awaiting the outcome of her dilemma with little more than her faith to sustain her.

How simple, Julie thought. But then, every facet of the Indian's life was pure and simple. It struck Julie how complicated she'd made her own life—and all because of a lousy marriage. She'd let the memory of Mark's brutality become the basis of all her actions and reactions. She'd never accepted his cruelty, and so she'd never gotten over it. Why couldn't she face life as Mika was doing? Face life, be reborn.

The women gyrated, abandoning themselves to the drums, the hot night, the dust raised by their feet. Now pairing off with men they danced and danced, whirling to the haunting sound of the flute and the chanting....

Abruptly Julie's face flushed. The mood had changed, she realized. The dance was about rebirth. Physical rebirth. She shot a quick, sidelong glance at Ben, but his face was unreadable.

Sexual. The dance had become blatantly sexual—sweating brown bodies, mouths open, panting, cries of pleasure, of discovery. Men and women leaving, two by two, trailing off in the discreet darkness between the houses.

Julie looked down, embarrassed, feeling Ben's hand like a brand on her, heavy and hot. Her temples pounded, her belly writhed, flares of sensation burst within her, white-hot. She couldn't catch her breath.

The fingers of mist that groped the valley floor seemed to have slithered up the mesa and were probing the hard-packed earth of the courtyard, obscuring the moccasined feet so that the torsos of the remaining dancers appeared to float, legless. Tayosha was only a face on a bodiless head, a powerful demonic face.

Julie's head grew light and her breathing shallow. Mika was being reborn; hands were reaching out to touch her now as cries of joy split the night. The girl was smiling. The tribe was accepting her. Mika was alive to them again.

Rebirth.

"See," Ben was saying, "she's okay now. He pulled it off."

But Julie couldn't answer. She swallowed, blinked her eyes. Everything throbbed and swam in front of her. She felt nauseous, weak. Sweat popped out on her forehead.

"Julie?" Ben was saying. "You okay?"

She could only shake her head from side to side. The drums beat at the air, never letting up. A woman danced, bare-breasted, her torso glistening with sweat, and a man bent over her. Mika danced, too, turning slowly, keeping the rhythm with her feet, and Julie saw Hank, moving closer to her, his gaze locked hungrily on her.

Sexual tension flashed through the air like the burst of crimson sparks that shot up from the fire. Julie shuddered.

"I'm taking you back to our house," she heard Ben say. "Come on, you're as white as a ghost."

She felt Ben pull her to her feet, and then her legs seemed to give way beneath her, detached. She was floating—floating and moving, but Ben was propelling her, his arm around her shoulder, his side pressed heavily against hers. And the drums, they beat and beat.

The next thing Julie knew she was somewhere close to their house, doubled over, retching until she thought she'd rip in two. And all the while Ben was there, holding her head, wiping her brow, steadying her.

"It was that damn stew you had for dinner." He helped

her straighten, then held her against him. "You going to be all right now?"

"I...I think so." But it wasn't the stew. It was something else.

He held her there, immobile, for a long moment. Too long. Her chest rose and fell too fast, and inside her belly tiny thrills of sensation ignited, licking at her. She trembled with his nearness.

It hadn't been the stew. There was no acid taste, no bitterness, only a sort of sweet, thick taste in her mouth, as if she'd eaten too much candy and been instantly ill. She drank several cups of water when she got inside, then sat on the sleeping mat and put her face in her hands. What had happened to her? Her whole body felt light, as if she'd cast off weights she'd been carrying around for an eternity.

"Do you feel better now?" Ben asked, worried.

"Yes, better." She couldn't meet his eyes. "I'm so sorry..."

"Hey, it's okay."

She was embarrassed. He'd seen those men and women, heard their cries, sitting there right next to her—man and woman. The drums still pulsated outside in the night, reminding her. "I don't know what made me so sick, I don't know why..." Her voice trailed off, and she felt herself go pale, as if the blood in her head was pumping out the rhythm of the drum beats. For an instant she thought it was the aftermath of being ill, but when she saw the look in his eyes she knew. She was sick with suppressed need, with desire that had been so long buried inside her that it was washing over her like molten lava.

She tore her eyes away from his, ashamed, sure she was reading too much into his look, and searched frantically for words.

Her heart was beating so hard against her ribs it hurt. What was she doing, what did she really want? And there were the drums beating, beating on into the night, beating like her heart, pounding in her ears. That fog that filled the magic valley seemed to swirl up into her head, filling it with pictures of the Indians dancing, gyrating slowly, sensually, the brown skin, hot eyes, open mouths panting, the scent of flesh and smoke in the air, the sweet perfume of desire.

"Ben," she whispered, her voice raw with need.

He was there, driving all thought from her brain, his hands on her shoulders, his eyes dark with passion. His lips were at her neck, his beard brushing her collarbone. She clutched at him and her head lolled back. She moaned, abandoning herself to the drums and the mist of the night.

Her fingers entwined themselves into the thickness of his hair. She felt his mouth on her breast while a warm hand slid under her shirt, beneath her bosom and held its weight. A shock rippled through her limbs.

Ben stroked her everywhere, his hands gliding along her hips and across her belly, up to her breasts, down her back and spine until he gripped her buttocks and held her to him. He kissed her gently, his tongue moving against hers, probing her mouth. And he kissed her with urgency, his lips hard and insistent on hers, forcing her head back, his hands roaming her body in a fever of their own. And he asked her if she was ready as he pressed himself to her, his maleness a rock against her inner thigh. Oh God, she was ready, she wanted him inside her with a desperation that she never dreamed possible, but what was going to happen when she couldn't…when she didn't…

He entered her swiftly and painlessly, and she felt him deep inside her, his hips gliding against hers, their bodies becoming sweat-slicked as they moved in that age-old rhythm of love. She felt herself climbing and falling and climbing agian. Over and over. She was certain she was going to reach that height, so sure. Then she fell back, trying so hard, so hard.

Ben held her face in his hands. He was panting, but smiling. "It's okay…it's okay," he said again and again. And then minutes later she felt him shudder above her and inside her, and he groaned and rocked then finally collapsed on top of her.

She'd expected to feel ashamed or at least embarrassed. Instead, while Ben nuzzled his lips to hers and against her neck, his fingertips brushing the tips of her breasts, she felt strangely relieved and at peace with herself. It was okay, he'd said.

It came easily to Julie that night to unburden herself at last. She told him everything, things that she hadn't even known herself.

"I was married," she confessed. "His name was Mark. I loved him at first." She drew a deep, quavering breath and looked straight into Ben's eyes. "He used to hit me," she said without shame, and she felt Ben stiffen against her. "It's okay. After tonight I can accept it."

Ben's arms tightened around her convulsively. He cursed under his breath. "How could a man do that?"

And she told him about her sex life. "He never gave me a chance, and then, well, I guess I was scared of him. I held back."

"Maybe you were punishing him," Ben said in a whisper at her ear.

"Maybe I was."

"You aren't frigid, Julie, just wounded. I could kill that creep."

"No, no don't say that. If it hadn't been for Mark, who knows how my life would have turned out?"

"Is it so great?"

"It is…now," she said.

"You know, in time," Ben said carefully, "if you trusted me…I could help. We could be better together. A whole lot better for you."

"Oh, Ben," Julie said, adoring him, "what are we doing? Are we crazy?"

"Maybe."

He told her a lot that night, more than she wanted to hear, perhaps. He told her, so truthfully it hurt, that he wasn't sure he could ever love again the way he had loved his wife. But

Julie was special, he whispered, holding her close. Different than anyone he'd met.

"I'm never sure *what* to make of you," he said, a smile curving his lips. "All I know is that I can't get enough."

"What are we going to do?" Julie ran a finger softly down his cheek to his bearded jaw.

"I don't know," he said.

They both rested finally, Coyote on the threshold, Brady and Hank still with the others who would dance in ritual till the first rays of light filtered through the mist on the floor of the valley. Julie rested, dozing, her head in the crook of his arm, her hip still touching his. She dreamed of pagan ceremonies and of drums beating to the cadence of their love-making, of waking to begin the odyssey anew. She dreamed of having all the time in the world to be with Ben, to decide on a future, a future in which her values were changed, in which money and worldly possessions meant nothing. She dreamed of being utterly happy.

And then she dreamed about Hank, about his bursting into their little house, and about his angry face and his swearing.

Julie sat bolt upright. It was dawn and Hank was there, somewhere close by, and he was cursing.

"I'll kill him myself this time!" she heard him say, and she touched Ben on the shoulder.

"Wake up, Ben. *Wake up.*" She saw him roll over onto his back and struggle to open his eyes. "Ben," she said, alarmed, "something's happened."

In the next room she could hear Brady ask something and his son's answer: "It's rat face, the reporter. Phillips is back!"

CHAPTER THIRTEEN

BEN FELT HIS BLOOD freeze in his veins. Phillips was back! After what he'd done, he had the nerve to come back!

"Okay," he heard Hank say, "this time I'm gonna kill the guy!" The young man's hands were balled into fists; he looked like he could kill.

"Hold it," Brady said, barring his son's way. "Calm down. You can't do a thing. Let Tayosha take care of it."

"Tayosha, ha! He'll just let the creep go like he did last time!" Hank yelled.

"Please, Hank," Julie was saying, a hand on the boy's arm, "it won't help matters."

"He can't get away with it!" Hank was saying furiously.

The pueblo was in an uproar. Gone was the tranquillity, the sense of peace and belonging and perfect harmony. There were murmurings, small groups gathering, babies crying and young men muttering and scowling. Tension permeated the centuries-old cliff house, disruption, confusion. And all, Ben thought grimly, because of one lousy reporter.

He frowned at Brady. "Try to find out what they're going to do to Phillips."

"Maybe I shouldn't interfere," Brady began.

"Look," Ben said, "we've got to stay on top of this. God knows what that rotten little—never mind. I just don't want to sit up here doing nothing. I can't talk to these people, Julie can't. It's up to you."

"*I'll* go," Hank put in darkly. "If they're gonna stake him out, I wanna be there."

"You can go along with your father," Ben said, "but you'll do nothing. You understand me, Hank?"

The boy, seeing the look on Ben's face, nodded grudgingly.

"And let us know," Julie said, "please."

Ben rubbed the back of his neck with a hand and strode angrily back and forth in front of their house. "Didn't Phillips do enough? Couldn't he quit? Talk about *tenacity*!"

Julie put a shy hand on his arm, as if she were not used to touching a man comfortably, and he stopped pacing. "What will they do to him?" she asked. "Do you think he's in real danger?"

"I hope so," Ben replied harshly.

"Oh, why didn't he just leave?"

Ben pulled her close, felt the firm curve of her body against him as if it had been made to fit there. "Look, I didn't want to say this in front of Brady and Hank, but it's not really our problem anymore. Phillips just gave up all rights to our protection, as far as I'm concerned."

"Oh, Ben, I'm afraid it's not going to be so easy." She leaned her head against his shoulder, right in the hollow in front of his collarbone. He felt a sudden tightening in his groin, remembering.

What they'd shared last night had been miraculous. He wanted to wallow in memories, to talk about it with Julie, to sit and hold her hand and watch her brush her hair and smile at him. But Phillips had come back and destroyed the mood completely. For that alone...

"He's a horrible person," she was saying. "But I don't want to see him hurt."

"I'm not sure I agree with you on that, Julie," he said dryly. "I'd love to see him get his hide tanned."

They didn't have to say it aloud, Ben knew, but they were both keenly aware of the new tension in the air. There was an undercurrent of anxiety that ran through the pueblo like an invisible river. Ben felt an ache behind his eyes, a growing pressure. He hadn't had one of his headaches—those hangovers from having endured so many Gs when he'd been a test pilot—for a couple years. But then he thought wryly, he hadn't been in a situation quite like this, either.

The huge sun rose, casting long, somber shadows among the houses. It would be another hot day—hot and dry. Ben looked down into the valley. The night mist was gone, and he could swear the stream was narrower. What if it dried up? Did these people know how to dig wells? He pondered whether helicopters could lower enough water barrels to keep them going until it rained. And what would these Indians think of helicopters landing in their valley?

Brady came back, huffing up the last set of ladders. "They've got him in an empty house, under guard," he reported.

"Where's Hank?" Ben asked.

A thin smile curved Brady's lips. "Watching over Mika."

"He's got it bad, huh?" Ben said.

"Nutty kid," was all Brady replied, shaking his head. "He can barely talk to her."

"I think it's nice." Julie said in Hank's defence. "I think it's good for Hank, to care about someone a lot. And Mika likes *him* a lot, too."

"So what are they going to do to Phillips?" Ben wanted to know.

Brady lifted a brow. "I couldn't quite understand the words they used. Some kind of ceremony, I guess."

"Will they hurt him?" Julie asked.

"I really don't know, Miss Julie." And then Brady took off his hat, swung his braids back and mopped his brow. He looked from Ben to Julie. "We've got another problem," he began.

"Figures," Ben said, feeling the throb in his temples.

"I heard Phillips bragging that he's got help coming. Something about a camera crew on its way."

"Oh God," Julie breathed, "he called his paper!"

"Looks like it," Brady said.

Ben stayed silent, studying Julie's face. So much for keeping her valley a secret.

"They won't find this place," Brady was telling her, "I'm sure they won't." But she didn't look convinced. Ben could only reach out and brush aside a stray lock of her hair and try to reassure her wordlessly that somehow it would all work out.

But how? he wondered, half listening to Julie and Brady as they both talked, upset about this new and unsettling problem.

He was caught in a real quandary. For the first time in his life Ben really didn't know what was right. The Indians deserved their prerogative to remain secluded, and the thought of the *Nation's* troops descending on the pueblo—of dozens of Gary Phillips—made him damn good and mad.

And yet—all the evidence pointed to this truth—these Indians were of tremendous scientific and anthropological value. Ben had been trained as an investigator, not a judge of moral rights and wrongs. He was on foreign ground here, stepping into a quagmire, where seemingly solid ground sank under his feet.

"You'll help me, won't you?" she was asking. "You'll help me keep this valley safe?"

"How, Julie?"

"By keeping reporters like Phillips and his camera crew out of here." She stirred him with her surety and her ideals and that romanticism that couldn't be quenched.

He scrubbed a hand on the back of his neck. "Julie, I'm not sure either of us has the right to stop reporters or a camera crew from filming here. The press is protected by the first amendment. The world has the right to know." He spoke quietly with his brows drawn together, his head pounding now, uncomfortable with this truth of which he wasn't sure. And yet he'd been taught all of his life to collect facts and search out the truth. Damn, the truth again.

She was looking at him, aghast. "Ben, oh my God, how can you say that? How can you be so unfeeling?"

"I'm not being unfeeling. I'm trying to be objective. You're taking this too personally."

But her face reflected what she thought of his scientific objectivity. She grew silent and withdrew, her mouth pale and pinched. He wanted to pull her close and protect her from all the ugly choices she'd ever have to make in her life, but she was too distant, and he didn't have it in him to try to overcome her resistance.

For the first time since they'd met he felt a space between them, a chasm that seemingly was not going to be bridged by talking.

"Look," he said, rubbing his temples, "I'm going for a walk. It's not you, I just need some time. Okay?"

"All right," she replied. Then, seeing his fingers pressed to his temples, "Are you...are you getting sick, Ben?" There was genuine alarm in her voice.

"Just a headache, that's all. I used to get them when I flew."

"But..."

"I'm fine. I'll see you in a while. Okay?"

"Sure. Okay," she said doubtfully.

He walked and climbed throughout the pueblo that day, an invisible man, carefully unseen by anyone. He studied the brown faces, the cubicle houses, the women patiently grinding corn or building fires, sewing or climbing ladders with heavy jars of water. Illusion and reality. The cliff palace gave the illusion of being untouched by time, the people living innocently in a previous millennium, but what was the reality?

He wondered if it were, indeed, possible to sustain a falsehood as completely as these people seemed to be doing. His heart said no but his suspicious, analytical mind said maybe.

His head pounding worse by the hour, he wandered to every level, up every ladder, into every cul-de-sac of the ancient stone city. Nowhere did he see a slip, a bit of plastic or metal, a nail, a scrap of paper, a rubber band.

Could he allow this living, breathing relic of the past to be corrupted?

Tayosha's people grew and reaped their simple crops; they lived and died close to nature, part of it. They did not pollute nor did they live with any form of pollution. The Sun Father shone on them, the Cloud People wept, the Earth Mother fed them. Their cycles went on, their ceremonies celebrated the cycles. The sun, the moon, the stars moved in their ordained paths. They lived an ordered existence, at peace with themselves and their world. Until the white ghosts had invaded.

To whom did Ben have a primary responsibility? To these innocent people, the discovery of whom would mean devastation? Or to the outside world, his world?

Tension filled the pueblo and reverberated in every shadowed corner. The tribe had tried to ignore the invaders from the spirit world, but in the end they had not been able to. Phillips had seen to that; he'd sullied the valley with his devious schemes. What would Tayosha do with the reporter? What could he do?

Near the summit of the aged pueblo Ben sat and rested on a wall. Sweat trickled down the back of his neck and his damn headache persisted with a will of its own. Somewhere below him on that steep cliff was Julie. He'd have to go back and face her eventually, but he had no more answers now than when he'd left.

IT WAS ALMOST DARK by the time Ben returned to his own fire pit. The enormous sun was setting with the pink-streaked abandon of a painter gone mad, and the ground fog was beginning to curl at the foot of the cliff. The old stone city glowed, reflecting burnished copper, and the cooking fires dotted the pueblo like bright jewels. And somewhere, as if it were rising out of the heart of the very rocks upon which the pueblo was built, there was the muffled rhythm of drums, booming out the questions still throbbing in his mind, causing his head to pound in blinding pain.

Julie was there waiting for him, twisting her hands in front of her. "Where have you been?"

"Walking, thinking." Dots swam in front of his eyes. A real migraine this time.

"Brady," he heard her call, "where's that medicine?"

"Hey," Ben began, but none of them were having his protests. He drank the concoction Brady had gotten from Tay-osha—the medicine chief, Ben thought wryly through the haze of his discomfort. He just hoped the stuff didn't kill him. He sat there, feeling foolish, because Julie and Brady kept staring at him, waiting for some reaction, he supposed.

"Think I'll turn blue?" he asked sarcastically, but neither of them paid him any mind.

The odd thing was, in a few minutes the pain was a little duller, the pounding a little less. And in a few minutes more it was practically gone.

"Better?" Julie asked softly.

"I'll be damned," was all Ben allowed himself to say.

A lot had happened since Ben had disappeared. And none of it boded well for Phillips. Apparently Tayosha had come to a decision about the reporter and was soon to hold a meeting of the elders in the sacred kiva—a ceremonial underground chamber—near the central plaza. Already the drums summoned the people down from their homes, promising punishment and justice.

"I hope Phillips gets everything Tayosha has to dish out," Hank said as he started to climb down their ladder to join the assemblage.

The meeting looked ready to begin. All around Ben and Julie the muttering of the crowd grew louder and the drums answered. Cries rang out on the night air. Where were the drummers? Ben looked around but couldn't see anyone beating them. Tayosha stepped from the doorway of a nearby house then, dressed in his ceremonial finery, his feathers fluttering, one eye painted blood red, and behind him came men with flutes and rattles. And always the drums kept up a steady rhythm.

It was effective, Ben allowed himself to admit. Primitive but effective.

He heard Julie's sharp intake of breath then, and he looked to where she was staring. Gary Phillips burst from a nearby doorway, his face shiny with sweat, and clinging to him were four men, four grotesquely painted men. A steady stream of filth poured from Phillips's mouth. He dragged at the men, jerking, trying to pull away, the center of a surging mass of arms and legs and brown skin.

Julie stiffened next to Ben. He touched her arm, and she turned her face to him, frightened.

"There you are!" Phillips screamed, lunging toward Brady. "Tell these guys to let me go! Goddamn it, Brady! They can't do this! Tell 'em!"

Brady stared at him silently, with resignation.

"Tanner! Son of a bitch! Help me. Get these thugs off me. Who the hell do they think they're messing with?" He strained against the hands that held him, his pearl gray summer slacks filthy, his glittery violet knit shirt ripped.

"Hell, I warned him," Ben growled to himself.

More foul words. Ben turned away, uncomfortable in his role as spectator.

"Tanner!" The reporter's voice was a howl, a counterpoint to the flutes and drums. "Don't let 'em take me!"

Ben felt his skin begin to crawl. Tayosha was disappearing down into the kiva, and Gary was being shoved toward it, struggling, yelling, swearing.

"Ben," Julie said beside him, her voice cracking. "You *have* to help him." She put her hand on his cheek and looked into his eyes. "If things get out of hand, Ben, please. I detest him, too, but you have to help him if...if..."

A long moment passed. He could still hear Phillips yelling, an eerie echo, and Julie faced him, tense and afraid. He put a finger on her lips. "I'll do what I can," he said softly, and saw relief fill her.

"Hey, *kemo sabe*, come on, Hank and I are going down into that kiva," Brady said as he approached them. He looked totally unconcerned.

"Will they let me?" Ben asked.

"They can't see you," Brady replied dryly, "remember?"

"Yes, go," Julie urged, "then you'll be able to help."

"Help that creep?" Hank said. "If these Indians don't get him then I'm going to!"

Julie squeezed Ben's hand one last time. "Go on. I'll be waiting."

The kiva was large, hollowed out of solid limestone, maybe thirty feet in diameter. Men crowded around a fire built in the center of an earthen pit. Ben looked it over, a little nervous at being there, but nobody so much as flicked an eyelid at his entrance. He moved into a corner in the back, squatting, hoping to be unobtrusive in the semidarkness.

The walls of the kiva were covered with ancient handprints and hung with ceremonial animal skins that glowed redly, seeming to move, to come alive in the wavering firelight. The ceiling was blackened by a millennium of wood fires. There were niches cut into the walls for prayer sticks and fetishes, flutes and rattles.

Impressive.

Tayosha was chanting in the middle of the room, and the drums echoed hollowly. And there was Phillips, with Tayosha, his mouth shut for once, his rodent eyes shifting, big sweat rings under the arms of his shiny violet shirt. His eyes met Ben's for a moment then darted away in fear.

Smoke from the fire filled the kiva, escaping too slowly from the hole in the roof, the symbolic *sipapu*, or belly button, the opening into the world that the Indians' ancestors had crawled from originally. Ben tried to breathe shallowly, but the smoke was choking, blinding, making his eyes water and his stomach churn. Dizziness rocked him.

Cross-legged, Brady sat next to Ben, breathing in deeply, eyes closed. Why did he look so damn calm? Hank glanced around the kiva in awe and disbelief, his eyes moving but always returning to Phillips as if afraid the reporter would try to escape.

Tayosha chanted, swaying back and forth in time to the drums—the drums Ben couldn't locate—and the men answered in low, wailing cries, beating at the smoky air with their voices.

Reality, illusion. Ben tried to hold the concepts in his mind, tried desperately to decide which facets of this ceremony were reality, which illusion. But the smoke choked him, filled his head with thickness, and the ideas slithered away.

Gary Phillips looked as sick as Ben felt, his fingers twitching, his bright eyes searching the faces around him frantically for help, but everyone, Ben included, was expressionless, held by the rhythm, the chanting, the leaping flames, the smoke.

Time became strangely disjointed. It seemed to Ben that he'd been breathing in that smoke-laden air for hours, yet it was most likely only minutes before one of the elders stepped forward from the group, holding up a rabbit that was trussed up but still struggling. Abruptly Tayosha pulled a long, wicked-looking blade from his belt, and Ben sat up straight. He nudged Brady and whispered, "What's going on?"

"The medicine chief believes Gary is a *powaqa*, a sorcerer. He has two hearts, one animal, one human," Brady said. "He brings misfortune to the pueblo."

And then, when Ben glanced back at Tayosha, it was done. The rabbit no longer struggled. Ben whistled silently between clenched teeth.

Brady, unaffected, turned back to Ben. "Tayosha has killed Phillips's animal heart. Now Phillips will die."

Hank cast his father a skeptical look.

"Come *on*," Ben scoffed.

"That's what the medicine chief says," Brady said levelly.

"So they're not really going to harm Phillips, just scare the pants off him." Ben was satisfied. Then he glanced in Phillips's direction. Sure enough, Tayosha's knife had panicked the man. He began to thrash about, but the four men still held him. He was greenish-white, terrified, so terrified that Ben almost felt sorry for the slob and tried to steel himself against sympathy. A good scare was just what Phillips needed.

The drumbeat quickened and all the Indians watched Phillips expectantly. Suddenly he gasped, stiffened, grew rigid, clutching his chest, starting to moan. The Indians watched in stony silence.

Ye gads, thought Ben, Phillips was a suggestible jerk. He must have really sucked up the mood, the sinister setting. Well, he deserved every bit of it. Old Tayosha really knew his stuff. But before Ben could finish the thought, a scream rang out. Phillips lunged, threw off the men who held him and rushed toward the ladder leading out of the kiva. Surprisingly no one, not even his four captors, made a single move to stop him.

"Hey, he's getting away!" Hank whispered, and rose to follow the reporter.

Brady held him back. "No, son, let him go."

Hank shook off his father's hand, then apparently saw something in Brady's face, hesitated, and sank back silently.

"Maybe I better follow him," Ben said, remembering he'd promised Julie to keep Gary from harm. Perhaps someone was waiting for the reporter outside the kiva, someone with a long-bladed, razor-sharp knife like Tayosha's.

"No," Brady said. "The will of the gods, and *your* God, Ben, will be done now. Do not interfere."

"Hey, you don't know that someone..." Ben began.

"No one will lay a finger on him," Brady said in a voice filled with certainty.

Ben sank back onto his haunches. Brady should know. Besides, it wasn't Ben's place to disturb the ceremony by chasing Phillips, and it was true, no one had touched the man except to hold him still.

It was pitch-black when they emerged from the kiva. Reportedly Phillips was gone, having climbed down the ladders and disappeared into the night mist in the valley. Slowly, tiredly, Ben stood in the fresh air and drew it into his lungs. He could see Julie making her way through the crowd of onlookers, her face pale and drawn in the glow from the fires. He wondered just how he'd describe that scene in the kiva. He wasn't sure there were words for it.

"Ben," she said, rushing to him, "what *happened* down there?"

He took her arm, gave her a reassuring smile and began to lead her away from the crowd toward the ladders.

"Ben," she said, stopping him. "Tell me."

He tried. He really did. But it all sounded crazy. He saw her flinch when he mentioned Tayosha slaying the rabbit, but she'd wanted to hear it all. "But it was only an illusion, Julie," Ben said unconvincingly.

By the time they'd reached their own fire Julie was at least calm. She sank down and sighed. "He's gone then," she said, "thank God for that much."

Ben looked at her and shook his head. "I hope the poor sad guy is okay out there. Why in hell didn't he listen to me?"

"Oh, he'll be okay. Remember, he went in and out of the valley twice now. All by his lonesome," Julie replied.

"Yeah, I guess you're right. Forget him, the jerk. He's not worth—"

They both glanced up to see Brady appear, a troubled look to him. "That kid of mine is hanging around Mika's house. Says he's guarding her in case Phillips comes back."

"That's kind," Julie said.

"I'm not sure what it is," Brady said. "And I wish that little girl would quit acknowledging him. It just eggs him on."

"She's not so little," Ben reminded him.

Brady rolled himself up in his sleeping robe in the courtyard and was soon asleep, but Ben, despite his fatigue, was restless, still in the thrall of the ceremony.

"Tired?" he asked Julie.

"Jumpy," she answered. "What a day this has been."

Silence fell between them comfortably. The fire in the pit gave off a stream of red sparks into the night. The full moon hung directly over the pueblo, washing everything in silver, casting sharp shadows.

Ben looked up and studied the stolid face shining down on them. And then it occurred to him—a full moon again. It had been full a week, no, ten days ago. Impossible.

Had it been full when they'd driven to Los Alamos? He

couldn't recall, hadn't noticed, but it had seemed awfully dark when he'd been driving.

He couldn't bring himself to say anything about it to Julie. She'd think he'd lost his mind. He just hadn't noticed correctly last week; he'd been mistaken. So much had happened, how in hell could a guy be expected to keep track of the phases of the moon?

Julie sat quietly next to him, a contented look on her face. "It's peaceful here," she said.

The scent of her hair rose to his nostrils, bringing back to him without a bridging thought their lovemaking of the night before. He could feel the warmth of her, the silkiness of her skin tingling on the palms of his hands. The softness, the sound of her breath rushing in and out, her cries, her love cries.

"Julie," he said, "this whole thing is crazy."

"What's crazy?"

"This valley, these people, what they did tonight. You, me." He hesitated then blurted it out. "The moon."

"You've noticed," she said, a tiny smile turning up the corners of her lips.

He rubbed a hand over his eyes. "Yeah, I noticed. I wasn't going to say anything. Tell me I'm not nuts."

"You're not. The moon is always full here."

"It can't be."

"I know."

"Okay, forget that. There's some rational explanation. I'll check at the astronomy lab when I get back to Holloman."

"You do that," she said matter-of-factly.

"Julie."

"Yes?"

"I'm crazy about you."

She ducked her head shyly in the way that caused his pulse to leap.

"Come here." He pulled her closer and put an arm around her shoulder. She snuggled against him. "And you know what else I'm going to check on? Those forest fires. As soon as I get back.''

She said nothing.

"Okay, so you believe this weird place is magic. To me it's only another valley.''

"Is it, Ben?''

"Yes,'' he said firmly.

"Tell me more about the kiva,'' she said dreamily.

"Some bedtime story,'' he said, then grinned. "Besides, women aren't supposed to know those things. They're for men only.''

"Oh, really?''

"Yeah.''

"Then tell me about Phillips. Did he really buy into the symbolism of Tayosha killing the rabbit?''

Ben sighed, rubbing her shoulder softly with his hand. "I suppose that much is possible. There are stories...you've probably heard about voodoo dolls and that kind of stuff. To people who really believe in voodoo, sticking a pin in a doll can make them sick or even kill them. It's been documented. And curses. Look at the curse of King Tut's tomb in Egypt. All the archaeologists who disregarded it supposedly died young. Lots of scholars believe in that curse.''

"Do you?''

"No.''

She gave a little laugh. "You're consistent at least.''

"There's something to be said for consistency.''

She reached her hand around then and unfastened one of his shirt buttons to stroke his skin underneath.

"You still mad at me about this afternoon?'' he asked.

"I thought a lot about it, Ben,'' she said soberly.

"So did I.''

"I can't make you go against what you feel is right. I can't judge for you. You'll have to work it out yourself. But I'll fight you every step of the way if you try to open this valley up.''

"That's a daunting thought.''

"Good, keep it in mind," she said lightly, but he knew she meant it.

They could talk. Despite their differences they could communicate so well. Mutual respect, he guessed. He hadn't felt this way about a woman since Carol. Close, easy, confronted with all the joy and pain of caring, he sat there under an improbable moon in an implausible city and thrilled with the delight of holding Julie. It was a scary feeling, as if he were stepping off a sandbar into cold, deep water full of riptides and dragging currents.

It was wonderful, it was terrifying. Julie was a woman of strength and beauty and spirit, with a dash of tantalizing romanticism thrown in for spice, a perfect foil for his own perhaps too-strict pragmatism. She could take him down a peg or two when he needed it, too.

What would Laurie think of her? What would Julie think of his daughter? Somehow he could see them, fair head bent to dark, laughing, talking, confiding.

He caught himself. He really was coming unhinged. His whole life was being torn apart. First these Anasazi. A week ago he'd have bet his whole career no such people could possibly exist. Now he wasn't so sure.

And Julie. Were these gut-wrenching yearnings he had for her love? And what of her? She'd had a bad experience with that Hayden character. Could she ever really trust a man again? Could *he* trust a woman not to die, not to leave him bereft again?

He cradled Julie's head on his shoulder and wondered.

"Tired?" he finally asked.

"Half-asleep."

"Let's go inside and get some shut-eye."

"Um." She reached her hand up and ran her fingers over his beard affectionately, then straightened. "Let's."

They made love slowly, lazily, lingeringly. It was different, comfortable, as if they'd lived together a long, long time, as if they knew each other so very well, as if they belonged together. He recalled making love to a woman like this before.

The memory was faraway and dim, hazy around the edges and very, very pleasant.

They slept together, one robe under them, one over, entwined lovingly. Ben had a single thought just before he went out, a single, disturbing thought: the drums had finally stopped.

CHAPTER FOURTEEN

JULIE WAS AWAKENED by a strange noise coming from somewhere below them in the pueblo. It was a noise she'd never heard before, muted, female, like some sort of shrill lament. Yet it also sounded somehow triumphant.

She shook Ben's shoulder. Even as he pulled on his pants, still half-asleep, she felt a disturbing chill seize her, as if those mists in the valley below had crept into their tiny room.

Ben zipped his trousers. "Stay here," he said firmly. "God only knows what it is this time." He disappeared into the pearly dawn. It was only minutes later that he reappeared, filling the low portal, his expression hidden from her in the shadows. The chill she felt turned to fingers of ice crawling up her spine. "It's Phillips," he said quietly, "down in front of Tayosha's house..."

"Ben?" she whispered.

"Look, I'm afraid...Julie, he's dead."

The sun had not yet tipped the far rim of the mesa when they stood together in pensive silence and stared down into the courtyard below. At the lifeless body, the lips looking blue even at that distance—blue on a mouth that was open, frozen forever in surprise.

Julie knew she was quaking and felt Ben's arm go around her shoulder. Images began to shoot through her head like bullets: Phillips showing up at the ranch, trying to ingratiate himself with her, smiling too much; Phillips bouncing around the pueblo, bubbling with energy; Phillips trying to negotiate in the Los Alamos motel room while Mika huddled in a corner.

"Christ," she heard Ben say softly. "I should have gone after him. I knew it. I could have stopped him."

She wanted desperately to say something, to deny his statement, but the words clogged in her throat. It was true. In some insane, convoluted way, they were all responsible.

It was Brady who told them what had happened. "They found him like that," he reported. "Lying facedown on the scree up near the entrance to the valley."

"You believe that?" Ben asked.

"You're damn right I believe it, *kemo sabe*," Brady retorted. "Tayosha didn't lie."

"Okay, calm down," Ben said. "You've got to admit—"

"They found him already dead, not a mark on him, and his lips were blue."

"He deserved it," Hank muttered.

"But he's *dead*," Julie said. "How could he just have died?"

Ben rubbed his bearded jaw and stared at Brady for a long moment. "It *could* have been the ceremony," he said, as if to himself. "The power of suggestion."

"Just like that?" Julie asked.

"It's happened before. Assuming—" he gave Brady a quick look "—*assuming* that Tayosha's telling the truth, Phillips could have had a heart attack or a stroke. Let's face it, the guy was in lousy shape, scared out of his wits, and he probably ran all the way to the spot where he was found."

Brady was nodding. "Tayosha's got no reason to lie," he said. "It's the whites who lie all the time. Bad habit."

"What—what are they going to do with him?" Julie asked.

Brady lifted his shoulders. "Don't know."

"But we just can't leave him here. My God, he may have a family...a wife, children. They'll never know what happened to him."

"Wait a minute," came Brady's voice. "You're forgetting something. If we haul Phillips out of here, we're going to have to tell someone just what happened. How long do you think the valley will stay secret then?"

Julie looked at her foreman. He was right, of course, but to just leave Phillips, no matter how rotten he was...

Ben cupped her chin in his hand, tipping her strained face up to his. "I promise we'll think of something—we'll take care of it. Just give us some time to think this out. Okay?"

"Well, I know one thing I'm going to have to do," Brady stated. "I've got to get his car keys. That Continental of his will be sitting out there. It's got to be driven off the ranch and left somewhere."

"His keys," Julie said. "Where are they?"

"I assume in his pockets."

"Oh, no..."

"Go for it," Ben said tightly. "It can't hurt him now." Brady shrugged and made his way to where Phillips's body was lying in the plaza. Julie turned away, her stomach lurching. When she looked again, Brady was speaking to Tayosha, gesturing and pointing, listening, asking a question over and over. Four men came with a pallet made of poles, lifted the reporter's body onto it and trotted away with their grisly burden.

"They're going to bury the body," Brady told them. "As far away as possible. They're going to take him to that scree near the entrance to the outside world and bury him there."

"But nobody will ever know what happened to him," Julie said. "It's horrible."

Brady fixed her with his dark gaze. "You could tell them, Miss Julie. Call that newspaper and tell them."

She blanched. "I couldn't. It would be like murdering these people."

They returned to their house, each silently contemplating Phillips's fate, each registering a different response. Julie's face was pinched; she was deeply troubled. Ben appeared resigned. Brady was accepting, his faith in the innocence of these people unshaken. And Hank—like windows to his soul, his eyes showed frustration and resentment, misery, confusion, yearning.

Julie paced the area in front of their house, hugging herself.

"We have to leave," she finally said. "We have to leave right away. Look what we've done by coming here."

"Come on, Julie," Ben said. "We can't hold ourselves responsible for the things Phillips did."

"Oh, can't we? We led him here. We *are* responsible."

"He followed us. That's it. Bottom line."

"It doesn't really matter," she said. "We've tainted this society. We had no right."

"I don't believe that," Ben began.

But she was hardly listening. "If we could make it up to the Indians, maybe leave something for them, something valuable."

"For instance?"

"I don't know…medicine…metal."

"Tayosha's medicine," Ben said, "seems strong enough to me." He gave her a quick, wry smile. "And metal? What do they need it for, cars? Bridges? Skyscrapers?"

Julie sighed. "I know this sounds ridiculous, but what about the wheel?"

"They've gotten along for centuries without it."

"Sheep…horses?"

Ben shook his head. "Look at what they've done for you. You admitted you had to buy that valuable mare, and she about broke you. And why'd you need her? Because, Julie, you wanted to have something better than your neighbors."

"I *didn't*." But she thought a moment. "Well, yes, I guess I did. I wanted to breed the best stock around."

"And so would one of the Indians. Then you'd have jealousy. Range wars. And you have to irrigate to graze horses, or cattle for that matter. They couldn't support those animals here," Ben added. "It'd destroy the ecology of the valley."

"What about sheep?"

"Same thing."

"Forget animals," Julie said thoughtfully.

The list went on and on. But for each benefit they might leave the Indians, there was surely going to be an insidious consequence.

"Listen," Brady said, "the Anasazi need nothing from us. Can't you see how perfectly in tune they are with their environment? They have their spirituality, they've kept their ties to nature that we've completely forgotten. Why do you want to leave them the very things that have corrupted the rest of us?"

Julie let out a long breath. He was right, of course. "I only wanted to help," she said.

"If you *really* want to help," he said, then looked from her to Ben, "then you can keep their secret, keep them from being destroyed by our greedy society."

"Yes," Julie breathed, "I'll do that much. I promise."

For all the tragedy their coming to the valley had brought, it had served one purpose: Brady had been touched profoundly by seeing the spiritual traditions of his tribe come to life. He had been living in neither the material, future-oriented white man's world nor the tradition-laden, mystical, Indian one. He'd existed in a gray area, a vacuum between them, not finding succor in either. It was no wonder at all his wife, a Hopi who clung to tradition, had left him. And, Julie realized, it was no wonder as well that Hank could find no meaning to his life, either.

She thought about Hank, a lost soul, a rebellious young man who was about to have his heart broken. But he couldn't stay there, and he couldn't return to the ranch and come back into the valley at his whim. If Julie knew nothing else that sad morning, she knew that no one from the outside world must ever come back into the valley. They'd done enough damage already.

But who was going to tell Hank?

She spoke to Ben about it. "Brady's his father, he'll just have to explain," Ben said.

"But the boy's going to be crushed."

Ben turned to her and laid a finger on her cheek. "We all have to face pain," he said. "No one can make it any better when the time comes." He gave her a crooked smile. "And there's something else we're forgetting," he said, "a whole lot worse than telling Hank. We're conveniently forgetting that Phillips has got a camera crew on the way, and they're expecting the story of the century.''

The time came to confront Hank. He'd been hanging around in front of Mika's house all morning, trying to talk to her, knowing he had to leave soon. She'd come out and spoken to him, and Julie could see how miserable the young girl was. Mika liked Hank a lot; anyone could see it. They held hands and stood close, whispering, although God only knew how they managed to communicate. To Julie, they looked just like any high school couple standing in front of their lockers at school, clasping hands, oblivious to the other students in the halls. Young love.

But then Mika's mother came out and took her daughter's arm. After that the young girl stayed inside, guarded by her mother and her sisters. Tayosha was taking no chances with a second kidnapping.

"Please," Hank begged Brady, "tell her I want her to come with me. I'll get a job. We can rent a house in Farmington. Tell her. I'll treat her real good, Pop. I'm in love with her!"

Brady sighed. "She can't come with us. You know that."

Ben and Julie waited, ready to leave, embarrassed by the boy's desperation. The young could be so blindly naive.

"*I'm* not leaving then," Hank said firmly.

"She's safe here, Hank," Brady told him gently. "Be sensible, son. You're from two different worlds. You'd only hurt her worse."

"I'd *never* hurt her." Julie saw tears glisten in his eyes.

"Okay, then," Brady said, "what do you think you're doing right now? You think this is easy on her?"

"How about me?" Hank retorted.

They argued. A part of Hank knew he had to go, but he had no tools to deal with the reality of his situation. Julie had known the boy was fond of Mika and that he felt protective of her, but she hadn't guessed just how deeply involved he'd let himself become.

"This is your fault," Hank told his father. "You kept me

out on that ranch so I could watch you drink and ruin your life. Now that's all I have to go back to! And now for the first time in my life, I care about somebody and she cares about me. And you tell me I can't stay here!''

Clearly Brady was shaken. "It'll be different now, I promise.''

Tayosha remained outside his stone house, sitting cross-legged, stolid, expressionless. Julie knew he'd heard the arguing, and she was certain he understood what was going on. The medicine chief's wise old eyes rested on Brady as he spoke to his son. She hated to butt in; still, all the explaining in the world wasn't going to make Hank feel any better. "Brady," she said, approaching him, "we have to go.''

He nodded, and looked at his son. "I'll tell Tayosha," he said. "At least *he'll* be relieved." Brady smiled ruefully and put a hand on Hank's shoulder.

Keeping Coyote on his leash, she and Ben waited outside the low walled enclosure at a respectable distance. But Tayosha couldn't see them or hear them anyway, so she wasn't sure it mattered.

"Brady," Julie called, "tell him that we're sorry about Phillips. Can you make him understand?''

"Perhaps," Brady said. "I don't know if he's in the mood to listen.''

Brady turned toward Tayosha who sat there with an unreadable expression on his face, his eyes staring straight ahead, fixed on the far wall of the mesa. Julie heard her foreman speaking to the old man. Then finally Tayosha replied something. His voice sounded tired.

"I wish I could talk to Tayosha," Julie whispered to Ben. "Just once. I wish I could make him understand." And then she couldn't help herself. "Brady," she said just loudly enough for him to hear, "what is he telling you?''

"He says other ones from the evil spirit world are bound to come here now," Brady replied.

"No," Julie said quickly, "tell him that's why we're going, so that no one will miss us and come looking.''

After a time, Brady turned to her again. "He doesn't trust you to keep the secret of his valley."

"How can I make him trust me?"

"By promising to guard the portal to the spirit world."

And then reality came crashing down on her and she remembered: the bank, the foreclosure proceedings, Jack Murdock, the Western novelist. She was about to *lose* the ranch!

"I know," Brady said, watching her face closely. "You can't make the promise. I think Tayosha knows it, too."

"Baloney," Ben said. "He can't know what's been going on."

"He knows plenty," Brady retorted, "even if he can only sense it." He pivoted his eyes to Julie. "What am I going to tell him?"

Julie sighed, miserable. "The truth, I guess, Brady. We owe him that much."

"The truth, he can understand," Brady said pointedly.

As Brady spoke to the old man, Julie watched Tayosha closely. He appeared sad but resigned, as if he'd known all along that his valley was soon to be exposed to the outside world. She felt like a traitor. And she felt so helpless.

"I told him about your ranch," Brady said finally.

"About the bank and Jack Murdock?" she asked.

He nodded. "To Tayosha," Brady said, "it means you've run out of goods to trade to stay on your land. He thinks in simple terms. But he gets it."

"*I'll* give you the money," Ben said abruptly. "You can't afford to argue about it anymore."

But Julie's shoulders sagged. "Oh, Ben," she said, "how long can it last? A year? Two? To keep the place going, I'll need more than a loan. I'm sorry. But—" she mustered a smile "—I'll never forget your offer."

No one seemed to notice Tayosha disappear, but then he had a way of coming and going like a wraith. One minute he was sitting there, the next he was simply gone.

"Then that's that," Ben said, frowning. "I think we've been dismissed."

She felt horrible. They'd come to this valley so innocently and now, it seemed, they'd done irreparable damage. She remembered the camera crew Phillips had sent for, and her heart felt like lead in her breast. And then her thinking flip-flopped, and she became angry at Tayosha for mutilating her animals in the first place. If he'd stayed in his valley where he belonged…

He appeared again as if from out of the smoke of his fire pit. Julie felt goose bumps raise on her flesh despite the heat. And then she saw that he had something in his hands, something wrapped in animal hide. She nodded at Brady, urging him with her eyes to see what the old man was up to.

Carefully Tayosha unfolded the corners of the hide. It was the kachina doll, the same one that Phillips had stolen. The Southwest Indians still made kachina dolls; they represented the hundreds of spirits that linked man with his creator. Kachinas formed the clouds, brought rain and fertility, provided all man's blessings. This one had been dated at 1295 A.D., Julie recalled, an ancient, priceless relic of this lost civilization. What was Tayosha doing with it?

Brady spoke to him. Tayosha bowed his head, holding the kachina out in front of him, mouthing alien, reverential words. He talked and talked, explaining something it seemed, and then Brady spoke and gestured, and his face registered wonder.

What was Tayosha doing? "Brady," she said anxiously, "what's going on?"

But Ben was smiling. "I think," he said, "that Tayosha is making a sacrifice to keep his valley safe."

"I don't…"

"He's giving you the kachina," Ben said.

Julie was astounded. She gazed at the seven-hundred-year-old figure made of wood with bone and turquoise inlay, draped with feathers and fur, and knew her mouth was hanging open. Why, the kachina would fetch a fortune from the right collector—far, far more than her ranch was worth. She could…she could sell it and…she'd be rich! *My God*, Julie thought, this was a miracle, a gift more valuable than a treasure of Spanish gold!

"Well," Ben said, still smiling, "are you just going to stand there, or are you going to accept the gift?"

"Oh, wow," she breathed, "I don't know what to say."

Tayosha was holding the kachina out, toward *her*, toward the evil spirit that he couldn't see or hear, that didn't exist. She drew in her breath, staring at the kachina doll, then slowly raised her eyes. The old man was looking at her, right *at* her, not through her! His gleaming dark gaze was fixed on her, and he was holding the figure out, saying something.

"Tell him, Brady," she breathed, "tell him thank you. Tell him I will be the guardian of his valley."

Carefully, as if she were receiving a gift from his gods, Julie reached out and took the precious figure and then held it protectively to her breast. She was sure that when her hands met Tayosha's he'd emitted a kind of energy from his fingertips to hers, a cool energy like an invisible white light. But then it must just have been the excitement of the moment. Tayosha was only a man, after all.

For all Julie's happiness, despite the myriad thoughts crowding her mind, she was not impervious to Hank's pain. He'd waited through all this close by, his troubled gaze on the doorway to Tayosha's house. But Mika never reappeared. Once he'd muttered to himself that he was going to stay there, but then he'd kicked at the hard earth and tightened his jaw, and his split eyebrow had given him a menacing look. It occurred to Julie that he was returning to a world as alien to him as this one was and far more hostile, that Hank had never adjusted to his Indian roots in a white man's environment. She knew, that like many of the Indians of the Southwest, he probably never would. His children, or perhaps their children, would finally be assimilated into modern society, but Hank was of a generation only a hundred years removed from having been conquered and oppressed. A cloud of doom seemed to hover over the young man, and she felt tears press against her eyelids. If it were possible, Julie would have given the entire United States back to the Indians at that moment.

Their leave-taking was poignant. She felt as if every member of the tribe acknowledged them now, as if all those dark, solemn eyes followed them down the ladders and onto the trail leading east along the valley floor until they disappeared into that hazy purple distance. They walked slowly and silently, each with his own thoughts, each impressing in his mind the images and memories of the magic valley. Julie felt strange. She felt as if with every step those images were fading in her mind, erasing themselves no matter how desperately she tried to keep them clear and sharp in her head. A moment of panic seized her: the valley was vanishing behind them.

She spun around and gazed back. The cliff house was still visible, yes, but the inexplicable mist that groped upon the valley floor seemed to be rising, obscuring the lower part of the cliff pueblo, making the upper terraces rest like a city on a cloud.

It looked deserted. All those T-shaped doorways and windows were staring blankly back at her. And, as before, she thought of them as black, empty eyes. Then, as they marched on in a silent file, she took one last look backward and it was gone, the ancient pueblo tucked into the ledge of the cliff swallowed once more by time.

They reached the narrow passageway leading to the outside world. Julie tried not to think about Phillips, about his being buried somewhere nearby, about all the misery he'd caused. She merely walked behind Ben, following his footsteps up the scree and tried to hold the last image of the Anasazi to her. She'd remember them more clearly in time, she kept telling herself; it was just that she was trying too hard.

They moved through the crevice slowly, still as noiseless as the rock faces that enfolded them. Julie glanced at the spot on the wall where they'd first seen the smear of blood from her sheep, but there was nothing there now. It must not have been the right spot, she guessed.

And there it was, the outside world, Tayosha's—what had

he called it? Oh, yes, the evil world, the world of spirits, *her* world. Funny how she kept forgetting that now.

Ben, Brady and Hank had stopped ahead and were all three gazing into the distance. She stood beside Ben and marveled at the clarity of air, the precision of line in the far-off mesas, the brilliance of sun and sky. She stood there and drew in a lungful of air then let it out slowly, calmly. She had a purpose now, a goal, something to keep her going. And her ranch was safe or would be, she knew, as soon as she found a buyer for the kachina.

She glanced sidelong at Ben. It had been such a short time since they'd met, since they'd first stood together over the mutilated carcass of her mare. She never would have thought, not in a million years, that the tall, arrogant stranger would have captured her heart, could have set her free from the bondages of her past. Yet he had. For all his abrasiveness, for all his stubborn determination, she'd found in Ben Tanner a friend, a lover, someone she could trust. And now they had a goal in common, a shared experience that no one would ever believe.

She studied his lean, handsome features as he gazed out across the vast expanse of land, and she felt her heart swell with love for this man. Everything was as it should be between them, she mused. But then suddenly she asked herself: was it, though? Wasn't she forgetting one small detail? She'd sworn to Tayosha to keep his valley secret—and she planned on keeping that trust forever. But what about Ben? He'd never made that commitment, had he? And she wondered, a fist of anxiety balling in her stomach, would Ben keep the secret, too?

CHAPTER FIFTEEN

THE JEEP was where they had left it, a shock, an incongruous metallic creature squatting on the barren landscape. Julie felt numb, stunned, trying to grapple once more with the switch in reality. It struck her anew how the light outside the valley was different—clearer, brighter, the sky bluer, the shadows more distinct.

Coyote danced around the Jeep, gave a delighted bark and jumped into the back seat where he sat panting, his tongue lolling out. She wished she were able to adjust so easily, to accept. Sadness lingered in her. She'd never return to Tayosha's pueblo, never see the Ancient Ones again. It was too dangerous for them. Only Gary Phillips's body, buried near the entrance to the valley, would stand guard over it forever.

Brady and Hank hadn't spoken a word between them. Hank was utterly miserable, Julie knew. How awful that he'd had to leave Mika; she was the only thing in the world he'd ever cared about, and one of the few to care about him. That a special love had sprung up between them was as clear as day.

"Well, folks, here we are," Ben said with false bravado, feeling in his pocket for keys.

Julie watched the sun glint off the chrome keys. How had anyone come up with the idea of a strip of notched metal that fit into a slot? Why?

Hank and Brady climbed into the back of the vehicle, Julie got in the front. Ben gave the gas pedal a push, turned the key in the ignition, and it coughed once then roared into life, spitting out a cloud of black smoke. Julie winced.

Ben gave her an apologetic glance.

The vinyl seat was hot from the sun and slippery, giving off a musty plastic smell that seemed unbearably sharp. And the exhaust and gasoline fumes were so penetrating. She was oversensitive to every odor, the feel of every man-made substance, flinching from the barrage of sensations that were old but somehow new to her.

"You'll get used to it," Ben said quietly, reading her mind. "We all will."

"You feel it, too?" she asked, relieved. "The difference?"

He nodded and covered her hand with his, and Julie's heart melted with love for him.

The familiar land rolled by, sunbaked and rough, but she saw it with new eyes. It was hers to keep in trust forever so that Tayosha's people would be safe. She could never sell it nor let it be used by anyone who might discover the cut into Red Mesa. She knew that with absolute certainty, and she knew, too, what it might cost her.

She bounced on the hot seat and clutched Tayosha's kachina. It was still wrapped carefully in the deer hide, but she'd get rid of the wrapping. Someone might wonder about it, ask questions. Julie had to be careful about things like that now.

Red Mesa fell behind. She'd never look at it again without remembering. And there were so many memories, but already they were growing hazy and indistinct.

She was afraid to ask, but she had to. "Ben," she said, and he turned his eyes on her. "Ben?" She touched his arm and asked, "You'll keep the secret, won't you?"

He fixed his gaze on her for a moment, solemn, inscrutable, then turned back to his driving, but the question hung between them, tangible, quivering with significance, all the way back to the ranch.

"Well," Brady said, "I guess that's that."

"I guess so," Julie said. She knew Brady didn't trust Ben to keep the secret. She knew her foreman was tempted to reason with Ben, to beg him. But he wouldn't. There was too much of the Indian stoicism in him, the sense of powerlessness in the face of fate. White men discussed and argued and negotiated, and in the end things turned out the way destiny decreed. No, Brady wouldn't ask.

"Guess you'll be leaving soon, *kemo sabe*," was all Brady said, "now that the mystery's solved."

Ben gave him a long, appraising look. "Yes," he said, "I will be. It's been a hell of an experience. I'll give it that."

"You could say so."

Hank said nothing. He went into the bunkhouse without acknowledging anybody or anything, his face frozen in pain. Julie started to follow him, to offer sympathy, to try to alleviate the boy's anguish, but Brady stopped her.

"He'll get over it," he said. "Just let him be."

"Will he, Brady?"

"He has to, Miss Julie. He's reaching for a star."

Julie turned away and walked up the porch steps tiredly, suddenly drained of energy. She opened the familiar screen door, heard it bang behind her. Everything looked the same yet different. The gleam of glass and metal and plastic, the hum of the refrigerator. She had to discover it all over again, accept it.

"Julie?" Ben was behind her, close, his warm breath stirring her hair.

She stopped, bowed her head, waiting.

"It's over now," he said. "We did our best."

"*Is* it over, Ben?"

He put his arms around her, pulling her back against his chest, and she leaned her head on him. They stood that way for a long time, silently looking out the window that faced west to Red Mesa. She could feel his heart beat against her back, slowly, heavily. She felt safe there, held by him, full of happiness and a singular kind of ache.

She forced herself to speak. "The camera crew is coming."

"They won't find anything."

"His car. It's out there somewhere."

"Brady and I will go out and move it."

"What if they call in the police to look for him? What if—"

"Sh." Ben tightened his arms around her. "No one will ever find Phillips. I promise you."

She turned in his arms and searched his face, loving the strength of it, the laugh lines, the newly grown beard, the beauty she saw in its planes and angles. His eyes were that smoky dark blue, shadowed, his brows drawn. Boldly she put her hands up, one on each cheek, and guided his mouth down to hers. And still the fateful question hung between them. Yet, oddly enough, Julie wondered if the question, the unspoken answer, didn't make them hold on to each other even more closely.

Oh, how she loved him.

He drew away from her and smiled lazily. "I'll bet I need a shower," he said.

She nuzzled her face into his beard. "Mostly you smell like smoke. I like it."

"And you smell like sunshine and honey."

"Ben..."

"Should we shower together or separately?"

Julie felt her skin tingle in the heat of the day. Her cheeks flushed. "Together?"

"Sure. There's a drought, remember? Think of the water we'd conserve."

The water was cool and delicious. And after his gentle prodding, and much teasing, Julie shampooed his hair and washed his back. He sighed, over and over. "Um, don't stop...there, scratch right there...um."

Then it was her turn. Ben poured shampoo into his palm then began to work it into her hair, his fingers scrubbing her scalp until she closed her eyes in ecstasy. He had black curly hair on his chest and she soaped it and curled it around her fingers. His arms and neck were tanned, but his body was pale. She ran her hands, slippery with soap, over his back, his ribs, down his hips, his thighs. She felt no shame, no modesty with Ben, and was surprised at herself. Mark had always made her feel embarrassed. But Ben made her feel beautiful.

"God, that feels good," he said, throwing his head back and standing under the water. "Civilization has its benefits."

"One or two," she whispered.

His hand ran over her shoulder, down over her breast, her waist, and slid over the curve of her hip. "*That* feels good, too."

Water ran into her eyes, and she blinked it away. "You'll stay at the ranch for a little while, won't you?"

His hands stopped their roving; his face hardened. "As long as you need me. We'll get this camera crew taken care of. Don't worry, Julie."

She wanted to cry out that she needed him forever, that she'd die if he left her, but she couldn't. That question loomed between them without solution, and she might have to fight him to keep the valley safe. She had to steel herself against that eventuality. And Ben knew it. Oh yes, he knew it only too well.

But the knowledge made Julie treasure the moments they had together even more. Each minute was a shining silver globe to be held in both her hands, precious, perfect, full of light and sparkle, and when she turned it the globe flashed and gave off brilliant images and sensations. But it was terribly, tragically fragile, the silver globe, and soon it would shatter into a million knifelike shards that would cut her and make her bleed.

Their play turned gradually into a heated, feverish search of mouths and hands and quick caresses. Julie tried to let all thought flow from her, wash down the drain with the water that streamed off their naked bodies. He pressed her to the wall of the slippery stall and gripped her thighs just below her buttocks, raising her, forcing her hips upward until she could feel his hardness between her legs, probing. Then he was inside her, gliding upward, pushing. She opened to him like a velvety flower and gasped as her breathing quickened, yet it was still too new to her, and her sensations, strong as they were, became overpowering. She couldn't handle it, not yet.

Ben's movements became more urgent. "It's okay, it's okay," he panted into her ear, understanding. "Later, give it time, it's okay," and he shuddered inside her then, stroking her, kissing her, clutching her to him. "It's okay, you can't try too hard…it's going to happen for you. I promise."

But would it?

Moments later, quietly, she moved away and stepped out of the shower, pulling a towel around her. "I'll fix dinner," she said, feeling breathless and uneasy. "What do you want?"

"A big steak and baked potato. Chocolate mousse. A nice Bordeaux," he said from the shower.

"How about beans and franks and a beer?"

"I was afraid to tell you that's what I really wanted." He turned the shower off and stood there streaming water.

She handed him a towel. She could get used to him here in her house, in her shower, in her bed. She tingled all over at the thought, at the memories, at the promise he'd just made. He'd said they could be good together—if she trusted him. Oh God, how she wanted to trust him.

The familiar, everyday motions of opening cupboards, locating cans, turning the stove on, cooking, setting the table, were automatic yet unique. She marveled at the can of baked beans. Someone had plowed the earth, planted seed, reaped a crop. Someone else had cooked and flavored and packaged the beans. Someone had advertised, money had changed hands. It was all so incredibly complicated, removed from its source.

"Interesting label?" Ben asked, coming into the kitchen, leaning a shoulder against the door frame.

"I was just thinking," she said vaguely.

"This is hard for you, isn't it?" he asked gravely.

"Yes, it's hard. I feel lost. Between worlds."

"My little romantic."

She looked at him and said carefully, "I'm not *your* anything, Ben."

His eyes switched away.

They ate at the kitchen table. Not talking much. Eating

thoughtfully, tasting the flavors, the spices, the salt. Julie had never noticed before how much salt there was in the food.

The stove was so smooth, so white. Julie ran the sponge over it while cleaning up, then ran her hand over the surface. The refrigerator door vibrated, a machine. Her house was full of machines running, vibrating, humming.

Ben was drying dishes and putting them away. Should she beg him to stay and keep the secret with her? Did he love her enough?

He put the dish towel down and turned to her. "All done," he said.

"Thanks."

"I should thank you. I'll make sure you get reimbursed from my expense account. As soon as I get back to Holloman."

"I don't want money," she said. "I don't need money. It isn't worth anything."

"Julie," he said, "I didn't mean…"

"Are you going to write a report when you get back? All neat and tidy, full of facts explaining everything? Are you?"

He turned to her slowly, tall and strong and beautiful in her homely kitchen.

"I don't know," he said. "I just don't know. I need time to think, time to sort things out. I have to figure out what's right. You can understand that, can't you?"

"I *know* what's right."

"How fortunate you are," he said dryly.

"I'm sorry." She knew she was pushing, hated herself for it.

"Look, Julie, my job has always been to unravel the mysteries of the earth, not to cover them up. I'm trained, conditioned, to expose facts, gain knowledge. That's where I'm coming from."

"This is different."

"Maybe. I'm not sure." He scrubbed a hand through his hair. "I care about you. A lot. But we've got a problem. If I write my report, if I tell the world about the valley and the people there…well, I guess there wouldn't be much hope for us then, would there?"

"No," she whispered, "I guess not."

"Damn!" He paced away from her, then back, held her arms in his big hands, dug his fingers into her flesh. "I can't let my feelings for you enter into my decision. I can't decide on that basis. Do you understand?"

"Yes," she breathed, knowing at that moment that she loved him, that she trusted him absolutely. "I can't ask you to keep the Anasazi's secret for my sake alone. You have to know it's the right thing to do."

"Yes, I do."

She collapsed against him, burying her head in his chest, clutching his shirt in her hands. "Oh, Ben," she whispered, "what are we going to do?"

He stroked her hair, the way one might comfort a child, then he lifted her head, holding her face in his hands. "Can I stay with you tonight?" he asked softly.

She nodded, speechless, beset by too many emotions. It was easier to give up, to give in, than it was to hold so many conflicting feelings inside her at once.

His lips were on hers, warm and firm. She could taste him, smell the soap on his skin and shampoo in his hair. Her head whirled with the explosion of familiar sensation within, the touch of his mouth, his hands hard on her shoulders. She closed her eyes and kissed him, opened her mouth to let him find the sweet nectar inside. His hands kneaded her shoulders.

"The lights," she whispered against his lips.

Darkness. Warm, intimate darkness. She led him to her bedroom, but he stopped her on the threshold, pulling her close, nibbling at her throat until waves of raw pleasure coursed through her veins.

"Julie," he whispered.

She put her hands under his shirt and felt his skin, smooth, hot, with the fuzz of hair. She wanted him so badly she was nearly sobbing.

They left a trail of clothes on the floor, dropped carelessly.

He lay next to her on the bed and moved his hands over her skin, touching a breast, brushing it with the back of his hand. The pulse in the hollow of her throat leaped convulsively, and she gasped as his mouth moved over hers with more demand. Then his lips left hers and he was kissing the curve of one breast. Her nipples grew taut. He kissed first one then the other, slowly, lingeringly, with infinite patience.

His nakedness in the hot night was beautiful, making Julie feel lovely herself. She could see in the faint light her whiteness against his tan, her slenderness against his male hardness. He kissed her everywhere, in sensitive places she never realized she possessed. Her spine, the white curve of her hip, behind her knees, even her ankles. Every inch of her flesh was ripe, ready to be plucked by his mouth, to be savored by his tongue.

He entered her at last, filling her, making her complete. He was gentle, careful with her, remembering his promise. His body covered hers, and he moved slowly, almost languidly, waiting for her, patiently, patiently.

Julie moaned, heat built in her, familiar heat. She loved this man, trusted him. He understood. She felt her breathing quicken and her belly ache. She reached for the feeling, felt it kindle in her, stronger and stronger. Ben filled her, bent his head to a nipple, whispered in her ears. The tide rose, unalterable, compelled by forces stronger than her. Her body rode the tide, lifted closer and was tossed, gasping and crying out, over the edge with him.

"Oh, Ben," she breathed finally, shaken. Her fingers were white, clutching at him so hard.

He held her close, sweat-slicked, content. "Yes?" he asked lazily.

Wonder filled her. Tears dimmed her eyes. "Ben. Oh my God."

"I know...I know."

She'd never be able to make him comprehend the marvelous thing that had just happened to her, that *he'd* made happen to her. An enormous load lifted from her shoulders. She wasn't frigid. She could love like a normal woman!

She buried her face in his beard and felt her tears dampen it. "Oh, Ben..."

He only kissed her forehead and rolled aside, pulling her with him. "Don't cry."

"Can we stay like this forever?" she asked.

"Sure, forever," he agreed, and she loved him even more for the lie.

CHAPTER SIXTEEN

JULIE JERKED AWAKE the next morning, disoriented, her heart pounding. Her arm was touching warm, bare flesh. Ben. The night before flooded her with a jumble of images, rudely shattered by the shrill summons of the phone.

She swung her legs out of bed, grabbed at Ben's shirt that lay on top of the pile of clothes on the floor. "I'm coming," she said hoarsely, then cleared her throat.

Barefoot, she hurried into the kitchen, pulling on his shirt. "Hello?" She had to clear her throat again. "Hello?"

"Julie? I've been trying to get you for days. This is Thatch Fredericks."

"Oh, Thatch, sorry, I've been…ah…away."

"I hate to call so early. Sounds like I got you up."

"Yes, well, we…I got back late."

"I see. Julie, I'm sorry to badger you, but August first is just around the corner, and I have to know what you're going to do about that loan."

"The loan." Julie's head spun. She'd forgotten all about her problems—money and loans and Jack Murdock. She had to pull herself together; she couldn't lose the ranch, not now.

"I'm looking at your file right here. Your balance is forty-two thousand, and it's been the same for a year. I'm going to have to ask that you reduce the principal by at least ten percent, Julie. That's four thousand two hundred dollars by August first. That is, of course, plus interest for the past six months."

"Listen, Thatch," Julie interrupted. She paced as far as the telephone cord would allow, her brain working, gaining momentum. "Something's come up. Actually, that's where I've been for the past two days. I've found a…an artifact on my land. Very ancient. Anasazi. It's been carbon-dated at 1295 A.D. It's worth a lot of money. I need a few days to get it to an art dealer. Scottsdale. That's where I'm going."

"An Anasazi artifact?"

Julie glanced over at the sideboard where the kachina figure lay. It stared back at her inscrutably, full of power, full of promise. "Yes," she said. "All I need is a…say a week. I'll pay off the loan. Every penny."

"I'd have to see this artifact," he said suspiciously. Then, "You understand."

"Sure, I'll drop by as soon as I can. Today. Well, maybe tomorrow."

"Julie, are you sure this artifact of yours is on the up-and-up? I mean, there have been cases…"

"I found it myself. On my own property. It isn't fake or stolen, and it doesn't belong—" she had to swallow to get the words out "—to the Indians. It's absolutely legal."

"Okay, bring it in. Not that I'm any expert. And I'll extend your loan for a week. At that point I'll be forced to start foreclosure proceedings if I don't receive from you a total of, let's see here—" she heard the sound of an adding machine clicking in the background "—ah, um, that comes to six thousand three hundred dollars and loose change. Of course, that included the interest. Is that satisfactory?"

"Yes, fine. Perfect. Thank you, Thatch."

She hung up and took a deep breath. She had a week. A precious week. And then the ranch would be safe, and Tayosha would be safe—forever.

"Julie?"

Slowly she padded back into the bedroom. Ben lay there, his hands clasped behind his head, his legs long under the covers.

"I heard. Was it the fellow from the bank?"

"Yes."

He watched her carefully. "Any problems?"

"No, it's okay," she said, sitting on the side of the bed.

"I'll lend you the money. The offer still stands."

She shook her head. "I've got a week. I'm going to Scottsdale, Arizona. All the big art dealers are there. I'll sell the kachina."

"You're sure."

She turned to him and smiled. "I'm sure. Thanks, though. Thanks a lot."

"Come here."

She curled up next to him in the warm rumpled bed, and he stroked her hair back from her face. "I'd forgotten about the bank. I'd forgotten everything," she said.

"Rude awakening, huh?" He brushed her lips with his. "I like my shirt on you better than on me. The color suits you."

She looked down at herself. The blue shirt gaped open in front, and her legs were bare. She tried to pull it together.

"No, don't. I like it," Ben said.

"It's indecent."

"No, it's beautiful."

She turned her face into his chest and smiled, breathing in the scent—his mingled with hers. "Hungry?" she asked.

"Starved."

Brady showed up as they were finishing breakfast, holding hands across the table, discussing what to do about the camera crew from the *Nation*.

"Morning, Miss Julie," he said at the screen door.

She straightened, withdrawing her hand. "Oh, come on in, Brady,"

"Coffee?" Ben nodded toward the pot.

"No, thanks. Had some already."

Julie took a last sip from her cup. "How's Hank?"

"Pretty quiet," Brady replied.

"Poor kid," she said.

"Hank and I, we figured to take the truck out and look for Phillips's car, drive it somewhere on the highway near town and leave it there," Brady said.

Julie looked down at her hands. "What do we tell the camera crew?"

"That we saw Phillips, he's been hanging around. Found nothing, no more animals mutilated. He headed back toward Trading Post. That's all we know."

"What if he told them about the kachina?" she asked.

"He didn't have a chance before we got it back," Ben said. "But if he did…well, we'll just say we don't know anything about it."

"I hate to lie," Julie said.

"I'd say we don't have a hell of a lot of choice," Brady offered, but he was looking at Ben, assessing him.

"Look, Brady, the last thing I want is for the *Nation* to get hold of this story," Ben said heatedly.

"Okay, *kemo sabe*, just wondering."

The question remained unspoken, however: what are you going to do, Ben? What are you going to decide?

THE CAMERA CREW arrived at lunchtime. They drove up in a rented van and pulled to a stop in front of Julie's house. The driver got out, coughing and waving away the cloud of dust he'd stirred up.

Julie watched the man walk up the two steps of her porch, looking around in disbelief, and raise his hand to knock. She opened the door before he had a chance. "Yes?" she asked.

The man was tall and skinny, pale as a ghost, with a wispy ginger beard, dressed in white pants and a sweat-stained T-shirt. "Is this the Someday Ranch?" he asked uncertainly.

"Sure is."

"Well, I'm Al Patterson, with the *Nation*…"

"You a friend of Phillips?" she asked.

For the first time the man seemed to relax. "Yeah, Gary sent for us. I've got a whole crew in the van. Cameras, the works. He phoned three days ago and told us to meet him in Trading Post, New Mexico."

"Haven't seen him in a while," Julie said. "I told him to get off my property and not come back."

The man swore. "We've been waiting in the godforsaken town all day! He had a story, he said. One of Phillips's typical scoops. What in hell's going on around here? I hope this isn't another one of his wild-goose chases."

Ben came out on the porch and stood next to Julie, his arm draped casually over her shoulder. "Well, sir, I don't know what story he was referring to, but there's not much happening around here, is there, Julie?"

"That Phillips! Always screaming about spaceships and stuff. Told us some story about animals with their heads cut off and Anasazi Indians. Crazy," Al Patterson said.

"Yeah, we had a couple of animals die. The drought," Ben said. "That's all."

"And the Anasazi Indians disappeared six hundred years ago," Julie said, straight-faced, "in case you didn't know."

Patterson shook his head. "That damned Phillips. Dragging us out here in this heat! For nothing! I'm gonna kill the sucker when I get my hands on him. Hey, you seen him around here today?"

Julie shook her head. "No, sure haven't. I figured he was gone for good." She told the truth.

Patterson's shoulders slumped. "Hey, you think we could get something to drink? We're dying. Waiting all day in that one-horse town. Maybe Phillips'll show up after all."

Julie gave Ben a quick, panic-filled glance.

"Sure, fellas," Ben said in an artificially hearty voice. "We've got beer, anyway."

"Okay, great, just a sec." Patterson went back to the van and returned, followed by two other men. One was heavy, red-faced, perspiring. The other was young and red-haired and freckled. They all wore what Julie thought of as city clothes—creased, shiny pants, loose polo shirts, thin-soled loafers or canvas deck shoes.

"This is Francis Holder." The heavy man. "Joey Torres." The young one.

"Julie Hayden," she said, nodding at them.

"Ben Tanner." He shook each man's hand, pumping it.

"Too bad you fellas had to come hoofin' it all the way out here on a wild-goose chase. Sit down. Have a beer."

She didn't want those men in here! Gary's friends. Oh, God. And she had to smile and lie, and Phillips was buried out there, dead. Oh, she knew what Ben was doing. He was trying to disarm any suspicions they might have. But Julie almost didn't care; she wanted those men gone!

Ben gave them all beers. "You sure you're old enough to drink?" he asked Joey Torres with a wink, while the boy blushed and protested.

"I'm twenty-four," he said. "I've been working on the paper for three years. I can't help looking young."

"Boy, it's hot," Francis said, wiping at the sweat that trickled down his temples. "Dry, but hot!"

"It's the drought," Julie said.

"Yeah, read about it," Patterson replied. "We had one two years ago. Atmosphere's going nuts."

"I bet you guys are hungry," Ben said. "It being lunchtime and all."

"Well…"

"Sure. Julie, you can fix these boys some sandwiches, can't you?"

Her eye caught his; she begged, his glance remained firm. *Fix them lunch,* it said, *and they'll leave.*

"Oh, sure," she said, glad at least to have something to keep her hands busy.

It struck her as she was putting mayonnaise on the bread. Brady and Hank weren't back yet. What if they drove up in Gary's car? Oh my Lord. But these men, they didn't know Gary had rented a car or what it looked like. Or did they? But Brady wouldn't do that. Hadn't he said they'd take it out on the highway? That is, *if* they found it. But of course they'd find it. It had to be close to the entrance to the valley. Phillips wouldn't walk any further than he had to.

The men ate, had more beer, perspired into handkerchiefs, talked to Ben. Still no Brady.

Julie, all nervous and jittery, sat down with the group,

catching Ben's eye on her from time to time as if he were afraid she'd break down and tell the camera crew what had happened. She gritted her teeth and tried to follow the conversation.

"Phillips has a reputation," Al was saying. "He makes big bucks. Always has a hot story going. Remember the serial murderer in New Bedford, Massachusetts? Gary covered that story. Upped our circulation that week by 200,000 copies. And all that Elizabeth Taylor business. Thin, fat, into the booze. He loves Taylor. She'd good for a story a week."

"He's an obnoxious little twerp," Francis Holder said.

"Sure, but he gets his stories. Used to be a straight news reporter, you know. But he's done better at the *Nation*."

They knew Gary well, had known him for years. What would they do if they knew the truth? But they'd never know. No one would ever know. She wished she could tell them, so at least he'd have a decent funeral, so his family would know. His family.

Casually, her heart pounding, Julie heard herself ask, "Was…is Gary married?"

Joey Torres laughed. "Gary? You gotta be kidding."

Immense relief flooded her. "No family at all?"

"Nah. I think he has an old mother in a nursing home. Never goes to visit her, though. He's a real self-centered kind of guy."

By two-fifteen, Julie was ready to scream. Brady wasn't back, and Ben was handing more beer around, seemingly unconcerned, best buddies with the three New Yorkers. Why didn't these men give up and leave? If they didn't, Julie was feeling more and more strongly that she should tell them where Gary was, steer them in the right direction. Phillips was a human being. Didn't they owe his friends, his coworkers, the knowledge of his death?

She sat there in her stuffy kitchen, smelling beer and male sweat, trying desperately to smile and listen and not think, watching the clock hands crawl slowly, so slowly.

"I gotta tell you about the time Gary covered the Olympics

in Los Angeles,'' Francis Holder was saying. "He got into the locker room of the ladies swimming team. I'll tell you…''

Julie massaged her temples. It was so hot, so still; dust raised in little tornadoes out in the driveway. The drooping cottonwood hanging over the porch rustled feebly. And Gary lay buried, his body under the rocks. He'd lie there forever.

A car drove up and stopped outside. Julie sprang to her feet. Brady was back! She gave Ben a wild look and went to the screen door.

No, it was Ken Lamont. What on earth did he want? She stepped outside. "Hi, Ken. What's up?''

He took off his hat and stood there on her porch looking solemn. His small mouth worked. "Gee, Miss Julie, I hate to upset you. See you have visitors…

Her heart twanged with apprehension. "What is it?'' Brady? Hank? Phillips? But no, it couldn't be. No one knew…

"Well, Brady and Hank just come into town and found me. Seems they ran across that reporter fellow that was botherin' you…''

The sky reeled. Julie put out a hand to steady herself.

"You okay, Miss Julie?'' Ken asked, concerned.

"Fine. Sure. I'm fine. It's the…it's just the heat,'' she breathed.

"Well, it's that reporter, Phillips. Brady and Hank, they found his body. Out by Red Mesa.'' Ken looked at her, playing with his hat, turning it in his hands. "Poor fella is dead.''

"Dead?'' she whispered.

"Yeah, dead as a doornail. Looks like a heart attack.''

"What…what happened?'' Her thoughts whirled, making no sense of anything Lamont said. Her lips felt wooden when she tried to talk. Her hands shook. She was aware of Ben coming to stand beside her, of the screen door slamming, of a sudden horrible silence.

"Deputy Lamont,'' Ben said. "Is there a problem?''

"Only for Phillips, and he's past caring. He died. Brady and Hank found him.''

"So, what happened?" Ben said hastily.

Ken Lamont shrugged. "His car was stuck in a ravine. I figured the damn fool was trying to push it out. Guess the heat got him."

Ben shook his head. "Terrible thing. Awful. I thought the man had gone back to New York days ago."

Julie leaned against a fence post, hugged herself. Nothing made any sense. Why would Brady go to Lamont? How had the body gotten outside the valley? She felt Ben's hand on her shoulder, his fingers firm.

"Awful, isn't it?" Ben was saying. "Strange thing is, his camera crew is here, Deputy Lamont. Right inside. Looking for him. What do you think of that coincidence?"

"Downright providential. They can tell us what to do with the body. I left Brady and Hank watching over it."

Julie straightened. "We better take them out there then, don't you think?"

"If they want to go. Someone's got to identify the body. Well, we all know who it is, but it's better to have an old friend do it. Makes my report real tidy."

"You want to tell them what happened?" Ben asked. "Poor guys, they'll be heartbroken."

"Yeah, I'll do it. It's my job, all the nasty stuff," Ken Lamont said.

He went inside and Julie could hear him talking. There was a short silence then protests, voices raised in disbelief, questions. She looked at Ben, her eyes huge with confusion. He shook his head and raised his shoulders, cautioning her silently, *Don't lose it now.*

She had to go along, of course. Ben tried to convince her to stay at the house, to relax, but she couldn't. She had to see with her own eyes this ultimate mystery—the second dying of Gary Phillips. Ken Lamont took the three New Yorkers in his car. She went with Ben in his Jeep, across the same hot, dusty miles they'd just crossed yesterday, under the looming, frowning face of Red Mesa. If she looked, Julie could see the pillar of rock that hid the cut. She wouldn't look.

There was her truck. Brady leaned against the door, and Hank sat in the shade, reclining against a tire. Both stood slowly when they saw the two vehicles approaching.

"Where is he?" Al Patterson asked. "Where did you find him?"

"There." Brady pointed. The black Continental was nearly hidden, at the bottom of a shallow wash.

The three men stood on the lip of the arroyo and stared. Julie stared, too. Ben stood next to her, and she heard him grunt, then he turned away.

The body lay beside the car, facedown, covered with dust, the shiny violet shirt a spot of color, almost like blood on the bleached ground.

"We didn't touch him," Brady said. "Found him just like that."

Julie turned away, met Brady's impassive gaze, questioned him with her own. Not a muscle ticked in his lined, brown face; only a black eyebrow lifted.

She knew then. She knew who had moved the body. Tayosha. He'd had it dug up and carried through the crevice in the mesa and put here, by the unthinkable machine that must have given him a moment's pause. But Tayosha, canny old man, would have known the machine and Gary Phillips belonged together.

If they searched, if they let Coyote loose, he'd follow a path of moccasin tracks right up to the base of the mesa, right around the spire of stone, right into the heart of the rock itself.

Brady nodded infinitesimally.

"Oh my God," she heard one of the New Yorkers say in his nasal accent. "It *is* Phillips! The poor son of a gun."

The camera crew finally left. It was dusk by then, because they'd had to fill out reports and sign papers. Phillips's body was wrapped in a tarp in the back of Ken Lamont's vehicle. The closest funeral parlor was in Farmington. The deputy would take the body there, where it would be prepared and flown back to New York. The *Nation* would foot the bills, Al Patterson had promised.

"Damn! I told him he should watch the cholesterol. And no exercise," Francis Holder had said. "Who am I to talk? Thirty pounds overweight. Scary. Real scary."

"He wasn't so old," Joey Torres had said. "What, forty-two? That's all. That's not old."

"Well, thanks for your help, everybody. Maybe it was a good thing we were out here, after all. Strange, isn't it?" Patterson had said.

"Weird," Joey had remarked.

"What a way to go," Holder had added.

"And no story. Not even a lousy line of copy," Patterson had lamented.

They drove off into the darkness, following Ken Lamont, their lights making tunnels in the dust that swirled behind the deputy's vehicle.

Julie sank onto the top step of the porch and lowered her face in her hands. She shuddered.

Ben sat beside her, put his arm around her. "It's over. They're gone."

"It was awful."

"I know." He pulled her head into his shoulder. "You did fine, Julie."

"Couldn't they tell? Couldn't they tell it was all a lie?"

"No. Why should they?"

"You know who did it, don't you?" she asked.

"Yes, I know."

Julie tried to conjure up Tayosha's face—the knowledge-able old eyes, the eerie paint, the seamed brown skin—but his features would not coalesce in her mind's eye. She was left with an indistinct, receding image. It frightened her for a minute, the thought that she might be losing her mind, but the fear washed away quickly. It was better to forget, really.

A strange sound made Julie lift her head, a low hollow sound, far off to the west. "What was that?" she asked.

"I don't know."

It came again, a rumble, a distant tremor. A cool breeze

touched her face. The sun was setting in brilliant layers of purple and orange and billows of pewter. Dark gray.

"Clouds," she whispered.

A flash split the sky. Lightning. Moments later the rumble of thunder came again.

Julie stood up. "It's going to rain," she said, full of wonder. "Ben, it's going to rain!"

She pulled him up, grabbing his hands, grinning. The wind was picking up, whipping her hair around her face. A cool, refreshing wind.

Brady came out of the bunkhouse, went straight to the pickup and started cranking up the windows. "Damn thing'll get soaked," he grumbled.

"Brady! It's going to rain!" Julie called out.

"About time."

A fat drop of water splatted into the dust, then another. The smell of damp dirt filled Julie's nostrils; her hair blew into her eyes.

Hank emerged from the bunkhouse, looked up, held his hand out to catch the drops. Brady stood there, too, watching the clouds race in. The cottonwood tree whispered restlessly, its branches rattling.

Ben grinned and kissed Julie's upturned lips. "I suppose you'll say it's the kachina," he said.

But she only smiled as the precious rain fell, wetting them, falling harder and harder until even the broad face of Red Mesa disappeared into the blur.

CHAPTER SEVENTEEN

BEN COULD READ THE QUESTION on Julie's lips: will we ever see each other again? But she was too proud and still too inhibited. If he had the time, if this business about the Anasazi and keeping their secrets wasn't still wedged between them, then Ben would work on erasing those inhibitions. If there was just time.

She stood alongside his Jeep, the brim of her straw hat tugged low on her forehead so that he couldn't discern her expression. Only the freckled bridge of her nose showed, and those lovely lips, full and curved, expectant.

Ben put the key in the ignition. "I'll call," he said. But for the first time he wondered—was he kidding himself? Perhaps this was goodbye—and she knew it—but he was only just now coming to that painful realization.

"So long," Julie said too easily, "take care, Ben Tanner."

"You, too." He put the Jeep in reverse. "I *will* call," he said again, but he knew now how empty and trite that statement must sound.

It seemed a hell of a long drive to Albuquerque, where Ben planned on stopping to see Laurie. He was beset with self-doubts, a wholly new experience for him. And he felt that his decision on the Anasazi was a weight too great for one man alone to shoulder.

Ben drove through Trading Post, past the bank, past Mrs. Hickman's grocery store. Ken Lamont's car was parked out in front. What a piece of work Lamont was, small-town cop, hardly a rocket scientist. But he meant well and, Ben was sure, the guy was honest. The town could do a whole lot worse. In fact, he thought as he turned south on the main highway, he'd take a dozen Lamonts anytime over corrupt, big-city officials. Yeah. And he guessed he was going to miss this little place where people spoke their minds and were hardworking. It reminded him a lot of the small town in Washington state where he'd been born and raised. You bet he was going to think often of Trading Post, New Mexico, and of Julie Hayden. Too often, he knew.

Ben drove and he thought, his brow furrowed deeply above his dark glasses, his jaw working until it ached. The Anasazi. A discovery of this magnitude should be made public. Hell, in that hidden valley there was a bottomless store of information for archaeologists, anthropologists, biologists, geneticists, linguists, not to mention art historians and Anasazi specialists. He thought of all the questions that could be answered at last, the riddles to be solved after so long. And what about the benefits to the Indians in that valley? There was modern medicine to cure their ills, education, money from the government. What right did Ben have to sit as judge and jury on this matter? What right did Julie have?

He made Albuquerque by early afternoon and caught Laurie in between summer classes. She laughed at his beard and tugged on a couple of gray hairs that showed in it as they walked together to the local pizza spot.

"Is this *all* you kids eat?" he asked. "Don't they teach you anything about nutrition?"

"Come on, Dad," Laurie said, bouncing along, "give it a rest."

They had cool, tall Pepsis in red plastic cups and bubbling hot pizza with the works. Ben pulled a long string of cheese off his beard and watched his daughter devour her food like a starving college kid. He felt proud. Oh, she wasn't the prettiest girl there, but Laurie had that competent yet shy, vulnerable air that he adored, that apparently other males were attracted to as well. He hoped they appreciated her.

"My phone rings off the hook," she bragged. "It's not at all like high school."

"You're getting your work done, aren't you?" Ever the concerned single parent.

"Of course I am. Mellow out, Dad." She gave him a smile. "So, tell me all about the UFOs. You got any little green men in cages in the back of the Jeep?"

"Dozens." Ben drained his Pepsi, chewed on the ice, and signaled the waitress for another.

"Seriously. What did you find out? Who mutilated that animal?"

"What makes you think I found out anything?"

"'Cause you're my dad and I know you, and you wouldn't be heading back to Holloman if you hadn't found out."

"Very astute."

"That's me." She polished off her third wedge of pizza. "So? What happened."

He stared over her shoulder for a moment into the middle distance. How *was* he going to explain? UFOs seemed a simple and believable explanation in comparison to the truth. He shook himself. "I'll explain everything," Ben began, "but until I decide what I'm going to do about this, it's our secret. Can you keep this to yourself? It's pretty big."

Laurie grew serious and nodded. "If it's important to you, I won't breathe a word."

He knew his kid, and he knew she meant it. "We found a tribe of…of Anasazi, Laurie, and—"

"Of Anasazi? Come on, Dad, you're putting me on."

He told her everything, from the moment he'd arrived at the Someday Ranch to this morning when he'd left, besieged by doubts. The only thing Ben skirted around was his relationship with Julie Hayden. He wasn't sure Laurie was ready for that item.

"Wow," she kept saying. "Wow!"

What Ben saw as a huge dilemma—whether or not to keep the Anasazi secret—seemed no problem whatsoever to his daughter. She couldn't quite grasp his inner battle, but then she was only eighteen, and things were always clear-cut at that age.

"Dad," Laurie said, leaning across the table, "you can't be serious! You can't expose those people!"

"I'm not God," Ben said. "It shouldn't be my decision at all."

"What about Miss Hayden?"

"Julie," he said, casually pronouncing her name, "has decided to keep the secret. So has Brady, and his boy, Hank, the one who went to Los Alamos to help get Mika back."

"So you're the only holdout."

"Looks like." He shrugged.

"I can't believe it," she said. "It's so *obvious*, Dad. Here you tell me what a perfect society it is, and then in the next breath you want to introduce them to nuclear waste."

"I didn't say that," he grumbled.

"But that's just what would happen, and a whole lot more."

They talked, or rather Laurie did most of the talking, her disbelief that her father even thought there was a choice growing by the moment.

"You *can't* expose them," she said, sitting back in the dark vinyl booth and folding her arms across her chest in a snit.

They walked silently back to campus in the heat of the afternoon. He wished he'd never told her. Then again, he'd needed to hear all that, and not just from Julie and her Indian crew. He scrubbed a hand through his hair and walked along beside his daughter and wanted to tell her right then and there that in his heart he knew she was right. But then decisions of this magnitude couldn't be based on emotion.

They stopped in front of the building that housed the English department. "I gotta go," Laurie said, turning. Then she hesitated. "So what's with you and this Julie Hayden, anyway?" Laurie looked down at her pink crush socks and white Reeboks.

"What do you mean?" Ben asked innocently.

"Come off it, Dad. You about glowed red every time you said her name. I'm not stupid."

Ben let out a long breath and shifted his weight. "I guess you aren't," he said.

"So?"

"So, nothing. I liked her. I like her."

"Do you…love her?"

Oh brother. "Laurie—" he began, but then abruptly clammed up. "Yeah," he said, "I suppose I do." He couldn't meet her eyes. She was going to hate him, she was going to call him a traitor to Carol's memory, she was—

"That's great," she was saying. "I mean it, Dad, it's about time, don't you think?"

He didn't know what to say.

"Is she nice?"

"Oh, sure, very nice."

"Is she pretty?"

"Why, yes, sure."

"Are you going to see her some more? Have you got plans? You know."

Ben felt that twinge start in his head. "I don't know. We didn't decide anything."

"Why not?"

"Get off it, Laurie," he snapped, but she only grinned. "Sorry," he said.

"I mean, Dad," she said quietly, "how many men your age—" Ben grimaced "—get a second chance like this? I say go with it. Go with your feelings. You're too uptight."

"And *I* say," Ben put in, "to mind your own business and scoot on into class before you're late."

"End of conversation, huh?"

"You got it, smart-ass."

He made Holloman Air Force Base by six p.m. and unloaded his gear. It was hot as Hades out, blistering hot, not a wisp of cloud in sight. Sweat ran down the back of his neck and dampened his T-shirt as he hauled his things into his apartment. Inside the air was still, close, breathlessly hot. And his air-conditioning had been on the blink, hadn't it? He thought about Trading Post, about the wide open spaces and about the Someday Ranch, about last night's rain shower. How good it had felt, the big wet drops splattering on the hard-packed earth, the quick, cool wind that had blown before the dark clouds, the feel of the rain on his skin. And Julie's smile. Oh yes, he thought about that, all right.

His mailbox was crammed with the usual stuff: catalogs, junk mail, circulars, bills, his paycheck. There was also a report from Ed Niestrom, the scientist to whom he'd sent the samples collected at the first mutilation site on Julie's ranch. He wondered, as he opened the envelope, if something significant had shown up—something like a piece of fringe from Tayosha's moccasins, a drop of blood. Maybe Tayosha had cut himself. Suppose Ed had run that blood through the whole gamut of tests, found the peculiar DNA in it...

But there was nothing, only a note from Ed:

Sorry Ben, couldn't find a damn thing unusual in the samples. The soil contained residue of insects, ants, horse manure—nothing bizarre. There were trace minerals common in that area. As for the samples of torn flesh, I did find one that scavengers hadn't mauled. Looked to have been cut by a very sharp blade, though not typical of the pattern of a steel instrument. I found that odd. The edge was approximately one-eighth of an inch wide, and I'm guessing about twelve inches long. Purely a speculation. The cut was made by a right-handed individual— big help there, right? The blood samples were strictly from a horse, mare, don't know the age. I can run the DNA if you like. Let me know. Sorry again. Not much help. Stop by someday, stranger.

                                        See ya, Ed

Ben put the note down on his coffee table and kneaded his beard in thought. If Ed had found something out of line, then Ben would have had to include it in the report to his boss, but Ed had saved him that trouble.

He fixed himself a T.V. dinner then sat down on his couch and switched to the news. The usual stuff. Tension rising in the Mideast, an oil spill in the Gulf of Mexico, a known drunk in Santa Fe who blew away his wife and kids then put the gun to his own head. And then there was the weather. A few showers expected in the northwestern corner of New Mexico, due to a shift in the jet stream, minor relief from the drought that persisted. Ben wondered if Tayosha's Cloud People were going to be as kind to the rest of the state as they'd been to the Trading Post area last night.

He smiled, shaking his head, amused.

And then there was mention of a forest fire northwest of Durango, Colorado, but due to the northerly track of the jet stream, the smoke and ash were traveling toward Nebraska and perhaps as far north as Wyoming.

Of course, Ben thought, the weatherman could have been wrong. The smoke haze in the valley had to come from somewhere. After all, there were all sorts of local air currents.

He switched off the T.V. and tossed the remote control down next to his half-eaten dinner. In the morning he'd write his report to Jon Reveal. And in that report were supposed to be the unbiased findings of Ben Tanner, good ol' Tanner, devil's advocate, pragmatist, cynic at heart. But his findings would be straightfoward, honest, detailed...unbelievable.

Ben knew he could delay writing that report. Hell, some guys put off writing their reports for months, but Ben wasn't like that. The damn thing would be hanging over his head like a specter. No, that was no way to solve the problem.

His other choice was to write up a report blaming the mutilations on an Indian tribe—Hopi or Navajo—who had gotten into mutilations for ceremonial purposes, a cult or something. A partial truth, enough to satisfy Reveal and close the file.

He could do that, but it went against the grain. Ben reported fact, absolute fact, wherever he saw it. It was his job, all tied up with his pride, his view of himself.

He groaned, punched at a pillow, which he tossed at a corner of the couch, then he stretched out. He put an arm across his eyes and willed his body to relax. Outside, overhead, he could hear a pair of F-16s making their approaches to the airfield. How uncomplicated life had been then, when he'd still been flying. Uncomplicated, exciting, fun. But those days were long gone, weren't they? Of course, Ben mused, there was always the prospect of buying his own plane, a little lightweight job, sporty but manageable. Maybe a Cherokee. Think how easy it would be to fly on up and visit Julie...

Come on, Ben, he thought, *you're dreaming.* When he filed his report with Reveal that would be it for him and Julie. Over, kaput. She'd never want to see him again when all those scientists arrived at her door seeking permission to cross her land to get at the Anasazi.

He peeked out from under his forearm and spotted the telephone. He wanted to call her, to hear the lilt of her voice, to hear her laugh. But she'd ask him about his decision—or maybe she'd be tactful and say nothing. Either way the question would hang there. He better not call.

Julie. It had been good to feel a woman's body next to his again. It had felt warm and soft and safe. He'd denied himself for so long he'd almost forgotten. Now he knew, though, he knew he never wanted the cerebral, celibate life again. The trouble was, just any woman wasn't going to do. Ben was a one-woman man. Julie Hayden had come into his lonely life and brought a ray of hope. But now, how was he going to make it work?

Hand in your resignation, buddy. Run back to her, grab the gift and hold on for dear life.

Sure. And he'd remember forever the chance he'd had to unveil the discovery of a century, remember till his last days that he was the one to keep the truth from the world. He wouldn't be the one to help advance modern science, to help the Indians themselves. Why had this decision been dumped in his lap?

The sun set in a brilliant display of orange and red and purple. Ben's stuffy apartment grew dark, the shadows crawling out from beneath tables and chairs, creeping out of the corners. He stared up at the ceiling, at a chip of paint around the light fixture, until he could no longer see it. But there was something there, superimposing itself over the ceiling. It looked like a great house of stone, of sandstone, a cliff house, nestled in an overhang on a sheer canyon wall. He laughed to himself, thinking, *You old coot, Tayosha, you're doing this, you're sitting over your fire right now, conjuring this image up, playing with my head.*

He let the image grow, however, unafraid. He could see the colors of the mesa, the rich hues of a vanished civilization, the earth tones muted by soft reds and ambers, soft loam browns and tans that were bleached by the sun and wind. The colors of the high desert. And in those colors was the cliff house, the palace that had grown into the canyon wall over the many centuries, melding into the stone, forming a harmonious union with the land itself.

Ben lay there and saw clearly the mute remnants of a lost civilization, a society that had supposedly completed its life cycle hundreds of years before the first Europeans had set foot on this continent. The huge dwelling Ben saw was empty, and he could almost hear the desert wind singing through its dark, abandoned rooms, whispering against crumbling walls of sandstone, digging at the ancient remains of a vanished people, The Ancient Ones, as the Indians of today called the Anasazi.

It struck him then with the force of a thunderbolt: Was he seeing the fate of Tayosha's world?

Ben slept on the couch that night then rose stiff and tired the next morning. He rattled the air-conditioner, thumped it with a hand, gave up. He made coffee, then he sat down at his cluttered kitchen table and began to type out his preliminary report. He filled half a sheet of paper, pulled it out of the carriage, crumpled it and tossed it aside carelessly. He rubbed at his beard, sipped on the steaming hot coffee, put another piece of blank paper in the machine.

Let's go, Tanner. Start punching the keys. Get it done.

He typed all morning, reread his tale dozens of times, tried to avoid the guilt that was eating at him. Julie, and his daughter, too, were romantics. In time they'd see the fallacy of their thinking, realize that a discovery of this significance belonged to the entire world. They'd know, they'd...forgive him.

At one he showered and shaved—wouldn't want Reveal to think he'd gone native, lost his edge—and dressed in clean khaki trousers and a white polo shirt. He dropped the six-page report into a file folder, locked up the apartment and hopped into Nelly. He'd feel better, much better, when the job was done. He drove across town toward the Air Force base.

What an unattractive town this was, he thought as he steered, a man-made scar on the face of the desert, a loud, noisy place where the air smelled of jet engine exhaust and greasy burgers. Funny, but he'd never noticed that before.

Ben parked in a reserved space in front of the squat, whitewashed building and walked toward Reveal's door. He had his hand on the knob when a light breeze ruffled his hair, making him turn automatically to check the sky. Incredible, he thought, but there were several dark-looking clouds to the northwest, hovering over the mountains. Was it actually going to rain? Maybe Tayosha's medicine really was working. He smiled at himself. Or maybe, Ben thought, the clouds were a symbol of the old man's wrath.

He opened the door, shrugged off thoughts of Tayosha and rattling bones and smoke-filled kivas, and headed straight toward Reveal's office.

To hell with guilt, he told himself, he was doing his job the only way he knew how.

CHAPTER EIGHTEEN

IN AUGUST it rained often in the afternoons, a normal weather pattern. The drought was over. Julie returned from Scottsdale and drove up to Farmington the next day to open a large savings account at a bank there. She thought it was better that way, Trading Post was so small that everyone would know and talk and speculate, and that wouldn't be such a good idea.

She walked into Thatch Frederick's office in Trading Post that same afternoon and said hello politely, sat in the chair across from him and pulled out her checkbook.

"How much do I owe you?" she asked evenly.

"I'll have to get the payoff amount for you. Can you wait just a minute?"

"Sure, I'm in no hurry."

She wrote the check, handed it to him, waited while he got all the papers stamped and signed. It was as if another person in her body were doing these things and she was only watching, smiling smugly.

"Well, I do thank you, Julie. I stuck my neck out for you, and my faith was well-founded. Anytime you'd like to do further business, I'd be glad to oblige. Loans for new farm equipment, whatever. I know how hard it is for small ranchers these days."

"Thank you, Thatch," she said, gathering up the papers and checkbook, "but I'm fine for now, just fine. Everything worked out real well."

The old pale blue pickup bounced and rattled all the way back to the ranch. My God, she could buy a new one, a brand-new truck. Or would that be extravagant? She'd have to think, to decide. Maybe she'd wait and see how much interest piled up. She never wanted to touch another cent of the principal if she could help it.

Dark clouds boiled up in the west, and a few raindrops splatted on the truck's cracked windshield. Another afternoon shower. Her alfalfa field would make it now, and with a little irrigation she'd be set. She'd ordered a new irrigation system while she was up in Farmington—modern, more efficient, and the pumps were guaranteed for five years.

She'd had lunch with her mom, Julie's treat, and told her about the kachina and her new-found wealth.

"Oh, honey, I'm thrilled! Why, now you can buy a house here and take it easy. Meet some nice young men, have a social life."

The image of Ben that last morning had flown into her mind—the sadness in his eyes, the beloved, familiar lines of his face, the beard that was thicker and blacker by the day. She'd shaken her head. "No, Mom, I'm staying on the ranch. Upgrading. That's what Dad would have wanted."

Her mother had put a hand on hers. "Your father would have wanted you to be happy, Julie."

She'd swallowed, felt tears sting her eyes. "I *am* happy, Mom."

"Are you?"

She was, she should have been. Except that the man she loved was gone, and she didn't know if he'd ever be back or if they were enemies. "Sure, I'm happy, Mom. Now that the loan's paid off."

But her mother had looked at her doubtfully.

It had been two weeks since Ben had left, Julie thought as she drove.

And she'd waited each and every second of those fourteen long days for the phone to ring, to hear Ben's voice, to hear that he'd made up his mind. Maybe he'd tried to call while she'd been in Thatch's office just now. Maybe he hadn't.

She was relatively certain of one thing, anyway. So far Ben

had kept the secret. If he hadn't she'd have been inundated by newsmen, scientists, gawkers.

Of course, there was another possibility. Maybe Ben had turned in his report, and his boss had decided to keep it under wraps for the time being.

Maybe.

She pounded her fist on the steering wheel. Darn him! Why hadn't he called?

Ben Tanner. She conjured up his image and wondered if he'd shaved off his beard, wondered if he was really as tall and lean as she recalled, wondered what he was doing at that moment.

Call me, Ben. For godsakes, call me!

Brady was fixing the gate that led into the alfalfa field. He waved to her as she drove past on her way up the long driveway. Where was Hank? she wondered. He was still depressed, totally withdrawn, and she was really worried about him. He spent his nights drinking and his days with morose hangovers. He was lost, brooding, ripped apart by the discovery of his roots, unable to accept them, unable to have the only thing in the world he wanted. Brady had said Hank would forget, but he hadn't, not yet.

She carried the bags of groceries into the house and set them on the counter, wiped her upper lip with the back of her hand. It occurred to her once again that she could get a new truck with air-conditioning and power steering, a big one that'd haul a ton of hay at a time.

She put the groceries away. In every corner of the kitchen Ben's ghost persisted. He sat at the table, his long legs stretched out in front of him. He stood by the sink, drying dishes. He spoke into the phone, opened the refrigerator for a beer, stroked Coyote's back, kissed her for the first time.

Had he even made his decision yet?

She couldn't believe he hadn't phoned. Not a word. Two weeks and not a word. Maybe he'd decided he didn't love her. Once he'd gotten back to his other life at Holloman, seen a photograph of Carol to remind him, spoken to his daughter.

A grown daughter. Did grown children resent their parents' relationships? She didn't know about Laurie, but Julie wouldn't mind in the least if *her* mother remarried.

What terrible questions was Ben facing? If only he'd share his pain with her. If only he'd call or drive up in his old Jeep, hop out, smile, take her in his arms. After all her years alone, it had only taken her two weeks to get used to loving a man so much that she felt like half a person without him, as full of pain as if she'd lost an arm or a leg. Or her heart. She needed him near her, she needed to see him and touch him, to hear that particular tone of voice he had, to breathe in his smell.

Julie leaned on the sink and looked out the window. She'd finally fallen in love with a man she trusted implicitly but, ironically, a matter of conscience kept them apart. Such an abstract thing, but it had so many ramifications in their lives.

Oh, how she longed to pick up the phone and dial his number. How she wanted to ask him, to say, "Come live with me. Love me, Ben. Help me keep the Anasazi's secret. If you loved me, you'd do it." Isn't that what people in love did? They gave up important things for each other.

Brady appeared at the screen door. "Fixed the fence, Miss Julie. Want me to check on the sheep in the north pasture?"

But Julie was still staring out the window, musing. "Hey, Brady, what would you think if I bought a new truck?"

"A new truck?"

"I could afford it. One with air-conditioning."

"Well, sure, whatever you say."

"You don't sound enthused."

"What's wrong with the old one?"

She turned to face him. "I thought I'd give it to Hank," she said. "Make him feel a little better. You know he hates asking if he can use it every time he wants to go somewhere. I thought...well, maybe giving him more responsibility..."

Brady shook his head. "That's real nice of you, Miss Julie, but I'm not sure it'll do any good."

"We've got to try something," she said. "He can't go on like this."

Brady took his hat off and rubbed a weary hand across his eyes. "I spoke to him about going to live with his mother for a while. He won't."

"You know," she said carefully, "there's a mental health clinic in Farmington...."

Brady gave a harsh laugh. "You're kidding. Hank?"

"I just wish—"

"He'll have to find his own way, Miss Julie."

"What if he doesn't?" she asked anxiously.

Brady shrugged. "We can't do it for him."

"Brady," she said earnestly, "I can't bear to see him destroy himself like this. Look, would he consider going back to school? Junior college, maybe. I'll pay for it."

"I'll talk to him about it, but I'm afraid he's not in the mood right now to consider anything like that."

"Please, ask him. He could go to Santa Fe or Durango, whatever he wants. Tell him he can have the truck."

Brady looked at her a long time. "You're a good person, Miss Julie. Your daddy would be proud."

"Oh, stop, it," she said, embarrassed. "It's purely selfish on my part. I can't bear to see him so miserable."

"Sure, Miss Julie."

A few days later a horse trailer delivered the new brood mare Julie had bought. She was a pretty thing, dark bay with a white foot and a star.

"What do you think?" Julie asked her foreman.

"Nice."

"We'll breed her next spring. I thought that stallion of Red McKay's."

"He'll do," Brady agreed.

"Maybe I should get my own stallion," she mused.

"A pain in the neck," Brady said.

"Yeah."

Hank came out of the bunkhouse, blinking in the bright

sunlight. He looked vaguely green, and his clothes were rumpled, as if he'd slept in them.

"Come on over here," Julie called to him. "Take a look at our new mare."

He sauntered over, his scuffed boots kicking up puffs of dust. He glanced briefly, uninterested. "Nice," he said.

"You want to ride her? I don't know how well broke she is."

"Nah."

"You give her a name yet?" Brady asked, disregarding his son's truculence.

"Yes," Julie replied. "I gave her a name."

"What is it?"

"Mika."

Hank's head snapped around. He drew in his breath and balled his fists. "What'd you name her that for?" he asked angrily.

"To remember," Julie said.

"Goddamn it, I don't *want* to remember!" Hank cried.

"Hank," his father said, "you have to—"

"Aw, shut up, the both of you. I know what you're trying to do! Trying to be nice. School, the truck. Sure, but it won't work. There's only one thing I want and I can't have it! So what good does all this other stuff do?"

"Don't talk to Miss Julie that way," Brady said tightly.

"That's okay, Brady. Hank, I'm sorry. I was only trying—"

"Don't try. I don't need your help. I don't need anything you can give me." Hank whirled and ran, stumbling, back to the bunkhouse and slammed the door shut behind him.

"Oh God," Julie whispered.

BEN CAME THE NEXT DAY. He didn't phone and he didn't drive up in his Jeep. Julie heard a noise, a low droning at first, then it got louder. An insistent whining noise. She walked out of the house, stood on her porch and searched the sky. If it was an airplane, it sure was low. Maybe the pilot was having engine trouble. It happened around here once in a while, but if the pilot couldn't make it to the small Farmington airport, he'd usually land on a field somewhere, or even the county road.

The drone increased, and then she saw it when the sun glinted off the windshield. A small two-engine plane, red-and-white, flying in low from the east, descending until it was skimming the ground.

Julie watched, astonished, as the plane's wings rocked slightly, and it came down on the flat expanse of empty pasture, bumping, bouncing lightly once then taxiing neatly to a stop. She just stood there, slack-jawed, unthinking, until she saw the pilot climb down and step onto the ground.

Suddenly she was running, racing toward the bright-colored plane that sat so incongruously in the middle of her field, racing, tearing open the gate, and Coyote came streaking by her, barking like a maniac. She was panting, stumbling over the hillocks of dry grass. And he was striding toward her, his teeth white in his sun-browned face, grinning, holding his arms out.

They met in the middle of the field and clung together, while Coyote danced and barked around them. "Ben," she whispered, "you came back."

He pushed her away and searched her face. "Guess I just figured out that I can't live without you."

"Good!" she cried, bursting with joy.

"Did you notice my baby?" he asked.

"Gorgeous," she said.

"I'm *not* a baby," someone said from across the field.

Julie's head jerked around.

"Oh," Ben said sheepishly, "that's my other baby."

Julie looked. A young girl stood there, tall, slender, with curly dark hair and strong features.

"Dad, maybe you'd like to introduce us. I mean, this is really embarrassing," the girl said.

"Oh, sure. Laurie Tanner, this is Julie Hayden."

Julie extricated herself from Ben's arms. "Laurie. Gosh, it's good to meet you. I've heard so much about you."

Laurie came toward her. She walked just like Ben, Julie noted, lithe, so sure of herself. What if Laurie hated her on sight? But the young girl strode right up and gave Julie a hug.

"I've heard so much about you, too," Laurie said. "And all about your ranch and the valley."

Julie switched her gaze to Ben swiftly, questioning. But he nodded and smiled, and she knew Laurie could be trusted. "I'm so glad. And I'm so glad you're here. Please, come on over to the house, come on in and let's talk."

She walked back to the house arm in arm with Ben, loving the feel and smell of him, remembering all over again every one of his gestures, the tone of his voice. She'd remembered him, of course, going over in her mind every moment she'd spent with him, but it was the generalities she'd recalled in her lonely vigils, not the subtleties that made up the man, and it was the subtleties that struck her now.

"Oh, Ben, it's so good to see you. And the plane. Is it yours?"

"Sure is. All mine. I bought it today."

"Today?"

"Yep, and I had to take it for a test drive, so to speak."

She laughed out loud. "A test drive? Up here?"

"Well, that's just an excuse. Actually, it was quicker than driving."

"I bet."

His eyes bored into hers. "I wanted to see you. I had to."

She couldn't believe he was there, filling her house with his presence, chasing away the ghosts. He sat at the table and sipped from a Coke while Laurie had lemonade with Julie.

"I love to fly with Dad. What a great trip we had up here," Laurie was saying. "What a nice place."

"Yo, *kemo sabe*," came a voice from the door.

"Hey, Brady, come on in," Julie said. "Look who's here. And this is Ben's daughter, Laurie."

"How's it going, Brady?" Ben asked. "How's Hank?"

"It's going, and Hank's…well, he's not real pleased with things."

"Sit down, have a beer," Ben said.

"Sorry, I got work to do. And I don't drink…anymore."

"Hell, Brady, have a Coke then," Ben replied.

"Later, *kemo sabe*. Now, I gotta drive out and look at the horses. Maybe Laurie would like to go along, see the ranch and all," Brady suggested.

Laurie looked at her father then at Julie then back to her father. She grinned knowingly. "Sure, Brady, I'd love to see the ranch. Nothing I'd like better."

She left with Brady, the screen door slamming behind her. Julie just sat and gazed at Ben, reveling in the sight of him, like a starving person before a table laden with food. His hand was on hers, warm and reassuring, and his eyes met hers, full of unspoken messages.

"I missed you," she breathed.

"I know. And I didn't call. I should have. I just—" he drew his brows together "—I just didn't know what exactly I was going to say."

"And do you know now?"

"Yes." His eyes switched away, and Julie felt that familiar tightening in her chest.

He squeezed her hand. "I was worried about you. The ranch. Your loan and all."

"Oh, it's all taken care of. I sold the kachina in Scottsdale for a lot of money. A lot. Brady was a great help. He swore we found it on my land, so we weren't breaking the Indian artifacts law. I've got the money in sound investments, and I paid off the loan. The ranch is safe."

"Good," he said. "Good."

Julie smiled. "And I had to call Jack Murdock and tell him my place wasn't for sale. He was real disappointed."

"He'll find another place."

"I suppose he will."

"Julie, I figured you'd have called if something happened,

but did you ever heard from Gary Phillips's paper? Anyone asking questions or anything?"

She shook her head, got up and rummaged through her junk drawer. "No, not a word, but here, I've got to show you this. Terry got this in at his store and called me." She pulled out a folded newspaper.

"What's this?"

"The *Nation*, July twenty-eighth edition. Look, Ben." She unfolded it and held up the front page. Heavy black letters across the top of the page screamed: Reporter Taken by Aliens, Dies Mysteriously in Desert.

"Ye gads," Ben said. "I don't believe it."

"Gary would have been proud, don't you think?"

Ben shook his head wonderingly. "Proud as punch."

"I still feel awful about Gary. I feel like we could have done something."

"Like what?"

She moved her hands. "I don't know. Something."

"I've thought that myself. If I'd gone after him that night...but we did our best. We did what we thought was right. I guess that's what we have to live with."

"I can live with it, Ben. I've done what I could. There's the money I invested. But it's not mine. It belongs to the Indians, to Tayosha, really. I won't even need all the interest, so every year the capital will build. I'm just the guardian." She looked to Ben for approval, but she couldn't read his expression. He must know that she was asking him what he'd decided. She quaked inside, afraid of his answer, loving him so much....

He took her hands in his and studied her face. Time ticked by in endless suspense. She loved him, yes, but that wouldn't help, not if he had betrayed the valley to the world. Her heart stopped, swelled, refused to beat.

"Julie," he said, his voice soft and a little sad, but decisive. "I thought a lot about this thing. I talked to Laurie. I wrote my damn report, got every fact straight." His mouth twisted in a wry smile. "Good report, too."

"Ben…"

He went on. "What bothered me the most was this—who am I, a simple mortal man, to keep this discovery from the world?"

"I know, but—"

"And then, on the other hand, who am I to introduce Tayosha and his tribe to the modern world? It works both ways." He shook his head in irritation. "It's been driving me nuts."

Julie held her breath.

He frowned and glared at her. "I burned the report, Julie," he said angrily. "Burned it."

Her heart beat again, bursting inside her. "You did?"

"I wrote a new one, some bunk about local Indians wanting the animal heads for ceremonial purposes."

"But, Ben, that's *true*," she said.

"Yeah, sort of."

"You didn't lie."

"I left out a whole hell of a lot, Julie."

"Oh, Ben, I'm so glad!"

He grinned self-deprecatingly. "I guess Tayosha's spirits willed it," he said. "Strong medicine."

"I love you, Ben Tanner," she said, smiling radiantly.

"That's not why I did it, Julie."

"I know, but I love you anyway."

"Yeah, well, I love you too, Mrs. Hayden."

She made a face. "I never really was Mrs. Hayden."

"Well, how about Mrs. Tanner then?"

"Oh, Ben…"

"Now, I've got it all figured out."

"I can't leave here, Ben, and you have your job."

"I quit my job."

"You what?"

"I'll be called in as a consultant if they need me."

"Is this what you want, Ben? Really want?"

"A publisher wants me to do a book about UFOs, and I have my Air Force retirement pay and a consulting job here and there. Sure, it's exactly what I want, Julie. As long as you come with the package.''

She closed her eyes, hoping this wasn't all a dream.

"What d'you say? Marry me, Julie. We'll live here. And I'll fly my plane. You know, just to keep my hand in.''

"Oh, Ben, I'll marry you today if you want.'' She stopped abruptly. "Does Laurie know?''

"Sure she knows. She told me to grab you before I got too old.''

Julie laughed, carefree, full of delight.

"It's a good thing you said yes, because I gave up my apartment in Albuquerque,'' Ben said.

"Pretty sure of yourself, buster, aren't you?''

"I've been accused of that before, yes, ma'am.''

"We have to tell Brady and Hank,'' she said. "And Laurie. And my mother.''

"We can drive up and see your mom today,'' he said. "Or maybe we should fly to Farmington.''

"Fly to Farmington!''

"Sure, why not?''

The pickup arrived then, rattling to a stop outside. Julie could hear Laurie say something, then Brady's answer. Suddenly she turned shy. "Oh, you tell her, Ben.''

He stood and pulled her up. "Come on, let's face 'em together.''

He kept his arm around her as they walked outside. Laurie looked up at them and smiled. "So, when's the date?''

Julie blushed. "Oh, we haven't really set one.''

"Saturday,'' Ben said.

"Saturday?'' Julie asked.

"Saturday's as good as any day.''

"I guess…oh wow, I guess it is.'' She laughed, overwhelmed, elated. "I better call Mom then, right away…and Brady…if we get married right here he'll have to help…oh wow.''

"Don't you think we better tell him?'' Ben suggested. "I can just hear him—'Yo, *kemo sabe*.'''

Julie took his hands in hers and squeezed them. "He likes you, Ben, he really does. It's just his way to be sarcastic."

"Don't I know."

They found Brady in the bunkhouse. He was sitting at the table, the one on which they always played poker, and he was staring down at a scrap of paper.

"Brady?" Julie said. "Guess what?"

But he never looked up, just kept his head down, looking at the paper. The hand that held it shook, Julie noticed.

"Brady?" Ben tried.

"He's gone," Brady said, stunned.

Julie drew in her breath. "Hank," she said, and it was not a question...

"He's gone back to the valley," Brady said wonderingly. "He's gone for good."

"Dad?" Laurie said at the door.

Ben motioned her to come in, and she stood silently with them, knowing instinctively that something momentous had happened.

"He knows he can never come back," Brady said. "He's gone to Mika."

Brady rose, the note still clutched in his hand, and walked outside. They followed. Brady was looking toward the west, toward Red Mesa. Julie's gaze followed his, turning toward the hidden valley of the Anasazi, to the place where a young, lost Indian would find love and fulfillment.

Ben squeezed Julie's hand. "It'll work out," he said, drawing her close on one side and Laurie on the other.

And suddenly Julie was sure it would.

EPILOGUE

LEGEND IN NEW MEXICO tells of two young Indian lovers murdered by their people for marrying outside their tribe. The Sun meant to separate the lovers' spirits forever by sending the man to the valley of rocks and the woman to the sky.

But the Moon Spirit saw the woman crying, pitied her and turned her into a star. The Spirit made the man into a river that flowed through the valley. And every night, the light from the star shone on the river and the lovers were joined.

A LETTER FROM THE AUTHOR

Dear Reader,

It was just last spring that I heard *West of the Sun* was to be included in WESTERN LOVERS. I was thrilled, as this book is one of my favorites and, I have to humbly mention, it won a *Romantic Times* award.

Every so often in life certain elements seem to come together magically. In *West of the Sun* I was able to answer—my own version, of course—a question that has baffled historians for years: What happened to the flourishing Anasazi civilization of the pre-Columbian Southwest, which seemed to vanish very suddenly and mysteriously around 1000 A.D.?

With this question in mind I chose a very special setting for the action of my story—the vast, isolated territory of northern New Mexico, a place that has always fascinated me with its ancient Native American mysteries.

I hope I've captured the feel of this magical Western setting, and that you can enjoy the journey of my hero and heroine as much as I did.

Happy reading and many thanks for your continued support.

Lynn Erickson

Harlequin Romance ®

Delightful
Affectionate
Romantic
Emotional

Tender
Original

Daring
Riveting
Enchanting
Adventurous
Moving

Harlequin Romance ®—
capturing the world you dream of...

HARLEQUIN *Presents*

The world's bestselling romance series...
The series that brings you your favorite authors,
month after month:

Helen Bianchin...Emma Darcy
Lynne Graham...Penny Jordan
Miranda Lee...Sandra Marton
Anne Mather...Carole Mortimer
Susan Napier...Michelle Reid

and many more uniquely talented authors!

Wealthy, powerful, gorgeous men...
Women who have feelings just like your own...
The stories you love, set in exotic, glamorous locations...

HARLEQUIN *Presents*

Seduction and passion guaranteed!

*From rugged lawmen and
valiant knights to defiant heiresses
and spirited frontierswomen,
Harlequin Historicals will
capture your imagination with
their dramatic scope, passion
and adventure.*

*Harlequin Historicals . . .
they're too good to miss!*